P9-BYH-821

Live and Let Growl

Books by Laurien Berenson

A PEDIGREE TO DIE FOR

UNDERDOG

DOG EAT DOG

HAIR OF THE DOG

WATCHDOG

HUSH PUPPY

UNLEASHED

ONCE BITTEN

HOT DOG

BEST IN SHOW

JINGLE BELL BARK

RAINING CATS AND DOGS

CHOW DOWN

HOUNDED TO DEATH

DOGGIE DAY CARE MURDER

GONE WITH THE WOOF

DEATH OF A DOG WHISPERER

THE BARK BEFORE CHRISTMAS

LIVE AND LET GROWL

Published by Kensington Publishing Corporation

Live and Let Growl

LAURIEN BERENSON

KENSINGTON BOOKS
www.kensingtonbooks.com

KENSINGTON BOOKS are published by

Kensington Publishing Corp.
119 West 40th Street
New York, NY 10018

All Kensington titles, imprints and distributed lines are available at special quantity discounts for bulk purchases for sales promotion, premiums, fund-raising, educational or institutional use.

Special book excerpts or customized printings can also be created to fit specific needs. For details, write or phone the office of the Kensington Special Sales Manager: Kensington Publishing Corp., 119 West 40th Street, New York, NY 10018. Attn. Special Sales Department. Phone: 1-800-221-2647.

Kensington and the K logo Reg. U.S. Pat. & TM Off.

Library of Congress Control Number: 2016933896

ISBN-13: 978-1-4967-0338-5
ISBN-10: 1-4967-0338-3
First Kensington Hardcover Edition: August 2016

eISBN-13: 978-1-4967-0339-2
eISBN-10: 1-4967-0339-1
First Kensington Electronic Edition: August 2016

10 9 8 7 6 5 4 3 2 1

Printed in the United States of America

Live and Let Growl

Chapter 1

I was moving fast.

The ground below me was little more than a blur. Scenery flew by with astonishing speed. I was running. . . .

No, not running . . . riding. I was on the back of a horse. I could feel the smooth motion of the muscular body beneath me. I could hear the creak of the leather saddle, and the steady, rhythmic sound of hoofbeats striking the turf.

Their pounding cadence pulsed through me. It drew me in and made me one with the motion. It propelled me onward, as if this heady race was the only thing in the world that mattered.

Where was I? I wondered. What was happening? Was I racing toward something—or was I running away?

I had no answers. All I knew was that I could feel the sharp bite of the wind on my face and a sensation of freedom humming deep inside my bones.

The feeling was heavenly.

It was addictive.

One thing I was sure of—I wanted more.

All at once a pale mist rose on the path ahead of us. Its silvery tendrils lifted and swirled, obscuring all view of what was to come. I found myself leaning forward in the saddle. I gazed in vain between the tips of two dark, pointed ears.

I could see nothing. The vista before me was still blank . . . and suddenly forbidding. In the space of a second, the breakneck speed at which we were traveling lost its appeal.

Frantically I reached for reins, but couldn't find them. My fingers felt thick and stiff. Useless. I screamed into the wind. I told the horse to stop but my words had no effect.

Then the mists shifted and drew apart and I saw that behind them lay only darkness. A void of nothingness. It looked as though my steed and I were racing toward the edge of the world.

Abruptly my stomach plummeted as the ground disappeared from beneath us. My hands flew upward, groping in the air, grasping desperately for purchase that wasn't there. My heart pounded with the sudden knowledge that I couldn't save myself. And then I was falling, helpless as I plunged downward and tumbled into the unknown below . . .

I awoke with a gasp and bolted upright in bed.

My heart was beating wildly in my chest. Mouth open, I was desperate for air. Fire clawed at my lungs. My insides still churned with the sensation of falling. Though my eyes were open wide I couldn't see a thing. Everything around me was black: inky and impenetrable.

I still had no idea where I was.

Clutching the bedcovers in frantic fingers, I swiveled my head from side to side. A moment later, my gaze alighted on the amber numbers of the bedside clock. Three-oh-two, it read.

Slowly my mind processed the number. With effort I made the connection to what it meant. Compared to my recent speed, I felt dull and sluggish as I worked to reorient myself. I gulped in a breath of cool air and shifted my shoulders, trying to ease their tension.

There was no horse. There was no wind. There was no

yawning crater waiting to suck me down into its gruesome depths.

I'd been having a nightmare. That was all.

I gazed around again. My eyes had adjusted to the darkness now. I could see the familiar bedroom surrounding me. I could feel the slight dip in the mattress caused by the weight of my husband, Sam, who was sound asleep beside me.

Relief washed through me and I blew out a long breath. I was safe. I was home in my own house, with my husband, my two sons, and my six dogs.

I heard a soft creak and turned to see the bedroom door nudged slightly ajar by a long black muzzle. My Standard Poodle, Faith, the dog who understood everything about me and who knew my thoughts almost before I did, was standing silently in the doorway.

Faith always sleeps on my older son, Davey's, bed. But now in the middle of the night, something had called her to me. The big Poodle was so attuned to my emotions that she had sensed something was amiss. As I glanced in her direction, Faith tipped her head to one side inquiringly. Even in the murky darkness, I could see the gentle gleam in her eye.

As our gazes met, Faith padded silently across the room. She stepped beside the bed and pressed her nose into my hand, offering her own special brand of comfort. As the Poodle's warm breath filled my palm, I finally felt my heart rate begin to slow. I cupped Faith's muzzle between my fingers and rubbed my thumb over her lips and cheek.

"It's all right, sweetie," I said softly. "You can go back to sleep."

Faith acknowledged the comment with a low swish of her tail but she didn't look convinced.

"Really," I told her. "Everything is fine. It was just a dream."

Faith lifted one front paw delicately and placed it on the bed in silent inquiry. I glanced over my shoulder at Sam. Covers pulled up to his chin, head burrowed deep in his pillow, he was too deeply asleep to realize that his sleeping arrangement was about to become even cozier.

I scootched over toward Sam and patted the space beside me. "Come on up," I whispered. "There's plenty of room."

Faith leapt up lightly. She aligned her body next to mine, lay down on the quilt, and pressed in close. As I settled down beside her, the Poodle's warmth enveloped me.

I closed my eyes and finally slept.

"I had the strangest dream last night," I said the next evening.

The comment was delivered to a full house. It was our son, Kevin's, third birthday. In honor of the occasion, I had invited some of our relatives to dinner.

In most families a gathering like that would lead to convivial celebration. Not mine, however. My relatives are equally as likely to set the house ablaze as they are to coexist in peace. There's nothing boring about the extended Travis/Turnbull clan, especially when my provocative and ever-entertaining Aunt Peg is part of the assembly.

So far we'd managed to make our way through most of the meal without incident. Minutes earlier, Kevin's birthday cake, alight with festive candles, had been presented to the room with great fanfare. Kev had shrieked and clapped his hands, bouncing up and down in his seat with glee when it appeared.

My younger son was a little hazy about what the concept of three years meant, but he knew all about chocolate cake. When I set the dessert down in front of him, Kev's first impulse was to reach for it with both hands. Luckily his older brother, Davey—a gangly twelve-year-old, teetering on the cusp between childhood and adolescence—was there to quickly intercede. Cupping Kevin's small hands in his own much larger ones, Davey also help his little brother blow out the candles.

The layer cake was cut and served and everyone dug in happily. If I were to be honest I would admit that most of the evening's success was undoubtedly due to Sam's calming influence. When it comes to my relatives, my husband is smart enough and affable enough not to sweat the small stuff. Things that cause me to roll my eyes and rail about the general state of insanity just make him shrug his shoulders and chuckle under his breath.

Lucky man. I wish I knew how he did it.

Sam was seated at the head of the table. On his right was my Aunt Peg. Now in the middle of her seventh decade, Margaret Turnbull is living proof that age is merely a state of mind. The woman possesses more than enough energy, ambition, and wit to run circles around me effortlessly. Unfortunately it's a circumstance she's not above exploiting to further her own ends. On the other hand, if it weren't for Aunt Peg I would never have discovered the intriguing appeal of the dog show world. Nor would I have Faith, or the other five Standard Poodles that currently grace and enrich our lives.

Completing the group seated around the table was my younger brother, Frank, and his family. For years Frank had been the feckless, thoughtless, bane of my existence. But now in his thirties, my little brother was finally grown up and married to one of my best friends, Bertie Kennedy. Their young daughter, Maggie, was seated between them. The child was keeping a beady eye on Kevin, seemingly determined to ensure that the birthday boy didn't get so much as a smidge more cake than she did.

Any minute now the sugar high was going to kick in, I thought as I gazed around the room. And then we'd really be off to the races.

And just like that I remembered my dream.

"I had the strangest dream last night," I said.

"Oh?" Aunt Peg looked up from her cake. "I read a book about that."

"About dreams?" Bertie asked. Her dark green eyes twinkled with amusement. "Or strange things?"

"Dreams, of course. Did you know that they're the way your subconscious works through problems while you're asleep?" Peg peered at me across the table. "Do you have any problems that need working out?"

She would ask that. There's nothing Aunt Peg enjoys more than involving herself in other peoples' troubles.

"Not that I'm aware of," I replied. "And certainly none that involve a horse."

"A *horse*?" Sam sounded surprised. I couldn't blame him. I felt the same way.

From across the table, Aunt Peg glanced at me sharply. I wondered what that look meant.

"That was what was so odd about it," I said. "In the dream, I was riding a horse. I've never done that in my life. The horse was galloping, we were racing like the wind. It's amazing how real it all felt."

"Real indeed," Aunt Peg muttered under her breath. I waited for her to continue but instead she resumed eating. Nothing could distract Aunt Peg from cake for long.

"Where were you going?" Bertie asked curiously.

"I have no idea. Everything ahead was foggy. I couldn't see a thing. We were just running."

"Maybe you were being chased by a zombie," said Frank.

"No." I laughed. "I don't think so."

"Was it a flying horse?" Kev asked. He has a book about Pegasus.

"No, just a regular horse. A very fast one."

"Maybe it was Willow!" said Davey.

Five years earlier, his father, my ex-husband, Bob, had surprised Davey with a palomino pony named Willow. Even though at the time Davey and I were living in a small house on a tiny plot of land, Bob apparently hadn't foreseen any difficulties with the care and management of Davey's new pet. As ponies went, Willow was lovely, but she hadn't lasted long.

"A pony," Kevin said with sudden interest. He had heard the story from his brother. "I want a pony!"

"Don't be silly." Aunt Peg sniffed. "Why would anyone want a pony when they can have Poodles instead?"

Poodles indeed. We not only had Standard Poodles, we were literally surrounded by them. And as Aunt Peg would have said, what was wrong with that?

Poodles come in three different sizes, but all share the same superb temperament. They're smart, they're endearing, and they have a superior sense of humor. Best of all, Poodles are people dogs. Wherever their family is, that's where they want to be.

Since the birthday celebration was taking place in the dining room, that meant that aside from the eight people sitting at the table, we also had six black Standard Poodles lying in attendance on the floor around us. Five of the six were even wearing party hats. The Poodles didn't look nearly as delighted about that development as Kevin did. In fact, judging by the expressions on their faces, they were feeling rather silly.

In my defense, the hats hadn't been my idea. Sam and Davey had snuck away and done the honors while I'd been busy greeting our arriving guests. But Aunt Peg's horrified gasp when she rounded the corner and saw the assembled crew—she being of the firm belief that Poodles are entirely too dignified to be treated frivolously—was gratifying enough to make me wish that I'd been a coconspirator.

All our Poodles are the Standard variety, the biggest of the three sizes. The top of Faith's head is nearly level with my waist, which positions her entire body within easy reach whenever she and I want to hold a conversation. That comes up more frequently than you might think.

Aunt Peg is Faith's breeder. Indeed she was connected in some way to nearly every dog in the room, her Cedar Crest line having set the standard for excellence in the Poodle breed since before I was born. A dedicated owner-handler in the show ring for decades, Peg had now scaled back her breeding and exhibiting commitments to concentrate on her burgeoning career as a dog show judge. As is true with many of Aunt Peg's decisions, that change in course has had the effect of keeping us all on our toes.

Faith's daughter, Eve, now lying beneath Kevin's chair in the hope there'd be spillage, was the second Standard Poodle I had brought to my marriage to Sam. He'd joined the union with two bitches of his own, Casey and Raven, both of whom were—like Faith and Eve—retired show champions. Sam was also the owner of GCH Cedar Crest Scimitar, also known as Tar.

Formerly an accomplished "specials dog," Tar had numerous Non-Sporting Group and Best in Show wins to his credit. Now, however, like the bitches, he was retired from the show ring and his long, plush black coat had been clipped off. He, too, wore the attractive and easy-to-care-for sporting trim, with a short blanket of dense dark curls covering his entire body.

Tar was a love. He was the sweetest, most well-meaning dog of the entire pack. But he was also the only dumb Poodle I'd ever met. Somehow, no matter what was going on, Tar always managed to be a beat behind the rest. Punch lines, along with other of life's intricacies, simply went right over his head.

Our newest addition and the only dog currently "in

hair" was Davey's Standard Poodle, Augie. Davey was responsible for Augie's care; and with Sam's help, he was also managing the young dog's show career. The collaboration was a successful one as Augie was already halfway toward the goal of accumulating the fifteen points he would need to be named a champion.

In deference to his long and oh-so-valuable topknot hair, Augie was the only Poodle not wearing a party hat. He didn't appear to be upset about the omission. In fact, I was pretty sure I'd seen Augie sniff derisively in Tar's direction when he thought no one was looking.

Having heard Aunt Peg reference their breed, several dark heads lifted as the Poodle pack turned into the conversation at the table. Ears pricked as they waited to see what would happen next.

"Don't care," Kevin replied firmly to Aunt Peg. "Have Poodles. Want a pony."

"Ponies are too big," I told him mildly. "Besides, you already have fish."

Kev's aquarium, a cherished Christmas present, was visible through the doorway in the living room. My son refused to be mollified. He thrust out his lower lip and started to shake his head. Despite the date on the calendar, we clearly hadn't yet left the Terrible Twos behind just yet.

"And you have cake," I added.

"Cake," Kevin echoed. His expression brightened as Sam reached over and slid another sliver onto his plate. "I like cake!"

"Don't we all," Frank said heartily. He reached over and helped himself to a second piece. "That's why I came tonight."

"And also because it's Kevin's birthday." Bertie leveled a glare at her husband. "Right?"

"Sure," Frank agreed easily. "That, too."

"Has it occurred to you," Sam said to me, "that maybe

the reason you were thinking about horses is because of Peg's judging assignment at the Kentuckiana Cluster next week?"

"No," I replied. That thought hadn't crossed my mind at all.

Aunt Peg's upcoming trip to Kentucky had nothing to do with me. Bertie, who was a professional handler, was also making the trip to the Midwest. With four back-to-back dog shows scheduled to take place in Louisville, and several clients whose dogs were looking for majors, she had entered a sizeable string to show. But with spring break starting in just two days—two whole weeks of vacation from my job as a special needs tutor at private Howard Academy—I was looking forward to nothing more strenuous than sleeping late and reading several good books.

"Speaking of which," said Aunt Peg, "while we're on the subject, I have an announcement to make. . . ." She paused and looked around, waiting until she had our full attention.

"Which subject is that?" asked Sam. "Kentucky?"

"Judging," Bertie guessed.

"Cake," Frank contributed, speaking with his mouth full.

"Fish!" cried Kevin.

"Horses?" I teased.

"Bingo!" Aunt Peg turned and favored me with a small nod.

Horses? That was a surprise.

Clearly I wasn't the only one who felt that way. The whole table fell silent with nervous anticipation. With Aunt Peg, you never knew which way the dice were going to roll. She might have wonderful news or it could be something truly alarming. I'd long since resigned myself to the fact that life with Aunt Peg meant existing in a semi-perpetual state of suspense.

"As it turns out, my trip to Kentucky has come along at a rather fortuitous time," she informed us.

"Why is that?" I asked.

"I have an asset in central Kentucky that I need to take a closer look at." Aunt Peg beamed at us all happily. "You are looking at the new owner of a Thoroughbred racehorse."

Chapter 2

For a moment, nobody said a word. Instead we sat around the table in a state of stupefied silence. It wasn't the first time Aunt Peg had succeeded in leaving us speechless, but it might have been the most unexpected.

As the rest of us struggled to process that information, Davey turned to his little brother with a wide grin. "It looks like you're in luck," he said. "Aunt Peg just got a new pony."

"Not a pony," Aunt Peg corrected firmly. "A racehorse. Albeit a retired one."

"Did he win the Kentucky Derby?" Frank asked eagerly.

"No, *she* did not. Although I am given to understand that she did win several other races during her career."

"A career that's now over," I said carefully. "Right?"

"I should hope so," Aunt Peg replied. "The dear girl is fourteen. That's forty-five in human years, in case you'd like to know. I went on the Internet and looked it up."

I suspected that was only the first of many things we would have to be researching in the near future.

Sam finally found his voice. "A racehorse," he said in a strangled tone. "How interesting. What precisely does a retired racehorse do?"

"In this case, she becomes a broodmare," Aunt Peg said

with satisfaction. She loves having the upper hand in a conversation. "And she produces little racehorses."

"Foals?" Bertie's eyes softened. My sister-in-law isn't a sentimental woman, so I was surprised to hear her sigh with what sounded like maternal bliss. "Your racehorse comes with *foals?*"

"Only one," Aunt Peg replied. "And it hasn't been born yet. She isn't due until next month. In the meantime, however, I would like to meet my new broodmare. I also need to check out her living arrangements and make plans for her continuing care."

"But," I sputtered, "where did she come from?"

"Anthony Stone," Aunt Peg said as if the name was supposed to mean something to us.

We all stared at her blankly.

Aunt Peg put down her fork, nudged her cake plate aside, and offered an explanation. "Anthony was a dear friend of my late husband, Max. A fascinating man, positively ingenious. Anthony was always interested in all kinds of unexpected things."

"Like racehorses apparently," said Sam.

"Precisely. When Max was still alive, he and I used to see Anthony quite often. But unfortunately in the intervening years since Max passed, Anthony and I have all but lost touch. I never received a Christmas card from him this year. I remember thinking that was odd. Even so, it came as a surprise to hear from his solicitor." Aunt Peg stopped and sighed.

"I'm sorry," I said.

"Anthony was such a vibrant man. The sort you think will live forever. But of course, he didn't. Nobody does, do they?"

Davey gazed at his great-aunt. "You will," he said with all the confidence of youth. In his world, a life without Aunt Peg was unthinkable.

"I should hope not," she replied briskly. "I have no intention of overstaying my welcome. But back to Lucky Luna—"

"Your horse's name is Lucky Luna?" Frank asked. He was clearly biting back a laugh.

"Indeed. What's wrong with that?"

"Oh, I don't know," said Frank. "Since it's a racehorse I guess I was expecting something majestic like Secretariat or Citation."

"I think Lucky Luna is a fine name," I said.

"Suck up," Frank muttered under his breath.

I reached over and kicked him under the table as hard as I could manage. We all like to think that we outgrow our petty childhood rivalries but, in reality . . . not so much.

Aunt Peg ignored us both. "Anthony explained in his will that he left Lucky Luna to me because he was certain that my extensive background in dog breeding would ensure I was well equipped to deal with the complexity of managing a Thoroughbred broodmare."

"That sounds more like a responsibility than a valuable bequest," I said.

"You may very well be right about that," Aunt Peg told me. "I must admit that I am clueless as to what to expect. Hopefully I will learn everything I need to know next week when I visit the boarding farm in Kentucky where Lucky Luna lives."

"I come, too!" cried Kevin.

"'Fraid not," said Sam. He lifted Kev out of his seat, pulled him over onto his lap, and wrapped his arms around him. "You're staying home with me."

"And me." I wet a napkin in a water glass and used it to clean Kev's hands before he could smear them across Sam's shirt.

"About that . . ." said Aunt Peg.

The sudden stillness in the room clued me in that something was up. I stopped what I was doing and looked around. "Yes?"

"You're going to Kentucky, too," Sam told me.

"No, I'm not," I said.

I was quite certain of that. I had plenty to do at home.

"Yes, you are." Aunt Peg nodded. She sounded equally sure.

"It's a surprise!" cried Davey.

It certainly was that. I looked around at my family. "What's going on?"

"You've been working hard since you went back to Howard Academy full-time in January," said Sam. "I thought you could use a break."

"And with HA's spring break falling at just the right time," Bertie added, "Sam set it all up."

I swung my gaze her way. "You were in on this, too?"

"Of course."

"*Everybody* knew but me?"

"That's how a surprise works," Davey informed me. My son didn't add the words, *Well, duh,* but they were certainly implied. "You're going to Kentucky with Aunt Peg."

"But . . ." I sputtered. "Who's going to take care of things here?"

"Not me," said Davey. "I won't be here. I'm going camping with Dad."

Of course he was. The trip was all arranged. He and Bob were going to be hiking a portion of the Appalachian Trail. Davey had been excited about the expedition for weeks.

"So it will be just me and the munchkin," Sam said easily. He bounced his knee up and down and Kevin gurgled with laughter. "Not to mention various assorted Poodles. Surely you think I'm capable of handling that?"

"Of course, you're capable. . . ." I said weakly.

"So then what's the problem?" asked Aunt Peg.

"Nothing . . . I guess. It's just unexpected. Why am I always the last person to know these things?"

"Really, Melanie." Aunt Peg sniffed. "If only you would

pay more attention, we wouldn't always have to be bringing you up to speed."

The first answer that sprang to mind was not entirely civil. Wisely I kept my mouth shut.

"Besides," said Bertie, "you have to come."

"Oh?" I arched a brow at my duplicitous sister-in-law. I couldn't believe she hadn't told me about the plans that were being made behind my back. "Why is that?"

"I'm taking a lot of dogs on this trip. I'm going to need your help."

The very idea made me laugh. Bertie was a successful and accomplished professional handler with a full roster of happy clients. She was also talented, hardworking, and the most thoroughly competent person I knew. In any given situation—especially one that involved grooming, prepping, or handling show dogs—I was much more likely to need Bertie's expert assistance than the other way around.

"That's right," Frank agreed. He slid his hand over his wife's and gave her fingers a gentle squeeze. "I've been trying to convince Bertie to cut down on how much she's been doing and she's finally starting to listen to me. After this trip, she'll be sticking closer to home until . . ."

"Until?" The word slipped out before I had a chance to stop and think. Because all it took was one glance at Bertie's happy glow and Frank's proud expression to know what he was going to say.

"I'm going to have a baby sister!" Maggie shrieked.

"Or maybe a little brother," Bertie amended quickly. "We don't know yet."

Before she'd even finished speaking, I was already up out of my seat and running around the table to gather her into my arms for a hug. I knew that Bertie and Frank had been trying for more than a year. Now I felt like shrieking myself. "*When?*"

"Not 'til late September. It's still six months away."

"Even so," Frank interjected, "Bertie needs to be taking care of herself."

"Frank worries too much," said Bertie. "He would wrap me up in bubble wrap for the next half year if he could."

"I don't blame him." Sam set Kevin down, went to the sideboard, got out a bottle of port, and poured glasses all around.

"As I recall, Frank tried that during your first pregnancy," I mentioned.

"Yup." Bertie laughed. "It didn't work then, and it's not going to work now."

"And it shouldn't," said Aunt Peg. "Coddling isn't good for anyone."

As if Aunt Peg would know. She'd never coddled anyone in her life.

"Under the circumstances, I'd be delighted to help out," I said to Bertie.

"I figured you would," she replied. "We'll have a great time."

"I've brought you a book about horses," Aunt Peg said to me. "We've got three days before we leave. I expect you'll be up to speed on the subject by then."

Lucky Luna, I thought. The excitement of Bertie's announcement had driven all thought of Aunt Peg's new broodmare right out of my head.

"Why me?" I asked. I might have sounded a little plaintive.

"Who else?" Peg wanted to know. "I'll be busy judging. Bertie has her dogs to show. You're the one who's on vacation."

True, I thought, brightening. And the Bluegrass state was home to horse racing, Southern charm, and the best bourbon whiskey anywhere. Not only that but while late

March still felt like winter in Connecticut, in Kentucky it would be spring.

Bertie was right. This trip was going to be great.

My first view of Kentucky wasn't at all what I'd been expecting.

That might have had something to do with the fact that I'd just woken up. Still a bit groggy, I opened my eyes and gazed out the side window of Aunt Peg's minivan at a monochrome world of tall gray buildings and six-lane highways, all of it backed by a dusk-darkening sky.

Aunt Peg and I had left her house in Greenwich before dawn that morning, setting out on our cross-country jaunt with Faith bedded down comfortably on the backseat. Aunt Peg and I shared the driving and the navigating between us. Faith served as perfect companion, arbiter of disputes, and occasional music critic.

We had made the 750-mile trip from western Connecticut to central Kentucky in eleven hours. If you think that sounds fast, you've obviously never been in a car when Aunt Peg is driving. During the final leg of the trip, I had alternated between bracing myself against the dashboard and closing my eyes. Which was probably how I had fallen asleep.

Now I sat up straight, shook myself awake, and had another look around. It was still disappointing. We appeared to be on a beltway that circled downtown Louisville.

"Where are the horses?" I asked. "Where's the Bluegrass? This just looks like a city."

"It *is* a city," Aunt Peg replied. She glanced up at an approaching highway sign and abruptly switched lanes. Somewhere behind us, I heard a horn honk. "Louisville is the largest city in Kentucky. Three quarters of a million people live here."

I frowned. "I was expecting something different. More . . . rural. More scenic."

"You missed that part. You've been asleep since Cincinnati."

"Even so," I argued, "I thought there'd be horses. What about Churchill Downs? And the Kentucky Derby?"

"The Derby is only one day a year. And Churchill Downs isn't open for racing at the moment. Honestly, didn't you read that book I gave you?"

"The book was about broodmares and reproduction," I said. "It told me every single thing that could possibly go wrong when mares deliver foals and scared the bejeezus out of me. But it didn't educate me in the slightest about horse racing. If the horses aren't here, where are they?"

"Mostly at Keeneland, I'd expect. They're getting ready to start their spring meet in a few weeks."

"Where's Keeneland?"

Aunt Peg lifted a hand and jerked a thumb back over her shoulder. "East."

Well, that narrowed things down.

Maybe it would be easier if I just went back to sleep, I thought. Maybe I could arrange to sleep for two weeks and then wake up once again in a world where things made sense.

Behind me, Faith whined under her breath. I threaded an arm between the two front seats and reached back a reassuring hand. The Poodle licked my extended fingers gently, then settled with her head nestled between her paws. I heard her sigh softly.

Faith was getting older now. I could see the first signs of graying on her dark muzzle and she'd lost the abundant energy of her youth. Once Faith would have been the first Poodle to chase a ball or dive into a pond. But these days she was more content by my side.

This trip's duration had seemed like entirely too long a time for us to be apart. Faith had agreed; she'd been excited when I'd told her that she was coming with me. I hoped the excursion wouldn't turn out to be too hard on her.

"The Kentuckiana Dog Show Cluster takes place at the Kentucky Expo Center here in Louisville," Aunt Peg said. "Starting the day after tomorrow."

"I know that." I withdrew my hand from the backseat and folded it primly in my lap. By my calculations—aided by a glance at the GPS—we were less than ten minutes from our hotel, which was right next to the Expo Center.

"Most of the horse racing and breeding activities in Kentucky are centered around the Lexington area, which is sixty miles east of us. That's where the famous farms like Claiborne, Spendthrift, and WinStar are. It's also where Keeneland is located."

"And Lucky Luna?"

"She's there as well. In a little town called Midway. Anthony had her boarded year-round at a farm called Six Oaks. I gather an arrangement like that is not unusual where racehorses are concerned. Much of the Thoroughbred industry is supported by the money that comes from absentee owners."

"It's odd to think of owning a horse and never seeing it." I couldn't imagine not wanting to see my dogs.

"These horses aren't pets," Aunt Peg informed me. "Many of them are worth a great deal of money. Even those Thoroughbred owners for whom horse racing is a hobby, still have to treat it as a business. Their horses are investments. With the sums that are involved, they have to be."

Clearly Aunt Peg had been studying up on the subject.

"Tell me about Lucky Luna's farm," I said.

"Most of what I've learned so far I've gotten from their Web site. They appear to be a full-service Thoroughbred farm with facilities that cover more than a thousand acres of land. They board broodmares and raise foals. They consign horses to the various sales. They have half a dozen stallions standing at stud, and they even have their own training track for getting youngsters started."

"It sounds like quite a place."

"It should be." Aunt Peg slanted me a look. "I've seen Anthony's bills for Lucky Luna's care. Which I might add, are shortly to become my responsibility. For what he's been paying to keep that mare in hay and oats, a top specials dog could enjoy a lengthy career at the very highest levels."

"Ouch," I said. We were talking about real money now.

"Ouch, indeed," Aunt Peg muttered. "Clearly this isn't a business one wants to approach with blinkers on. Nor to be involved in without knowing all the facts first. Before we left home, I did as much research as I could on my own. But now it's time to call upon the experts and see what they have to say."

Excellent plan, I thought. Except for one thing.

"Do we know any experts?" I asked.

Aunt Peg nodded with satisfaction. "Eleanora Gates Wanamaker."

That got my attention in a hurry. I was quite familiar with Ellie Wanamaker's name. Over the years, I'd read about her Gatewood Kennels in numerous Poodle books and magazines. I had pored over the pedigrees of her twentieth century champions and top producers in *Poodles in America*. Like Aunt Peg, Ellie had had a career in Standard Poodles that spanned decades. Unlike Aunt Peg, she had disappeared from the show scene long before I first became involved.

"Eleanora Gates Wanamaker is still alive?" I said.

"Of course, she's alive." Aunt Peg snorted. "Why wouldn't she be?"

I thought about articles I'd read, and the various pictures I'd seen of Gatewood Poodles that had been born as early as the 1970s. Faith was related to one of Ellie's Poodles—a dog that appeared many, many generations back in her pedigree.

"Because she must be very old," I said.

"She's younger than I am," Aunt Peg snapped.

Oh.

I didn't even have to turn around and look. I knew that Faith was shaking her head.

"Where does Ellie Wanamaker live?" I asked in a small voice.

"That's *Miss* Ellie," Aunt Peg corrected. "I've never heard anyone refer to her any other way. I gather it's a Southern thing."

"Miss Ellie," I repeated, feeling thoroughly chastised. "Where will we find her and why does she know about horses?"

"She grew up on a farm in Midway not far from Six Oaks. Her family has been in the Thoroughbred business for generations. We have an appointment tomorrow afternoon to have a look at Lucky Luna, and I have no intention of showing up unprepared. We'll be meeting with Miss Ellie tomorrow morning."

"Good work," I said.

"Indeed." Aunt Peg sounded rather pleased with herself. "Hopefully by the time we arrive at Six Oaks, we will be well armed with information about what to expect. Miss Ellie is sharp as a tack. I'm quite certain she'll be able to tell us everything we need to know."

Chapter 3

There were plenty of signs for the Kentucky Expo Center and we found our hotel easily. Bertie and I were sharing a room, but for the time being Faith and I had the accommodations to ourselves. Since the shows didn't start until Thursday, Bertie wouldn't be arriving until the following afternoon. Her grooming space was already reserved and she was planning to call me when she got to the Expo Center so I could help her unload and get set up.

Meanwhile, Aunt Peg had our itinerary for Wednesday's excursion to the Lexington area planned down to the minute. In the space of a single day, she intended for us to explore central Kentucky, visit with Miss Ellie, meet Lucky Luna, check out the broodmare's farm, and ascertain the extent of her new responsibilities. It all sounded like a tall order to me, but I learned a long time ago never to underestimate Aunt Peg.

Besides, I was on vacation. Hadn't people kept telling me that? As far as I was concerned, Faith and I were just along for the ride.

The three of us set out early the next morning, heading east on 64 toward Lexington. To my surprise, the first thing Aunt Peg did was turn off her GPS.

"Miss Ellie gave me directions," she said. "She was very specific. We're to be sure to take the scenic route. She wanted us to see and enjoy what she called the very best part of her home state."

We turned off the highway just below Frankfort and drove the last ten miles of our journey on local roads. Miss Ellie's directions were perfect. They took us straight into horse country. My gaze swung back and forth avidly as I tried not to miss a thing. Here, finally, was the Kentucky I'd been expecting: a wide blue sky, lush green fields, and Thoroughbred farms whose size could be measured in miles rather than acreage.

And the horses! I saw gorgeous Thoroughbreds everywhere I looked. Plump mares grazed contentedly. Foals leapt and cavorted around them. Herds of yearlings flashed by, racing across wide pastures bordered by four-board double fences. Centuries-old stone walls marked the property lines between farms.

"Pin Oak," I said, reading the signs as they flashed by. "Ashford Stud. Lane's End. I've heard these names before."

"I should hope so," Aunt Peg replied. "They're some of the most important names in the business. I'm guessing that one of the reasons Miss Ellie wanted us to come this way was so that we would see that there are other possibilities in case we're dissatisfied with what we find at Six Oaks."

"You seem to have had a high opinion of Anthony Stone," I said. "Do you expect to be dissatisfied with the arrangements he made?"

Aunt Peg glanced at me across the front of the van. "That's the problem. I'm such a neophyte at this whole business that I have no idea what to expect. I *hate* that feeling."

Under normal circumstances, Aunt Peg was the one telling everyone else what to do. It occurred to me that this was the first time in our long association that I'd ever seen her confronted by something she knew little about and forced to operate outside her comfort zone.

Welcome to my world, I thought.

We came to a small intersection and passed by several more farms before abruptly entering a quaint residential neighborhood. “This must be Midway,” Aunt Peg said. “We’re only a mile or two from Miss Ellie’s house now.”

“I thought you said she lived on a farm.”

“No, I told you that she grew up on a farm. One that her family has owned for many years. But Miss Ellie lives in town now.”

Even with Aunt Peg slowing the minivan to the speed limit, it didn’t take more than a minute or two to drive through the entire area of downtown Midway. There were train tracks through the center street and only a single stop light. Commerce appeared to consist mainly of restaurants and antique shops, but I also saw a leather store, a shop filled with Irish goods, and a drugstore advertising a real soda fountain.

“Midway is halfway between Lexington and the state capital of Frankfort,” Aunt Peg told me as she turned off onto a side street. “That’s how the town got its name.”

“How is it that you know so much about the state of Kentucky and yet still maintain that your knowledge of horses is lacking?” I asked.

“Geography is easy.” Aunt Peg sniffed. “That can be learned from a book. Horses are living, breathing creatures. I’ve devoted most of my life to the study of dogs and I still find that I’m learning new things all the time. I would have to be very foolish indeed to think that I might be able to understand all the details and nuances of broodmare ownership simply by reading about it.”

And yet . . . she’d given *me* a book to read. I just thought I’d mention that.

Ellie Gates Wanamaker lived in a Victorian-style house

on an acre of land just east of downtown Midway. The backyard of the home was stoutly fenced with both boards and wire and as soon as Miss Ellie opened her front door, I saw the reason why. A loud, lively pack of Jack Russell Terriers came flying through the doorway and streaming down the front steps.

I counted four at a quick glance. There might have been more. It *sounded* like more. Terriers have a lot to say.

I was standing beside Aunt Peg's minivan about to open the sliding door to release Faith when the racing, scrambling, shin-high horde reached me. The Jack Russells swirled around my legs, jostling and bumping each other, as each one vied for access to the best new smells I had to offer.

Two of the small, sturdy dogs were smooth, and two were rough coated. All were white with tan or black markings. All were keen, nimble, and muscular. And loud. Did I mention loud?

Cautiously I slid the van door open a sliver and pressed my lips to the crack. "I think you'd better wait here," I said to Faith.

"What's that?" Miss Ellie called down from the porch. She was a wiry woman with sharply defined features and a pugnacious expression on her face. Her spiky gray hair looked like it hadn't seen a comb in days. "Do you have a dog in there?"

"We do," Aunt Peg replied as I slid the door shut.

"It must be a Standard Poodle." She looked to Aunt Peg for confirmation.

Peg nodded.

"Does she get along with other dogs?"

Aunt Peg nodded again. If not for the JRTs who'd apparently decided that I was their new best friend, my presence would have been entirely superfluous.

"Then what are you waiting for?" Miss Ellie demanded. "Get her out of there and bring her inside. What's the matter with you, wanting to leave that poor dog sitting in a car?"

"I was trying to be polite," I muttered under my breath. It didn't make the slightest bit of difference. No one was listening to me.

"Peg Turnbull, it's been entirely too long!" Miss Ellie came down the steps and pulled her old friend close for a hug. "Why haven't you come to visit me sooner?"

"Why haven't you invited me?" Aunt Peg retorted.

Miss Ellie sighed. "Life," she said. "It just gets in the way."

I slid the door back once again. Immediately the two terriers nearest the opening hopped their front feet up onto the ledge and had a look inside. Faith, ready to disembark, tipped her head downward. The three dogs touched noses. Tails wagged all the way around.

I took that as a good sign and hopped her out.

"Oh my," said Miss Ellie. "That's a pretty Standard. It's been a long time since I've seen a Poodle as nice as that one. One of yours?" she asked Peg.

"Aunt Peg bred her," I said, cutting in smoothly. "But Faith has been mine since she was a puppy."

The pack of Jack Russells finished introducing themselves to Faith and took off across the yard. Faith hesitated for the briefest moment—looking to me for permission, which was quickly granted—then went flying after them.

"That's a champion," Miss Ellie said. It was a statement, not a question.

"And a champion producer," I told her proudly.

Finally the woman wrested her gaze away from Faith long enough to acknowledge my presence. Miss Ellie looked me up and down briefly, then stuck out her hand. Her skin was worn and leathered. She had a grip like iron.

"You must be the niece," she said.

"I am. Melanie Travis. It's a pleasure to meet you."

"Oh?" She cocked a brow. "Why is that?"

A forthright question. Miss Ellie looked like a tough cookie; even so, I hadn't expected to be put on the spot quite so quickly. It occurred to me that Aunt Peg and Ellie Wanamaker might have more than a little in common.

"I've read about you and your dogs in *Poodle Variety,*" I said. "You had wonderful Standard Poodles."

Miss Ellie lifted a hand and waved it dismissively. "That was a long time ago."

"Not *that* long," said Aunt Peg. "I have fond memories of showing against you when you came to the East Coast for PCA and Westminster."

"Not just showing against me," Miss Ellie pointed out, "but also beating me every chance you got."

"Of course." Aunt Peg just laughed. "That goes without saying. Although it didn't happen nearly as often as I would have liked."

"It's been over a decade since I lost my last Poodle," Miss Ellie told us. "And now, as you can see, I find myself surrounded by a band of little terrorists."

The terriers in question had led Faith on a great swooping tour of the front yard and were currently busy sniffing beneath the bushes on the side of the house. I hadn't seen another car pass by in the five minutes we'd been there but I was keeping a wary eye out just in case. Faith knew better than to cross a road, but if those JRTs flushed a rabbit, I was betting they'd be long gone before any of us even had time to react.

Miss Ellie must have been thinking along the same lines. "Let's gather up that bunch and head inside," she said, starting up the front steps and whistling for the dogs to follow. "Otherwise the neighbors will start sticking their heads out and wondering what all the fuss is about. I try to convince myself that living in town is easier at my age but, oh, there are days when I still miss the farm."

Dodging the terriers who eddied around our legs, we followed Miss Ellie into the house. She led the way to a comfortable living room with a wide stone fireplace and a rounded bow window that looked out over a tree-shaded backyard. Faith had returned back to my side and remained there as Miss Ellie shooed the Jack Russells on through the kitchen and out the back door.

Most of the homes I visit have multiple photographs on display. Usually they're an assortment of win pictures from dog shows. But Miss Ellie's large collection of framed photographs was different than any other I'd seen. Only half of them featured Standard Poodles. The remainder were of sleek racehorses, shown winning at numerous race tracks, each one topped by a jockey clad in a distinctive set of green and white silks.

I turned to motion Aunt Peg over to have a look and saw that she was standing by the fireplace, studying an oil painting that hung above the mantelpiece. The equine portrait featured a single chestnut stallion. The horse standing in the foreground and staring proudly into the distance. Though the stallion was still, there was a quivering watchfulness about him. It wasn't hard to imagine him taking flight and racing away across the landscape.

"Richard Stone Reeves," Aunt Peg said when I walked over to join her. "It's lovely, isn't it?"

"Wonderful," I agreed. "Who is the horse?"

There was a small plaque affixed to the bottom of the frame but before either of us could read it, Miss Ellie reappeared carrying a silver tray with a crystal pitcher and three glasses.

"That's Cockerel," she said. "My father bred him nearly thirty years ago. He was the best two-year-old of his generation. Injured before he could run in the Derby, he came back and won several good races at four before retiring to the farm to stand at stud."

"He's gorgeous," I said.

Miss Ellie nodded. "He was indeed. For a time it looked as though he was going to be the one to reverse Daddy's fortunes. But like so many other good racehorses, he turned out to be not nearly as proficient at siring good runners as he was at running on the track himself."

She set the tray down on a low table between two plump couches. "Sweet tea?"

"I'd love some," said Aunt Peg. She's never turned down a sweet in her life.

"Me, too." I sat down across from Miss Ellie and took the glass she offered. Faith turned a small circle on the rug and lay down beside my feet.

"Now I want to hear all about this new broodmare of yours," Miss Ellie said once we were all settled. "I'm happy to find you in my own backyard, but I must confess your news came as quite a surprise."

"To me as well," Aunt Peg admitted. "I believe I explained the circumstances under which Lucky Luna became mine?"

"You did. I know Six Oaks Farm well and I'm acquainted with many of their clients, but I don't believe I've ever heard of a man named Anthony Stone. Did he own many mares?"

"Probably never more than a handful," said Aunt Peg. "At the time of his death, there was just the one left."

"That explains it," Miss Ellie said with a nod. "Here in central Kentucky, the same families have been around for a long time. Everybody pretty much knows everyone else. So I wondered whether I might have previously run across your benefactor. But it sounds as though he was an outsider."

"Anthony was from Boston," said Aunt Peg. "But I gather he had a rather nice mare nonetheless. I've done some reading about Lucky Luna's pedigree. The solicitor told me she was very well bred. Her sire is a horse named Malibu Moon?"

"Yes, indeed." Miss Ellie smiled. "That works. And her dam?"

"Lucky Mary, by Storm Bird."

"Nice cross. Did she race?"

"Ten starts with four wins."

"Stakes caliber?"

"I'm afraid not."

They might as well have been speaking Greek for all the sense the conversation made to me. Wisely I kept my mouth shut and sipped my tea. It was very sweet.

"Don't worry about that," said Miss Ellie. "A winning mare from a good family can still be a valuable commodity as a broodmare. Who is she in foal to?"

Aunt Peg consulted a sheaf of notes she had pulled from her purse. "The stallion has an odd name. Let me look to be sure. Ah, here it is. Medaglia D'Oro."

Miss Ellie clapped her hands happily. "Well done!"

Peg looked up. "That's a good thing?"

"It's a very good thing. Medaglia D'Oro is an excellent sire. And also a very handsome horse."

"Does that matter?" I asked, surprised.

"But of course."

I shook my head. "But we're talking about horse racing. So the fastest one wins, right? No matter what they look like. So why would it make a difference?"

"You're assuming that Peg is going to want to race Lucky Luna's foal when the time comes," Miss Ellie told me. "But doing that would necessitate a large commitment of time and money. Under the circumstances, she might want to consider other options."

"Like what?" Aunt Peg asked with interest.

"One possibility is that Lucky Luna's offspring could be

offered for sale to a racing home next year when it's a yearling. Peg, take a moment and think back. When you initially heard about this mare, I'll bet the very first thing you wondered about was her pedigree. Am I right?"

"You are," Aunt Peg agreed. "Of course I was curious."

"That's because after all your years with Standard Poodles, you approach things from a breeder's perspective. But there are plenty of racehorse owners who have no interest in that side of things. All they want are horses that are ready to go to the track and run."

"Surely not as yearlings," I said.

"No, but that's the age when the majority are sold. And a handsome, successful stallion sires the type of offspring who have all the qualities that capture the buyers' attention at the sales."

"I hadn't even considered something like that," Aunt Peg admitted. "I'm afraid I hadn't thought very far ahead at all. All I meant to do was come and assure myself that Lucky Luna was being well cared for until I can decide what to do with her."

"You had better start considering things like that," Miss Ellie said briskly. "This time of year there are all kinds of decisions to be made. Is Lucky Luna booked to a stallion for this year's breeding?"

"She hasn't even foaled yet," Aunt Peg protested. "She isn't due until next month."

"That doesn't matter in the slightest. The books for the popular stallions fill up quickly. Many are already closed. And if you want to maximize your investment—"

"Good Lord," said Aunt Peg. She didn't sound happy. "I thought I was going to need to buy Lucky Luna a warm blanket. Or inquire about the quality of her hay. But now you're telling me that a mare I haven't even seen yet is in need of a suitable mate and I'm already behind in procuring one?"

"You asked for my advice," said Miss Ellie. "And you'd

be foolish not to listen to it. Fortunes have been won and lost with horses. Not only that, but the Thoroughbred industry has a way of steamrolling right over beginners. I should hate for you to be one of its victims."

"I would, too," Aunt Peg replied. She pulled out a fresh sheet of paper and prepared to take notes. "Let's get to work."

Chapter 4

"We'll begin with some background," said Miss Ellie. "Six Oaks is an old farm with a venerable name and a long history of achievement in the Thoroughbred world, but the property itself is currently owned by a partnership of foreign investors."

As she spoke, one hand slipped down from her lap and dangled a few inches above the floor where she waggled her fingers invitingly. Faith's head lifted. She had a look.

"Go ahead," I said softly.

The Standard Poodle stood up, and padded around the table between the two couches. Reaching Miss Ellie's side, she lay down with her body pressed against the older woman's legs. Before Faith had even gotten settled on the floor, Miss Ellie's fingers were already tangling in her topknot. As she continued speaking, Miss Ellie was smiling happily.

"It's not unusual for farms that have been around for a long time to pass into new, more energetic hands. Sometimes a family's younger generation doesn't share the same passion for horses. Or sometimes poor decisions have been made and the money runs out. As you might imagine, maintaining these farms is a huge undertaking. Some of them employ hundreds of people. It's big business and it requires a firm hand at the helm."

"Aunt Peg told me that you grew up on a family farm," I said.

Miss Ellie nodded. "Green Gates Farm. You'll drive past it on your way to Six Oaks. The two farms are right next to each other. They also share a training track that sits on an area of common land between them."

"How long has your family owned the property?" Aunt Peg asked.

"The original piece of land was purchased by my great-grandfather, Ellwood Gates, in the late 1800s. That property later passed to his son, Bentley Gates, my grandfather, who became a successful tobacco farmer. He tripled the size of the acreage and then, as the family story goes, decided to indulge his penchant for gambling by investing in a few racehorses. Those first few soon grew into a sizable breeding and racing operation.

"Today the business of the farm is mostly devoted to Thoroughbreds, though my two cousins who share management of the property also grow corn and hay and have a herd of Black Angus cattle. You'll see the green gates in the fences as you go by. They were my grandfather's trademark."

"It must have been an incredible place to grow up," I said.

"It was, indeed." Even as Miss Ellie agreed with me, I thought I saw her stiffen slightly. She withdrew her hand from Faith and replaced it in her lap. "It was wonderful being able to be a part of it all."

And yet she had left it behind, I thought. I wondered why that was.

"My son, Gates Wanamaker, manages the yearling division at the farm," Miss Ellie continued. "So many young people these days can't wait to escape from a place like this. They all want to go to the big city. But working with horses and assuming his role in the family's heritage is the only life Gates ever wanted."

"Speaking of horses . . ." said Aunt Peg. "Perhaps you could tell me more about what to expect when I go to see Lucky Luna?"

"Certainly." Miss Ellie paused for a sip of sweet tea before continuing. "I'd imagine that an account manager at Six Oaks has been assigned to look after you. That person may give you the grand tour. It's a magnificent place so they will want you to see it and be wildly impressed. Then someone will take you to see your mare. I'm sure I don't have to give you any tips about that. You know what a good, healthy bitch in whelp looks like. Just size up."

I was half tempted to laugh but I was glad I hadn't when Aunt Peg nodded solemnly. She was taking this whole enterprise very seriously. "What sorts of arrangements should I be making for the delivery of Lucky Luna's foal?" she asked.

"None," Miss Ellie told her. "The farm will take care of everything for you. If you're satisfied with what you see today, there's no need to make any changes. And in fact with your mare this close to foaling, it's probably safer not to."

Aunt Peg jotted down a note. "And you mentioned something earlier about a stallion?"

"You'll have to check with your account manager about that. The mare's former owner may have already made the decision for you. In that case, a contract will have been signed and, once again, the farm will know what to do to get Lucky Luna bred back when the time comes."

"And if there is no contract?" Aunt Peg was nothing if not thorough.

"Come back and see me again. I may not be part of the industry anymore but I still keep abreast of what's happening and who's who. If necessary, you and I can go stallion shopping."

"That sounds like fun," I said. "Can I come, too?"

"Absolutely." Miss Ellie smiled at my enthusiasm, before turning back to Aunt Peg. "There's one more thing you need to know. When you visit Six Oaks, you may find that Kentuckians can be rather dismissive of people who aren't from around here."

"I may be an outsider," Aunt Peg said archly, "but as far as that farm is concerned, I'm also a paying client."

"Yes, but with just one mare, you're only a very small one. Which means that they may or may not bother to take you seriously. So let me tell you this. If anyone gives you any trouble, you let me know, and by God I'll come and straighten them out. The Gates name carries some weight around here. Nobody will dare talk sass to me."

The expression on Miss Ellie's face was fierce. So much so that I suddenly found myself hoping we'd have an excuse for her to come and shake things up. *A Southern grande dame on the rampage.* That would be fun to watch.

"Thank you for the offer," Aunt Peg replied, "but I'm sure we'll manage just fine. After all, Ellie dear, you're not the only one who knows how to fight her own battles."

"I have every faith in you, Peg. But you may find that things are very different here than you're used to back home. Just keep me in mind, that's all I'm saying."

Miss Ellie sent us on our way with directions to a tavern in Midway where we could stop for lunch before keeping our afternoon appointment at Six Oaks. No one minded when Faith accompanied us onto the outside terrace. The waiter even brought her a bowl of cold water and adjusted the umbrella over our table so that Faith could lie down in the shade.

"Miss Ellie is quite a character," I said to Aunt Peg as we split a loaded pizza between us.

"She always has been." Peg nodded. "Miss Ellie and I were dog show friends for years. But, sad to say, when she stopped showing Poodles we allowed ourselves to lose contact. I know she was having some problems back then. Her husband was ill and subsequently lost his battle with cancer. And I believe there was another family issue that was causing trouble as well."

Aunt Peg reached up and slid the last slice of pizza onto her plate. "That's the problem when your whole social life revolves the dog show community. When someone drops out for whatever reason, it's as if they just disappear. Nowadays people talk on Facebook or Twitter. But we didn't have those options then. I'm sorry I didn't try harder to stay in touch with Miss Ellie. Hopefully that's an omission I'll be able to rectify on this visit."

From downtown Midway, the drive to Six Oaks took only a few minutes. As Miss Ellie had indicated, we first passed her family farm with its white board fencing and distinctive green gates. Then the fences changed from light to dark and half a mile later we came upon a pair of high, stone gateposts, bracketing an ornate double gate. A polished copper sign announced that we had reached our destination.

Aunt Peg pulled into the entrance and paused before the tall gates. After a moment they swung slowly inward to reveal a long driveway that was bordered by a double row of mature oak trees. The road meandered between bountiful green pastures filled with sleek Thoroughbreds.

Off in the distance, on the other side of a rustic, double-arch bridge, I saw several low stone buildings. A group of barns was visible beyond that. The entire vista was breathtaking. Someone had obviously taken great care to ensure that each man-made element served to complement the charm of the beautiful landscape rather than detract from it.

"Whoa." I blew out a long breath. "*Lucky* Luna, indeed. This place is amazing."

Aunt Peg was less impressed. "Perhaps that explains the size of the bills I've been told to expect. Don't forget, Lucky Luna is a horse. All of this grandeur is lost on her."

"But not on visiting clients," I pointed out.

Aunt Peg merely snorted under her breath in reply.

A sign outside the first building we came to identified it as the farm office. Aunt Peg parked the minivan in the shade. We rolled the windows down halfway, and I dug a rawhide bone out of the glove compartment. We left Faith chewing on it happily and went to check things out.

Inside the office, a receptionist was sitting in a front room that had the look and feel of a gentlemen's library. Aunt Peg explained the nature of our visit and was told that someone would be along shortly to help us. I studied the equine art on the walls while we waited. Aunt Peg sat down in a leather club chair and thumbed through a glossy stallion brochure.

"It occurs to me that I might need this," she said after a minute. Aunt Peg looked over at the receptionist. "May I have it?"

"Of course," the woman replied. "That's why they're there."

As Aunt Peg was tucking the brochure into her purse, the office door opened and a woman in her early twenties with a bright smile and a brisk, energetic stride came hurrying inside. Her curly hair was gathered into a French braid that reached halfway down her back and she was dressed in what appeared to be the farm uniform: blue jeans, solid boots, and a navy blue polo short adorned with the SIX OAKS logo.

She looked at the two of us and immediately approached Aunt Peg with her hand extended. "Mrs. Turnbull? I'm Erin Sayre, the assistant broodmare manager. Ben Burrell, your account manager, was called away but he should be back shortly. In the meantime, he asked me to show you around. Welcome to Six Oaks Farm. It's a pleasure to meet you."

"It's lovely to meet you, too," Aunt Peg replied. "This is my niece, Melanie Travis, who's traveled with me to

Kentucky. We're both looking forward to making the acquaintance of my new mare."

"I can imagine," Erin said cheerfully. "If you'll come this way, I'll take you right to her. Is Lucky Luna your first Thoroughbred broodmare?"

"First and only," Aunt Peg told her. "This is my initial foray into horse ownership. I'm hoping the learning curve won't prove to be too steep."

Erin strode to the office door and held it open for us. "I'm sure it won't," she replied. "We at Six Oaks will be here to help you every step of the way. I know Ben Burrell will take great care of you. But if you have any questions before then, feel free to ask. That's why I'm here!"

Erin led us outside to a dark blue pickup truck with the farm logo painted on both doors. As I walked by, I snuck a look into Aunt Peg's minivan. Faith was still busy with her bone. She glanced up, flicked her tail up and down in acknowledgment, then went back to work. She'd be fine on her own until we returned.

"Do you mind riding in a truck?" Erin asked. "It'll be easier if I drive. You can leave your car here and I'll bring you back when we're finished."

"Young lady, I have ridden in far worse conveyances than this one." Aunt Peg appropriated the front seat and left me to scramble into the back. "This will do just fine."

"We're on our way to the broodmare division," Erin said as she pulled the pickup back onto the driveway. Another gate separated the barns from the front buildings. Like the one at the road, it opened when we idled in front of it. "Lucky Luna hasn't foaled yet this year. I assume you know that?"

Aunt Peg nodded.

"She's due on April fourteenth, but that's an estimate not an exact date. Normal gestation time varies a great deal in broodmares."

"The same is true in dogs," Aunt Peg said.

"Oh?" Erin glanced over. "Do you have many dogs?"

"I have bred and shown Standard Poodles for many years," Aunt Peg told her. "I gather that's why Anthony Stone bequeathed Lucky Luna to me."

"I didn't know Mr. Stone," Erin told us. "All I know is that he owned a lovely mare. I work with lots of broodmares and Lucky Luna is one of my favorites. I'm sure you'll like her."

She guided the truck into an empty space beside a big, U-shaped, cream-colored barn. Large stalls, lushly bedded with straw, had doors that opened into the interior of the barn and big open windows that faced the outside. Most of the stalls appeared to be empty.

"All of our horses spend as much time outside as possible," Erin said as she jumped down from her seat. "That's the way horses would live in nature and it's much healthier for them. The rest of the broodmares in this barn are turned out now. But of course we knew you were coming, so we kept Lucky Luna up. Here she comes now with Sergio."

In the time it had taken us to cross a small path and walk into the barn's wide courtyard, word that we'd arrived had already preceded us. A groom, neatly attired in an outfit that mirrored Erin's, was coming toward us leading a tall bay mare from the other end of the shed row.

Even from a distance, it was easy to see that the mare was in foal. Her wide, rounded belly extended outward on either side of her body and swayed slightly as she walked. Lucky Luna had a big white star on her red-brown face and a kind look in her dark eyes. Those two facts, both evident at first glance, comprised the entire extent of my equine knowledge.

"Oh, she *is* pretty," Aunt Peg said as Sergio and Lucky Luna drew near. "And big, too."

"Sixteen one," Erin told us. Seeing my blank look, she added. "Horses are measured in hands, and a hand equals four inches. So Lucky Luna is sixty-five inches at the withers." She approached the mare and brushed a spot at the base of Lucky Luna's neck with her fingertips. "That would be here."

I nodded and tried to look more knowledgeable than I was. I don't think I had anybody fooled, least of all Lucky Luna.

The mare regarded me with a look of benign indifference as Sergio brought her around and posed her so her left side was facing us. He stopped Lucky Luna in place, and rocked her back and forth gently, until he was satisfied with the position of her feet. Then he stepped back out of the way to let us admire her.

"Not unlike stacking a Poodle," said Aunt Peg. Having watched the exercise with interest she sounded pleased.

"Stacking?" Erin repeated.

"Positioning the legs just so," I told her. "So that they can optimally be seen by a judge at a dog show. Show dogs learn to take a pose and hold it."

"Horses, too." Erin laughed. "At least ones that go through the sales ring often enough."

That was the second time that day someone had mentioned Thoroughbred sales. As Aunt Peg walked around the mare to take a look at her from all sides, I asked Erin how often they were held.

"All the time," she told me. "Keeneland and Fasig-Tipton are the two big sales companies in Lexington. In the spring, we have two-year-old in-training sales. In the summer and early fall, people buy and sell yearlings. In the winter, breeding stock changes hands. It's not unusual for one horse to be bought and sold several times throughout the course of its life. There's serious money to be made at the sales. Sometimes even more than you might make by racing."

"She has a lovely shoulder, doesn't she?" Aunt Peg asked.

Erin nodded in agreement. "Good bone, too. Lucky Luna is a beautifully balanced mare. You can really see her sire in her. If she has a foal that looks anything like she does, I'm sure you'll be very pleased with it."

"I'm pleased already," said Aunt Peg, stepping in closer. "May I touch her?"

"Of course," Erin replied. "She's yours. And she's a very friendly mare. They aren't all like that, but Lucky Luna is a pleasure to work around. Right, Sergio?"

"That's right."

As Peg approached Lucky Luna, Sergio slid his hand up the lead rope and tightened his hold. The precaution proved unnecessary. When Aunt Peg stroked the mare's soft neck, Lucky Luna simply flicked an interested ear in her direction, but didn't move otherwise.

"I think I'm in love," Aunt Peg said after a minute. She laughed in happy surprise. "I can't say that I expected that."

Erin just smiled. "As soon as you told me you had dogs, I knew it would happen. Horse people and dog people are all the same."

"Lucky Luna certainly looks as though she's been very well cared for," Aunt Peg said as she stepped back again. "I'm sure there are questions I should be asking, but right now I am perfectly content just to stand here and enjoy looking at her."

"That's the good thing about having your mare under the management of a farm like Six Oaks," Erin told her. "We have all the experts you need right here. Vet care, bloodstock advice, day-to-day care, and monitoring; we take care of everything for you. All you have to do is relax and enjoy the fun of owning a very nice mare. When we're finished, I'll take you back to the office and you can sit down with Ben to go over any remaining details."

"Aunt Peg was told that she might need to find a stallion to breed Lucky Luna to this year?" I asked. "Do you know anything about that?"

"I do, actually, and it's already been taken care of. The previous owner booked Lucky Luna last fall to a stallion at Lane's End named Candy Ride. We have the signed contract on file in the office. I assume that meets with your approval?"

"Should it?" asked Aunt Peg. She clearly had no more idea who Lucky Luna's potential suitor was than I did.

"Absolutely," said Erin. "Candy Ride is a very good horse and a super choice for your mare."

"Excellent," Aunt Peg declared. "One less thing to worry about."

I stared at her in surprise. Usually Aunt Peg wasn't happy unless she was micromanaging everything and everyone. So this was a change, and a pleasant one at that. Maybe this trip to Kentucky would be good for her. Maybe it would be good for both of us.

After all, it was spring break. One could only hope.

Chapter 5

"I'm a little disappointed," I said when Sergio had taken Lucky Luna back to her stall and the three of us were walking back to Erin's truck.

"Why is that?" asked Erin, pausing. "Was there something else you wanted to see?"

"Yes." I nodded. "Racehorses."

"You just saw Lucky Luna," Aunt Peg said. "She was a racehorse."

"Sure, once upon a time. But now she's retired. And pregnant. So she doesn't really count. I came to Kentucky thinking that I was going to see *real* racehorses and so far I haven't seen a single one."

Erin was smiling by the time I finished speaking. "I can help with that," she told me. "Hop in."

Erin started up the truck, and headed off in a different direction than the way we'd come. The new road conveyed us past yet more fields and farm buildings before finally coming to an end on the far side of the property.

"Here we are," Erin announced. Stopping the truck on the crest of a small rise, she lifted a hand and swept it wide. "Is that what you wanted to see?"

It was indeed. In the hollow below us sat a three-quarter-mile racetrack with a pristine dirt surface and waist-high white rails that glistened softly in the afternoon sun. As we watched, a trio of horses went galloping by. Their legs moved gracefully in unison. Long tails streamed out behind them. Three riders bobbed gently up and down in their saddles.

"This is the Six Oaks training track," Erin said. She put the truck back in gear and coasted down the shallow hill to a parking lot beside an airy, center-aisle barn. "It's where the young horses get started before they're ready to go to a real track, and where older campaigners get legged back up after a break. Most of the work usually gets done in the mornings, but with the Keeneland two-year-old in-training sale coming up, we have lots of buyers stopping by to have a look at the horses we'll be offering, so there are youngsters on the track at all hours. Would you like to get out and have a look?"

"I'd love to." I didn't even wait for the truck to stop moving before opening my door and scrambling out. "Can we go over near to the rail?"

"Sure, if you like."

"I don't want to disturb anyone."

"Don't worry about that," said Erin. "No one will even notice us."

She and Aunt Peg followed me across the grassy verge between the training barn and the track. Off to one side was another big field. This one was filled with curious yearlings. At least a dozen of the young Thoroughbreds had lined up along the fence to observe the activity on the track.

"I guess we're not the only ones who want to watch," I said with a laugh.

"Not even close," Erin agreed, but she was gazing in the other direction. "Look at the gap."

She gestured down the track and I saw an opening in the rail where horses could enter and exit the oval. Clustered nearby were several dozen observers. Some were talking, others were hanging over the rail. One man was videotaping the proceedings.

"Six Oaks shares this training track with a neighboring farm and it looks as though both farms are entertaining visitors today," Erin said, shading her eyes to have a look. "It's a full house. But we should be fine over here."

Our placement was better than fine, it was amazing.

As we approached the track's outer rail, another pair of young Thoroughbreds came thundering toward us. By comparison, the previous group had been loafing along at an easy pace. These two meant business. Both horses' legs pumped like pistons. Their riders sat motionless, hovering low over bowed necks. The two young horses, moving together, were the embodiment of power and finesse. Their hoofbeats pounded a loud tattoo as the pair went flying past us and down the stretch.

"Wow," I said on an exhale. My head whipped around to follow the action as the Thoroughbreds went by. "That's incredible."

"Isn't it?" Erin's eyes tracked the horses around the remainder of oval just like mine did. "I could stand here all day and watch them do that."

"Me, too," I agreed.

Aunt Peg had a question. "Is there a significance to the color of the cloths beneath the saddles? The first group all had yellow. This group was wearing green."

"You have a sharp eye," said Erin. "Most people wouldn't even notice that."

"Aunt Peg notices *everything*," I told her. The two colts were now on the far turn. Their riders were standing in their stirrups. They appeared to be pulling up. "Just so you know."

"I'll consider myself warned," Erin replied with a smile, before turning back to Aunt Peg. "Like I said, Six Oaks shares the use of this track with our neighbor, Green Gates. They breed and race Thoroughbreds just like we do. Actually they're one of our oldest competitors in the industry. But for the purposes of owning and maintaining a track, it makes sense for us to work together. The first group of horses you saw, the ones wearing yellow saddle cloths, are Six Oaks horses. The second pair, wearing green, come from next door."

"We've heard of Green Gates Farm," I said. "Aunt Peg and Ellie Wanamaker are old friends."

Erin's face lit up. "You know Miss Ellie? Isn't she great? That woman is a powerhouse. I only hope that I have half her energy when I'm her age."

"We just saw Miss Ellie this morning," Aunt Peg replied. "We stopped at her house in Midway on our way here."

"Oh," said Erin. Her smile faded.

"Is that a problem?" I asked.

"No, of course not. I mean, not really."

"But?" I prodded.

"I hope Miss Ellie didn't try to convince you to move Lucky Luna over to her family's farm. She's a wonderful mare and we love having her here."

"She did nothing of the sort," Aunt Peg said stoutly.

No, she hadn't, I realized. That omission hadn't even occurred to me earlier. But now I found myself wondering why Miss Ellie *hadn't* put in a good word for her family farm.

"That's a relief," said Erin.

We spent the next twenty minutes watching the activity on the track. It was all interesting to me. Horses came and went from the training barn, some of them singly, others in small groups. A few merely trotted around the well-cushioned oval, but most were galloping. Some, like the pair we'd seen earlier, appeared to be working at a fast rate of speed.

"They'll take a break now for track maintenance," Erin told us when the last set of horses was finished. "Have you seen enough?"

"Plenty," I said. "That was great. Thank you so much for showing it to us."

"You're welcome," she replied. "It was fun for me, too. I spend my days at the broodmare division, and I don't get to come to this side of the farm nearly enough."

Erin's truck was parked on the other side of the barn. As we approached the building a handler exited through its wide door, leading a fractious young Thoroughbred on a leather shank. Two men disengaged themselves from a group of people who'd been standing at the gap. The pair followed the chestnut colt to a level spot nearby where a pea stone–lined path formed a small walking ring. There, the handler posed the horse in much the same manner that Lucky Luna had been presented to us earlier.

Erin continued walking but Aunt Peg's steps slowed, then stopped altogether. It was probably reflex on her part. Once a judge, always a judge. She took a long look at the colt.

Standing several feet away and with their backs to us, the two men examined the colt together. Both appeared to be closer to Aunt Peg's age than mine. One man was tall and distinguished looking, with perfect posture and thinning gray hair that was precisely styled. The second man was wearing a ball cap pulled low over his face. He had a brawny build and sinewy arms, which he was using to gesture expansively as he spoke. I couldn't hear what was being said, but I guessed from their body language that the shorter man was engaged in pointing out the colt's merits while the other man leaned in and listened with interest.

Annoyed at being asked to stand still, the chestnut snorted and stamped his foot impatiently. Then he shook his neck from side to side and snaked out his head in a sudden burst of movement. Teeth bared, he aimed a quick nip at his handler's arm.

I gasped softly under my breath, but the handler barely reacted at all. Instead he simply flicked the end of the leather shank in the direction of the colt's nose and nimbly sidestepped the intended strike. Then, having obviously heard my quick intake of breath, the handler looked over at me and winked before turning his attention back to the horse in hand.

Absorbed by the chestnut's antics, it took me a moment to realize that a second handler had also left the barn and was now heading in our direction leading a muscular bay colt. While the chestnut was long-limbed, high-headed, and fiery, the newcomer looked plain by comparison. Striding along sedately beside his handler, the bay walked into the expected pose at the other end of the path, then dropped his head and pricked his ears politely.

The two men watched the second colt approach. Then they moved toward him for a closer look. The shorter man began to gesture again. Now that they were facing us, I could hear snatches of their conversation. The tall man was asking questions. The shorter one was mostly looking at the bay colt and shaking his head.

Erin, who'd gotten halfway to the truck before realizing she'd left Aunt Peg and me behind, had come circling back to find us. "Shall we?" she asked.

"Sure," I agreed. "Sorry to hold you up. It was just interesting to see the horses close up."

Once again I started to follow Erin away. Aunt Peg, however, was still looking back and forth between the two colts. She stayed where she was.

"He's recommending the wrong horse," she said.

I slammed on the brakes and pivoted back. "Shhh!"

"Don't shush me. I have something to say. That man . . . the one in the cap. He's recommending the wrong horse."

"How could you possibly know that? All these horses look alike."

Aunt Peg slanted me a look. "I remember a time when you said the same thing about Standard Poodles."

"Yes," I hissed under my breath. "And it took me a whole year to learn differently. You've only been in Kentucky for two days."

"That doesn't matter in the slightest. One either has an eye for a good animal or one doesn't. Form needs to follow function. A sound horse is like a sound dog; both are bred to perform. Surely you can see that."

"I hope you're joking," I muttered.

"Hardly. Take a good look at those two young Thoroughbreds. They're nothing alike at all. For starters, the bay is a better mover."

"How do you know?" I asked incredulously. "All we've seen them do is walk out here from the barn."

The expression on Aunt Peg's face was withering. "We watched those two colts gallop on the track earlier."

"We did?" That was news to me.

"Yes, we did. They were racing side by side. Don't you recognize them?"

Not a chance, I thought. These two looked more or less the same to me as all the others I'd seen go by.

"Aunt Peg, we have to go," I said in a low tone. "I'm sure the guy doing the talking over there is a horse expert."

"Then he should know that while the chestnut is more impressive at first glance, the bay is ultimately the better colt," she retorted.

And once again, Aunt Peg was back to micromanaging the world. I should have known that the brief respite wouldn't last.

"Excuse me."

I looked up. To my horror, I saw that the man in the ball

cap, the one whose opinion Aunt Peg had just been disparaging, was coming over to join us. I hoped he hadn't heard what we were saying.

"Who are *you?*" he demanded.

Yup. I swallowed a sigh. He'd heard us all right.

Aunt Peg straightened her shoulders. She drew herself up to her full height, a shade under six feet. Then she gazed down her nose imperiously. Usually I'm the one who's the recipient of that shriveling look. But under the circumstances, it didn't make me feel any better to see it aimed in another direction.

"I'm Margaret Turnbull," she said.

"And what do you know about racehorses?"

"I'm sorry!" Abruptly Erin reappeared. She insinuated herself between Aunt Peg and the man and asked, "Is there a problem?"

"No," I said hastily. "No problem at all. We were just leaving. Right, Aunt Peg?"

"I don't think—" she began.

I grabbed her arm and cut her off. "Yes, you do. In fact sometimes you think too much. But not today. Today we're not going to share our opinions with anyone. Are we, Erin?"

Looking baffled, Erin sputtered, "No?"

"Good answer," I told her.

I pulled on Aunt Peg's arm. And got no response. She just stood there like a large, unmovable mountain. The second time I tried a yank *and* a glare. If I had to make a third attempt to get her moving, I swear I was going to kick her.

Fortunately it didn't come to that. With Erin on one side and me on the other, we finally succeeded in hustling Aunt Peg back to the truck. To add to the ignominy of the situation, when I glanced back I saw that the handler who'd winked at me previously was now laughing at our predicament. Just perfect.

We'd barely gotten our doors closed before Erin had the truck in gear. She spun the vehicle around and aimed it back up the hill. Within moments, the track and the training barn had receded in the distance.

Then she looked at the two of us and asked, "What happened back there?"

"It was just a small misunderstanding," I said.

"My foot!" Aunt Peg harrumphed.

"Something's the matter with your foot?" Erin sounded dismayed. She leaned over and had a look. "Did you get stepped on by a horse? Dammit, I should have been paying more attention."

And thus we descended from mere ignominy into total farce.

"Aunt Peg's foot is fine," I said. "It's her mouth that's the problem."

As usual, I thought. It didn't seem necessary to voice the thought aloud.

"Who was that man?" Aunt Peg asked. "The one in the ball cap."

"His name is Billy Gates," Erin said. "He and his cousin are co-owners of the farm next door."

I stifled a small groan. This day was just getting better and better.

"And what was he doing back there?"

Erin shrugged. "It looked like he was trying to sell a horse."

"The *wrong* horse," Aunt Peg said firmly.

"Excuse me?"

Of course Erin sounded surprised, I thought. She didn't know Aunt Peg nearly as well as I did.

"And the other man," Aunt Peg continued. "Who was he?"

"I've never seen him before," Erin replied. "He's probably a client from out of town who's here to shop at the sale. Judging by what we saw, I'd guess that Billy is his bloodstock agent. Billy probably picked out a few nice colts for the client to look at ahead of time."

"I heard Mr. Gates tell the other man that the chestnut was the better colt."

Aunt Peg was like a Labrador with a tennis ball. She just couldn't let it go.

"Then he probably *was* the better colt," I said. Leaning up from the backseat, I looked across at Erin. "Wasn't he?"

"I don't know," she replied. "I wasn't paying that much attention."

"Aunt Peg doesn't know either," I said. "But that's never stopped her from having an opinion."

"I may be new to horses," Aunt Peg told me, "but I do understand the make and shape of a good, useful animal. It has to do with balance, and proportion, and a pleasing blend of parts. The chestnut might have been flashier, but the bay colt was an athlete."

"Even if that's true," I said, "you shouldn't have butted in."

I looked to Erin for support. After a moment, she nodded.

"Someone had to say something!" Aunt Peg insisted.

Never mind about the Labrador. Aunt Peg was more like a Bulldog, tenacious and stubborn. And apparently never wrong.

I supposed there was a bright side. At least we'd made our escape before Billy Gates had had us thrown out.

"You're probably glad we don't visit often," I said to Erin.

She turned and flashed me a quick grin. "Not at all. Most days are pretty routine around here. It never hurts to shake things up a bit."

"My sentiments exactly," said Aunt Peg. She sounded very pleased with herself.

So help me, I wish I'd kicked her when I had the chance.

Chapter 6

Erin drove us back to the farm's office and dropped us off in the small parking lot out front. I was sure she heaved a sigh of relief as she drove away and left us behind. Aunt Peg headed into the building where Ben Burrell was waiting for her. I hurried over to the minivan where I'd left Faith.

As I approached, I heard the sound of a sharp whine through the van's half-open window. Wounded censure, Standard Poodle-style. I deserved the rebuke. When we'd left earlier, I hadn't realized that we'd be gone for so long.

A second later, Faith's head popped up into view. Her long muzzle pushed out through the slender opening. Her tail was wagging so hard that her whole body undulated with delight. She woofed softly under her breath.

"I know, I'm sorry." Quickly I slid the door open. Then I climbed onto the seat and gathered the big Poodle into my lap. "That was all my fault."

Faith tipped her head back and gave me a look that was easy to read. *I know that,* she said.

As usual, my Poodle and I were in perfect agreement.

I was still sitting in the backseat of the minivan half an hour later when Aunt Peg emerged from the office. Faith's long, warm body was draped across my lap. My arms looped around her neck. Her head angled upward so that her muzzle rested in the crook of my shoulder.

"You baby that dog," Aunt Peg said with a snort as she climbed into the driver's seat.

As if that was a bad thing.

"You're just jealous that you didn't bring along a Poodle of your own," I told her.

Aunt Peg harrumphed under her breath, but she didn't disagree.

When we reached the outskirts of Louisville, I took out my phone and called Bertie. She had left Connecticut very early that morning, which meant that she should be arriving soon. If Bertie was almost here, I figured I'd have Aunt Peg drop me off at the Expo Center rather than going back to the hotel.

"Hey, it's me," I said when Bertie picked up. "Where are you?"

"Almost done," she replied.

"Done what?"

"Unloading. Setting up. I got in early and I'm finishing up at the Expo Center now."

I sat up straight. Jostled to one side, Faith exhaled a sigh of protest. I resettled her and frowned into the phone.

"What do you mean 'finishing up'? You were supposed to call me. I was going to come and help."

"About that," said Bertie.

"Yes?"

"I don't actually need your help."

"Of course you do. You said you did. You're pregnant, remember?"

"Oh please." Bertie laughed. "As if I could forget."

"Precisely!" I announced with satisfaction.

"Mel, I've been managing this business all by myself for years."

"I know that."

"Including during my last pregnancy," she pointed out.

When I'm pregnant, all I want to do is sleep. And wear stretchy clothes and no makeup. Not Bertie. As I recalled, she'd sailed through her previous pregnancy with all the aplomb of Helen racing triumphantly across the Aegean Sea to Troy.

"Yes, but—"

"I'm pregnant, not incapacitated."

To add insult to injury, I could hear noises in the background. It sounded as though Bertie was stacking crates while we talked. Me? All I was doing was sitting on a seat and holding a dog.

"It's a perfectly normal condition," she added. "Not only that, but it's barely twelve weeks. I'm hardly pregnant at all."

"That's not funny," I said. "If you don't need my help, what am I doing in Kentucky?"

"Enjoying your vacation? Taking a break? Having a good time? All of the above?"

True enough. Even so, I refused to be mollified.

"You set me up," I said.

"Actually Sam did that. And Peg. It was their idea. My pregnancy was just a convenient excuse."

"Wonderful," I muttered.

"So we're good, right?" asked Bertie. "I'll be done here soon. See you back at the hotel!"

The connection ended. I tucked the phone back in my pocket. Then I sat and stared at the back of Aunt Peg's head. She didn't turn around. My aunt, who could probably navigate New York City traffic and knit an argyle sweater at the same time, studiously kept her eyes on the road ahead.

"I feel manipulated," I said.

I saw Aunt Peg's smirk in the rearview mirror. "We wouldn't do it if you didn't make it so easy," she told me.

* * *

Bertie was right about pregnancy not slowing her down. With a full string of dogs to feed and exercise before the show started, she was up and out of the hotel room at sunrise the next morning. Aunt Peg would be judging half the breeds in the Non-Sporting Group on this first day of the dog show cluster, but since her duties didn't begin until nine A.M., she, Faith, and I followed along at a more reasonable hour.

"I have a surprise for you," Aunt Peg said as we made the short drive over to the Expo Center.

Of course she did. I should have seen the announcement coming. It was how most of my days started when I was with Aunt Peg.

"After we left last night, I called Miss Ellie to tell her about our visit to Six Oaks."

"That's hardly a surprise."

Aunt Peg slanted me a look. "Shush and let me talk. After Miss Ellie and I discussed Lucky Luna, we started talking about Poodles."

Again, I thought, not a surprise.

"It turns out that she hasn't been to a dog show in more than a dozen years."

Now *that* was unexpected.

"How very odd," I said. "Especially for someone who was once so involved in the sport. When Miss Ellie stopped breeding Standard Poodles, did she apply for a judge's license?"

That was the direction many former exhibitors chose when they were ready to cut back on breeding or handling. It was an excellent way to put years of hard-won knowledge to good use. It was also a means of giving back to the sport which was a lifelong passion for many of its participants.

"Not that I'm aware of," Aunt Peg replied. Which basically meant no.

"How come?"

She paused at the kiosk, waved her parking pass, and

then pulled through to the lot. "I don't know the answer to that. Perhaps you should ask her yourself."

"Are we going back to Lexington later?"

I had seen Aunt Peg's schedule. She had a full day's slate of dogs to judge. I wondered when we were going to fit in such a trip.

"Not at all. In fact, that's my surprise. Miss Ellie is coming here to the dog show." Aunt Peg smiled with satisfaction. "Mind you, it took some convincing on my part. At first she seemed quite reluctant to join us. For some reason Miss Ellie seems to think that she won't fit in with the current dog show crowd."

"Nonsense," I said.

"That's precisely what I told her. Ellie Gates Wanamaker was a fixture in the Midwestern dog community for many years. I'm sure at least some of her old friends will be here. Not only that but the entry in Poodles is enormous. She's bound to enjoy watching the judging."

Listening to our conversation from the backseat, Faith heard a familiar word. She lifted her head and cocked an ear inquiringly.

"Other Poodles," I told her. "Not you." As an unentered dog, Faith would be spending most of the day tucked inside a large crate at Bertie's setup.

"So now you won't be at loose ends all day while Bertie and I are busy working." Aunt Peg found an empty parking spot around the back of the building near the exhibitor's entrance. She pulled the minivan into it. "Instead I've found you a way to make yourself useful. You will have the rare privilege of escorting Miss Ellie around the dog show."

Loose ends, indeed, I thought. I should be so lucky. Despite what Bertie had said, I'd still been planning to offer her my services. Not only that, but I'd been hoping to watch the Poodle judging as well.

On the other hand, useful people were Aunt Peg's favorite kind. And spectating at the Poodle ring would be even more interesting with Miss Ellie by my side. Indeed, it occurred to me that perhaps I should thank Aunt Peg for the vote of confidence.

I never got the chance. As soon as the three of us stepped inside the large building, Aunt Peg was all business. "I have to go check in," she told me. "You'll want to keep yourself available. I told Miss Ellie to call you as soon as she arrives." And then she was gone.

Faith and I paused at the edge of the cavernous room to get our bearings. Even though I had never been to this particular venue before, the large pavilion already looked and felt familiar. Nearly all dog shows share a similar order and pattern of organization; and the vast hall where the show was being held appeared very much as I'd expected it to.

Twenty-two rubber-matted rings were arranged in back-to-back rows down the middle of the room. A wide aisle had been left free around the block of rings. Exhibitors would congregate there as they awaited their turns in the ring; spectators could use the space to pull up chairs and watch their favorite breeds.

Behind that busy area were the vendors' booths, offering everything from dog supplies to canine artwork and jewelry. Around the hall's perimeter was a narrow corridor available for grooming. Another larger, lighter grooming area filled the handlers' room next door.

Casual dog show attendees think that what happens in the show rings—who gets awarded what ribbon, who gets their picture taken when it's all over—is all that matters. But exhibitors know better. The amount of time that dogs spend being judged is miniscule compared to the hours that are devoted to pre-ring preparation. And much of that time is spent in the handlers' area.

There, exhibitors spend the day grooming, gossiping,

and hanging out with friends—all while sizing up the competition. By the time the judging arrives, it's not unusual for experienced exhibitors to be well aware of where they stand in the day's hierarchy of entries. The judge's opinion merely becomes confirmation of what they already knew—or at least suspected.

The action in the show ring might be the face of a dog show, but the grooming area is its heart. So that was where Faith and I went first.

There's something about the early morning buzz of energy at a show that always makes my senses tingle. People and dogs alike are busy. Everyone has a place to be and a job to do. But there's also a special zing in the air. Every dog show is a new adventure. And now, even though I wasn't showing myself, I couldn't wait to get started.

Faith's show days are long behind her but she remembered the drill. Head up and tail wagging as she took in the pavilion's sights and sounds, the Standard Poodle trotted along happily at my side. When I paused at the entrance to the handlers' room, looking around to see where the Poodles were set up, it was Faith who seemed to know, almost instinctively, which direction to head.

Or maybe she just smelled the hairspray.

The jumble and clutter of the grooming room was as familiar as it was welcoming. Exhibitors piled their crates on top of each other, nudged their rubber-matted grooming tables into the closest possible proximity, and left only slender aisles between setups. Tack boxes balanced on top of coolers. Storage space was any available crevice. The low hum of dozens of blow dryers served as customary background noise.

Everyone likes to be surrounded by friends, and dog show exhibitors tend to cluster by breed in the grooming area. So as soon as I spied a trio of Miniature Poodles standing on a row of rubber-matted tables, I knew we were going the right way. A moment later, Bertie came into view. Enviably statuesque with long, fiery red hair, my sister-in-law wasn't hard to spot—even in the midst of all this canine chaos.

Years earlier, when Bertie and I had first met, she'd been near the beginning of her handling career. Struggling to build a name for herself and to make a living, Bertie had had to accept any handling assignment that was offered. Now, however, she'd reached the point where she could afford to pick and choose among the opportunities that were presented to her.

Like most successful professional handlers, Bertie specializes in those breeds whose looks and traits she finds most appealing. My sister-in-law has always had an affinity for the Corgis, Shelties, and Shepherds of the Herding Group. But no one related to Aunt Peg could resist the lure of the Poodle breed for long.

Not that Bertie had ever had a great deal of choice in the matter. As I recalled, Aunt Peg had simply nudged the handler under her ample wing, then set about teaching Bertie all there was to know about presenting the three varieties of Poodles to Aunt Peg's own impeccable standard.

Considering that I'd had a several year head start on a similar education, you might think that I'd have been able to offer Bertie some pointers as well. But while I still struggled to scissor lines that were smooth as glass, or to spray up a topknot so that it looked entirely natural while standing straight up in the air, Bertie had effortlessly absorbed every nugget of information that Aunt Peg offered and then deftly gone on to create stylish trims that were all her own.

I have no idea how she accomplished that. In fact, if I hadn't liked Bertie so much I might have been a little bit resentful about it. Possibly even more than a little.

Today, however, the fact that Bertie had added Poodles and several other Non-Sporting breeds to her roster made my life easier. Not only did it mean that I knew where to look for her, it also ensured that she would be grooming near my great dog show friends, top Poodle handler Crawford Langley and his assistant, Terry Denunzio.

"Thank God you're here!" Bertie said as Faith and I approached.

Alarmed by the unexpected greeting, I quickly scooted Faith into an empty, floor-level crate. Snapping the latch shut behind her, I straightened and held out my empty hands, ready to go to work.

"What's the matter?" I asked. "Am I late? What do you need?"

Bertie had an apricot Mini Poodle lying on the table in front of her. She was line brushing through its wispy coat, the first stage of preparation for the ring. Now she leaned across the tabletop so that her lips were only inches from my ear.

"It's Crawford," she whispered.

"Crawford?" I was so surprised that I repeated his name out loud without thinking.

The handler was standing at the other end of the next setup. Though he was currently facing away from us, I'd suspected for years that Crawford had eyes in the back of his head.

"Shhh!" Bertie snapped. "Not so loud! He'll hear us."

"What's the matter with Crawford?" I whispered back, casting him a quick glance. He and I had been mates for years. I hoped it was nothing serious.

"He is driving me insane." Bertie grabbed my arm and squeezed it, hard. "You have got to do something. Because if this keeps up, I swear I'm going to have to kill him."

Chapter 7

Pregnancy hormones. Surely that was the problem. There was no other way to explain Bertie's outburst.

Crawford Langley was one of the first people I had met when I became involved in the dog show world. He enjoyed Elder Statesman status in the Poodle community, having reigned for years as one of its premier professional handlers. Crawford presented his Poodles in the show ring with an enviable mix of talent and flair. He knew how to make a good dog look better than it was, and he could make a great dog unbeatable.

Crawford was two decades older than I was, and it had taken us some time to become comfortable with one another. The handler was dignified and charming, and he always knew the right thing to say. In short, we had little in common beyond our mutual love of dogs. But beneath Crawford's reserved exterior was a man who cared deeply about his friends, and I was honored to count myself as one of them.

Terry Denunzio, on the other hand, was a whole different kettle of fish. Terry was not only Crawford's assistant, he was also his life partner. He was young, gorgeous, and flamboyantly out-there.

Terry cuts my hair and he criticizes my wardrobe. He always knows the latest gossip, sometimes because he's created it himself. I was well aware of Terry's propensity for stirring up mischief. So if Bertie had a complaint I wouldn't have been surprised to hear that it concerned Terry. *But Crawford?*

"Bertie, what on earth are you talking about?" I asked.

She looked over my shoulder and her eyes widened at what she saw. "Here he comes," she whispered unhappily. "You'll see."

I turned around. Crawford was threading his way toward us down the narrow aisle between his numerous grooming tables. The Miniature variety was first to be judged and Crawford had four Mini Poodles, all in various stages of preparation, out of their crates and waiting patiently on their tabletops.

He didn't look like a man with time to spare.

Nevertheless, as Crawford approached I gave him a big smile. Like many of my dog friends, we usually only saw each other when our show schedules meshed. And since Augie was our only Standard Poodle "in hair," and Davey, who handled him, was in the middle of basketball season, I hadn't been to many shows lately. At least a month had passed since Crawford and I had last seen one another.

He answered my smile with a glower and barked, "You're late!"

"No, I'm not," I replied uncertainly. It was unlike Crawford to be wrong about anything. "The show hasn't even started yet."

"Bertie told me she was counting on you."

"Umm . . . okay?" I sent my sister-in-law a quick, surprised glance. That wasn't what I'd heard.

Bertie's gaze slid away. She averted her eyes, staring upward as if something utterly fascinating was happening on the ceiling. (It wasn't.)

So . . . no help there. It would have been nice if she'd bothered to tell me what the heck Crawford and I were arguing about before opting out of the conversation.

"Bertie is in a delicate condition," he said.

Oh.

Only Crawford would have phrased the news that way. And overlooked the fact that Bertie was about as delicate as a longshoreman. But at least now I had an inkling what the problem was.

"She's pregnant," I said, just to see if Crawford would wince.

He didn't, but he did close his eyes briefly as if uttering a silent prayer. *Lord save me from women with explicit vocabularies.*

"I'm aware of that," I added. Just so we were all on the same page.

A moment earlier I had glanced at Bertie. Now I glared.

Instead of looking upward, she was now gazing down. Bertie's hands were clasped in front of her . . . and she was twiddling her thumbs.

Twiddling. Seriously?

Being familiar with the condition myself, I'm inclined to give pregnant women a lot of leeway. But Bertie was starting to test the boundaries of even my goodwill. I reached over and poked her in the side. I needed her to refocus on the discussion at hand.

"I had to tell him," Bertie said plaintively. Then she added in a low voice, "Morning sickness."

"I was afraid she had the flu," said Crawford.

"No such luck," Bertie muttered. Now that I was looking, she did appear to be a little green around the gills. "It was supposed to be over by now."

Crawford just shook his head. "Instead I find out that congratulations are in order. And that rather than staying home with her feet up, Bertie decided to gas up her truck and bring a dozen dogs to Kentucky. What kind of husband lets his wife do something like that? The guy must be an idiot."

"Bertie is married to my brother," I mentioned.

"It figures."

Ouch.

"Crawford, I'm *fine,*" Bertie said. "Really. So I threw up. It's no big deal. And I feel much better now."

Crawford arched a sleek gray eyebrow. "Are you still pregnant?"

"I should hope so."

"Then you're *not* fine. And you shouldn't be working."

I loved Crawford dearly but this was ridiculous. I thought of all the complimentary adjectives I'd applied to him and silently added another: *old-fashioned.*

"How would you know?" I asked him.

"What do you mean?"

"Last time I looked you were gay."

"Oh my God," a familiar voice squealed behind me. "Crawford is gay? When did that happen?"

I spun around and smiled in spite of myself. Terry always has that effect on me.

He was carrying a cardboard tray filled with several cups of coffee but he shifted it to one side so that we could lean in and air kiss each other's cheeks. It wasn't my makeup we were trying not to muss, it was Terry's. The man had on more eyeliner than I did.

"You're not helping," I told him.

"I should hope not," Terry sassed right back. "Is there a problem?"

"No," I said.

At the same time, Crawford uttered an emphatic *"Yes."*

Bertie just sighed. "I'm pregnant."

"Good news, then? Congratulations." Terry set down the tray on a nearby tabletop. Then he wrapped his arms around Bertie and hugged her close. "Are you sure you should be drinking coffee?"

There were three insulated cups in the cardboard holder. Terry must have taken her order before heading over to the concession stand.

"Not you, too," Bertie grumbled.

"What?" Terry managed to look innocent. "I just got here."

"Everybody has an opinion about something that should be my business."

"Can't help that," Terry said with a shrug. "It's what we do."

It was indeed.

Terry stepped back and shifted his attention my way. "If I'm reading the signs correctly, you're in trouble again. What did you do now?"

"Nothing!" I insisted.

"And that's precisely the problem." Crawford inserted himself back into the conversation. "Bertie told me I shouldn't worry because you were going to be here to help out and make sure that she didn't overexert herself."

"You threw me under the bus," I said to Bertie.

"Hey," she replied, reaching for her coffee. "Better you than me."

Sad to say, I couldn't argue with that logic.

"So here I am," I said instead. "At your disposal." Then a sudden thought struck me. "Except for one thing."

"Now what?" asked Terry, sounding delighted that our dilemma—seemingly solved only seconds earlier—was once more up for debate.

"Coffee break is over." Crawford cast a meaningful glance in the direction of his grooming tables. Then he looked back at his assistant. "Shouldn't you be working?"

All four of Crawford's Minis had their coats brushed out and scissored. But three needed to be sprayed up, and one still had its topknot and ears encased in the brightly colored wraps it would have worn since its bath the day before. I didn't need to check the show schedule taped to the raised lid of Crawford's tack box to know that even with both handlers applying themselves, they still had a lot of work to accomplish in a small amount of time.

Terry just grinned. Nothing rattles that guy. Plus, he's a whiz with hair. Terry can accomplish more with a Mini coat in ten minutes than I can achieve in an hour. Which is probably why he's Crawford Langley's assistant and I'm still a lowly owner-handler.

He stepped over to the closest table, picked up a pair of small, sharp scissors, and quickly popped the row of tiny rubber bands holding the Mini's topknot hair in place. Deftly he pulled the colored wraps free and set them aside. With a quick spritz of water he tamed the inevitable fly-aways, then used a pin brush to smooth out the long black hair.

"I'll work, you talk," Terry said to me. "Spill."

"Yes," Bertie agreed, back at her own grooming. "And speak up so we can all hear. What are you up to now?"

"It was Aunt Peg's idea—" I began.

"Of course it was," Terry agreed. He picked up a long knitting needle and used it to section off a small bit of hair above the Poodle's eyes, which he gathered into a super-tight ponytail. A second section quickly followed.

Terry was flying through the topknot. It was easy to see why. He didn't have to stop and redo mistakes, like I usually did.

"Aunt Peg," Bertie echoed. She didn't sound surprised. "I probably shouldn't admit this but road trips with that woman scare the crap out of me. Peg stirs up plenty of excitement at home. Take her to a strange place and you never know what might happen. Remember when we went to that judges' conference and she hooked up with a new boyfriend that she'd met on the Internet?"

"Really?" Terry looked up. "I don't remember that."

"That's because Richard didn't last long," I told him.

"Not even until the end of the conference," Bertie said with a laugh. "And now there's this thing with the horse."

"What horse?" asked Terry.

Even Crawford, busy spraying up a Mini farther down the line of tables, glanced over at us in surprise.

"Aunt Peg inherited a Thoroughbred broodmare named Lucky Luna," I said. "She lives at a breeding farm near Lexington."

"I love it!" Terry chortled.

That nugget of information would probably make his day—and keep him busy all afternoon. By the end of the dog show, pretty much everyone within shouting distance would know all about it.

"Peg with a racehorse," Terry said happily. "That's priceless. Is she going to ride it?"

"Definitely not," I told him. "Lucky Luna is ten months pregnant."

"*Ten* months?" Bertie raised a brow. Unconsciously she lifted a hand to her own stomach.

"Gestation in horses is eleven months and sometimes longer." Thanks to my book, I was a font of newfound knowledge. "Lucky Luna is due in April."

Bertie sighed. "I wish I only had a month to go."

"Don't we all," Crawford said under his breath.

"Yesterday Aunt Peg and I went to Six Oaks Farm to see her new acquisition," I continued. "And along the way we stopped to visit an old friend whom she hadn't seen in a long while, Ellie Gates Wanamaker."

"Miss Ellie?" Crawford's head snapped up. "She lives near here?"

"She does," I confirmed. "In Midway."

"Imagine that," he said. "I had no idea. It's been years since I've seen Miss Ellie."

Bertie looked over at Terry, who just shrugged. Neither of them had a clue. I knew why: Miss Ellie's tenure in Poodles had taken place long before either Terry or Bertie had become involved in the breed. Still, it was nice not to be the only ignoramus for a change.

"Who is Ellie Gates Wanamaker?" Terry mouthed silently to me.

"She was Gatewood Standard Poodles," I said. "Miss Ellie bred Poodles with great success for decades. She was a big deal twenty years ago."

"She was more than that." Crawford spoke up. "In those days, Miss Ellie was a veritable pillar of the breed. Everyone looked up to her. Her Standard Poodles were among the very best around.

"Miss Ellie didn't compete in our part of the country often. We might see her a few times a year at PCA and Westminster, and maybe Westchester. But when she did show up, we all knew we'd better shine our shoes and straighten our ties because it was going to take every ounce of talent and luck we had to beat her."

The three of us listened to Crawford's homage with varying degrees of bemused astonishment.

For one thing, Crawford is usually a man of few words. And for another, like Aunt Peg, he has been involved with the Poodle breed at the highest levels for decades himself. He's seen it all, done it all, and succeeded at most of it. So it takes a lot to impress him. I found it interesting that even years later, Crawford remembered Miss Ellie with such regard and appreciation.

"Miss Ellie sounds like an interesting woman," Bertie said. She appeared to be as surprised by Crawford's response as I was. "I'd love to meet her."

"In that case, I have good news," I told her. "Because the reason I can't stay here and help you is because Aunt Peg convinced Miss Ellie to come to today's show. I'm going to spend the day showing her around."

"Good luck with that," Crawford said with a laugh.

"What do you mean?"

"The Miss Ellie I recall didn't follow anybody around. *Ever*. I'd say that it's a great deal more likely that she'll lead you on a merry chase around the showground instead."

"Oh goody," said Terry, finishing up his topknot. "This should be fun to watch."

As if on cue, my cell phone vibrated in my pocket. I pulled it out and had a look. Miss Ellie had texted to say that she'd parked her car and was on her way to the Expo Center's west wing entrance.

"You're sure you're okay without me?" I said to Bertie.

"Absolutely. I'll be fine."

"Go," Crawford said. "Trust me, you don't want to keep Miss Ellie waiting." He cast a meaningful glance at Bertie. "I'll keep an eye on things around here."

"Thank you," I mumbled. "I think."

Terry lifted his hands and shooed me on my way. "Off to the races," he said merrily.

Chapter 8

Even though it was just past nine-thirty in the morning, the Expo Center was already crowded. Most of the people I passed as I skirted around the rings and hurried toward the entrance appeared to be exhibitors. But once I reached the wide lobby on the other side of the pavilion I realized that spectators were beginning to pour in as well.

It took me a minute to spot Miss Ellie in the throng. When I did, I raised my hand and waved. She smiled and veered in my direction.

Miss Ellie wasn't much taller than I was but she moved with such a firm sense of purpose that people simply seemed to melt back out of her way as she advanced toward me. Seeing her in action, I realized that Crawford had been right. Miss Ellie didn't look like she had any intention of following me anywhere. In fact, I'd probably be lucky to be able to keep up with her.

"Good morning, Melanie," Miss Ellie said as she drew near. "Peg told me that I was to put myself in your capable hands."

Let's hope you're up to the task, her expression proclaimed.

So now we both knew where we stood.

"I'm sure you know your way around a dog show," I told her. "But hopefully I can be of some use to you today."

Miss Ellie didn't bother to reply. Instead she simply strode past me, heading for the back of the lobby and the entrance to the large auditorium that housed the show rings. Caught flat-footed, I scrambled to catch up. The chase turned out to be brief. When Miss Ellie reached the opening, she stopped so suddenly that I nearly bowled her over from behind.

I hopped to one side and shot past her. It was a miracle I didn't fall on my face.

Miss Ellie didn't even notice. In fact, I realized as I righted myself, she wasn't looking at me at all. Instead, she was gazing out over the vista that appeared before us: matted, well-lit rings filled with beautifully groomed dogs of all sizes and shapes; exhibitors—some fretful, others composed—hurrying every which way around the room; dignified judges directing the activity in their rings and reveling in their position as arbiters of canine quality.

No matter how many times I'd seen that same spectacle, it never failed to thrill. It looked as though Miss Ellie felt the same way.

"It's been such a long time," she said softly. "But it never changes, does it?"

"Not the parts that matter," I told her. "Not the dogs, nor the people who love doing this. I bet you'll see lots of old friends here today."

Miss Ellie gave me an enigmatic look, then shifted her gaze back to the rings. The Miniature Poodle judging had yet to begin, but from our vantage point I could see that an assortment of breeds from each of the seven groups—Sporting, Hound, Working, Terrier, Toy, Non-Sporting, and Herding—were already in the rings. Choices abounded, all of them good. I wondered what Miss Ellie would want to see first.

For the first few minutes, however, the older woman was content to simply stand on the sidelines and take in the busy scene. Her gaze swept from one end of the long pavilion to the other, then slowly traveled back again.

"I've missed this," she said finally.

"I can imagine," I agreed. I had neither Miss Ellie's longevity nor her accomplishments, but if it ever became necessary for me to leave the dog show world behind I knew that I would feel its loss deeply. "If you don't mind my asking . . . why did you stop?"

"Something happened."

A non-answer if ever I'd heard one.

"What?" I prodded.

Miss Ellie turned and looked at me. When she spoke, her tone was tart. "A Southern lady would know how to mind her manners better than that."

I was probably meant to wither beneath her rebuke. But we Yankees come from strong stock. So instead I straightened my shoulders and said, "I'm sorry if I was rude. I'm sure you had a good reason."

"Dunaway," Miss Ellie spoke the name after such a long pause that for a moment I wasn't even sure she was speaking to me.

"Excuse me?"

"Champion Gatewood Dunaway, the best dog I ever bred. He was the reason."

"I've seen pictures of him," I said, thinking back. "Dunaway was gorgeous. You did a lot of winning with him, didn't you?"

"I most certainly did. He was a five-time Best in Show winner. I loved everything about that dog and the judges did, too. Dunaway was the Standard Poodle I'd always envisioned in my mind, the one I dreamed of producing every time I planned a litter. I knew that he would be the foundation of everything I bred from then on."

"But he wasn't," I said slowly. I knew that. There were several Gatewood Standard Poodles whose names were featured prominently in our modern pedigrees, but I was quite certain that Dunaway wasn't one of them.

"No, he wasn't," Miss Ellie agreed. "Dunaway was killed in a terrible accident. One that was all my fault."

"I'm so sorry," I said. "I had no idea."

Now I really wished I hadn't asked.

"Don't apologize," Miss Ellie said with a sigh. "I can understand why you were curious. Breeding good dogs is a way of life. It's something that gets in your blood."

I nodded, hoping she would continue. After a moment, she did.

"There was a car accident. I was driving home from a dog show. Dunaway had won the group, so of course we were there late for Best in Show. It was dark outside when we left and it was raining, too. The roads were slippery. To this day, I don't really know what went wrong. The only thing I know for sure is that I should have had Dunaway secured in a crate. But I didn't. He was riding on the front seat next to me."

We all knew that our dogs would be safer riding in cars in crates, I thought. But we all kept them close to us anyway.

"I walked away from the crash but Dunaway didn't." Miss Ellie's voice caught. "After that, nothing was ever the same. In the blink of an eye, all the hopes and dreams I'd had for the future of the Gatewood line were gone. Just snuffed out like they'd never existed at all. Oh, I kept on showing for a little while after that, but my heart just wasn't in it."

"I apologize for bringing up such a sad memory." I gave myself a mental kick. "Aunt Peg wanted you to come to the show and enjoy yourself. I never meant to get your day off to such a bad start."

"Bless your heart. I know you didn't mean any harm. Besides, everything I just told you was over and done with a long time ago." Miss Ellie lifted her gaze. She looked around the pavilion. "So Peg wanted me to have some fun, did she?"

I nodded.

"Then I would hate to disappoint her. We have a whole, huge dog show to explore. Let's get this party started."

Once Miss Ellie got going, she wanted to see everything. Our first stop was the ring where Aunt Peg was judging. Her Poodle assignment was later in the week; that day Peg's slate consisted of nearly a dozen other Non-Sporting breeds. When we arrived at ringside, she was sorting out a small group of French Bulldogs.

For most exhibitors, the goal in showing a dog is the accumulation of enough points to earn that dog the title of Champion. Points are earned within each breed by beating same-sex competition in the classes. Though a variety of different classes are offered, at most all-breed shows the majority of entries are in one of three classes: Puppy, Bred-by-Exhibitor, and Open. Dogs are judged first, followed by bitches.

Once the individual classes in each sex have been judged, the class winners return to the ring to vie for the award of Winners Dog or Winners Bitch. Those two competitors are the only ones who receive points toward their championships. The number of points earned is based on the number of dogs beaten on the day. The highest number of points a dog can win at any single show is five. The fewest—assuming that there is competition—is one. Within that fifteen point total, a dog must also win two "majors," meaning that he must defeat enough dogs to be awarded at least three points under two different judges.

The system sounds complex, but in practice it's actually quite easy to follow. When we arrived at Aunt Peg's ring, she was judging her Open Dogs. She devoted a fair amount of time to sorting through the five dogs in that class. Then, having already found her eventual victor, she made short work of awarding both Winners Dog and Reserve.

While Aunt Peg's ring steward got her bitch entry in order and called the Puppy Bitches into the ring, Peg came over to say hello to Miss Ellie.

"I'm so glad you came," she said.

"I am, too," Miss Ellie replied. "I didn't realize how much I'd missed all this until I walked in the building this morning and saw everything in front of me looking just the same as I remembered it." She added with a smile, "It felt a bit like coming home."

"As well it should have," Aunt Peg told her. "For many years, this *was* your home. And the dog community was your family. I know you've been missed. I hope Melanie is taking good care of you?"

"We're just getting started," I told her. "We've barely had time to see anything yet."

"Off you go, then." Aunt Peg shooed us away as if she'd been the one to hold us up, rather than the reverse. While we'd been speaking, her Puppy Bitch class had filed into the ring and the steward was sending us pointed looks. It was time for Aunt Peg to get back to work.

Miss Ellie and I strolled past several adjacent rings, taking our time and pausing here and there whenever something caught her eye. Miss Ellie had only had Standard Poodles but like most dedicated breeders, she appreciated a good dog no matter what breed it happened to be.

We'd been in the room about fifteen minutes when I started to sense a subtle shift in the atmosphere. At first a few heads turned in our direction. Soon they were followed by more. Whispered conversations began to spring up around us, their murmured words a low buzz that was just beyond earshot.

The dog show world has a telegraph that's as insistent and efficient as jungle drums. And all at once, I could feel its rhythm pulsing around the room. Word of Miss Ellie's presence was spreading rapidly. Before long, anyone old enough to remember her former dominance in the Midwestern dog show scene would be aware that she was back.

Some of the faces I saw around us registered delight. Others looked surprised—and perhaps even a little shocked—by Miss Ellie's unexpected appearance. Several people glanced our way with notable disinterest, then frowned and turned away.

At the outset only a few exhibitors came over to greet Miss Ellie. But as time passed, interest grew steadily and so did the press of people. Hands were shaken. Hugs were exchanged. Our casual stroll around the large room threatened to turn into a procession.

The first several times people approached, Miss Ellie took a moment to introduce me. But it quickly became clear that nobody cared who I was. It was the long-lost mistress of Gatewood Poodles who was the star attraction. After a few minutes, I simply stepped back out of the way and let Miss Ellie handle the commotion herself. She certainly didn't need my help.

A short while later I found myself standing near the Bedlington Terrier ring. I've always loved the look of that charming, playful breed so I was watching the action in the ring and paying only minimal attention to whom Miss Ellie was talking. I might not even have noticed the exhibitor who approached her at that point except for the fact that the woman was carrying a blue-shaded Bedlington in her arms and that she elbowed me sharply out of the way as she sidled in close to Miss Ellie.

When the woman spoke in a honeyed Southern drawl, I couldn't help but overhear. "Ellie, dear," she said in a confidential tone. "I just want you to know that I never believed those awful things I heard. I was sure they couldn't possibly be true."

Miss Ellie drew back abruptly. I saw the muscles in her neck tense. But when she addressed the other woman, the smile on her face was cloyingly sweet. "Why, thank you, Mandy Jo. How very broad-minded of you. Now if you will excuse me, there's somebody I simply must see."

Miss Ellie spun away and left the ringside so abruptly that it took me a moment to react. Then I quickly nudged my way through a small crowd of spectators and hurried to catch up. By the time I did, Miss Ellie's determined stride had carried her almost to the end of the building.

She turned as I came up behind her. The sickly sweet smile was still firmly in place.

"Oh, it's you," she said. The smile dropped away.

I didn't know whether I should feel insulted or complimented by that.

"Is everything all right?" I asked.

"Of course. Why wouldn't it be?"

"I heard what that woman said. And then you left in such a hurry—"

"It was nothing," Miss Ellie snapped. "Those terrier people are a tiresome bunch. I just decided I needed some fresh air."

Fresh air, my fanny, I thought. Miss Ellie had wanted to escape.

"If there's something I can do—" I began.

Miss Ellie stopped walking. She laid a hand on my arm. Her fingers patted me softly. "Why, bless your heart. Don't you worry about me. Everything is just fine."

That was the second time Miss Ellie had blessed my heart. The first time I'd misunderstood the expression's intent. This time I got it. Miss Ellie wasn't conferring a benediction upon me. Instead she was using the platitude to stonewall me—Southern-style.

"Oh how lovely," she said, looking over my shoulder at the nearest ring.

We'd paused beside the Briard judging. The dogs were big, and hairy, and totally adorable in a "Cousin It" kind of way. That was the entire extent of my knowledge about the breed. Miss Ellie's too, I suspected. But now she turned away from me and gazed avidly into the ring as if she was utterly fascinated by what she saw there.

Five minutes passed, and then ten. The Briard judging ended. Great Danes took their place. Miss Ellie continued to spectate from the sidelines. She didn't exactly have her back to me, but the way that she'd shifted her shoulders so that I could barely even see her profile seemed meant to act as a deterrent to conversation.

Maybe I'd misheard what that woman had said, I thought. Or maybe Miss Ellie had simply needed a break from the press of people who had eddied around us almost continuously since we'd first entered the room.

Here down at the end of the auditorium, things were much quieter. And now that the initial flurry of greetings had passed, the remaining exhibitors around us seemed less inclined to make overtures in our direction. I couldn't help but notice, however, that it didn't stop them from staring. And occasionally pointing and whispering.

I still felt the pulsing hum of the dog show telegraph eddying around us. But all at once, I was a lot less certain about what it might be saying.

I edged over to Miss Ellie's side, close enough that she had no choice but to acknowledge me. "Do you like Great Danes?" I asked when she tipped her head in my direction.

"I do indeed. Majestic dogs. Wonderful animals."

The same could be said for any one of several dozen breeds, I thought cynically.

"We can stay here as long as you like," I said. "But I just wanted to let you know that the Mini Poodles should be in the ring by now. Toys will be judged after that, with Standards this afternoon. I told a friend of mine that you were coming today. He was excited about seeing you again."

"Oh?" Miss Ellie's gaze narrowed fractionally. "Who is that?"

"Crawford Langley."

"Crawford's *here*?" Her expression eased. Indeed her whole demeanor relaxed. "I haven't seen Crawford in years."

"He's looking forward to renewing your acquaintance," I said.

"Dear man," Miss Ellie replied with a smile. "Of course he is."

And just that quickly, the majestic Great Danes were forgotten.

"What are we waiting around here for?" Miss Ellie asked. "Let's go see some Poodles!"

Chapter 9

Once again, we crossed the large room. And once again I couldn't help but be aware of the speculative glances that Miss Ellie drew as we walked through the crowds.

If she noticed those chilly looks, I saw no sign of it. Instead, with queenlike hauteur, Miss Ellie only paid attention to the abundance of complimentary attention that came her way. Several times she paused to return a smile or a wave. Once she even blew a kiss to an exhibitor holding a Bloodhound. The man looked thoroughly delighted to be the recipient of her regard.

Miss Ellie might have been deliberately oblivious to the mixed reception her appearance at the dog show had generated, but I most definitely was not. I found the situation puzzling, and more than a little curious. Which made me want to do some probing.

"You certainly know a lot of people here," I mentioned as I strode along in Miss Ellie's wake.

"Does that surprise you?" she inquired archly. "If so, it shouldn't. I spent the better part of three decades immersed in this world."

Miss Ellie had turned to look at me over her shoulder as she spoke. That was why she didn't see the pale, round-shouldered man who'd stepped into her path. He was holding a Newfoundland close to his side on a short leash. When Miss Ellie went barreling into the pair, the big black dog got caught between them. It yelped loudly in protest.

"Oh my!" Miss Ellie came bouncing back into me. I reached out and grasped her shoulders to steady her on her feet.

"Sorry," the man snapped automatically.

His hand reached down to shift the Newfoundland back out of the way. Then he glanced up and saw Miss Ellie's face. The man's eyes widened. His jaw went slack.

Miss Ellie looked every bit as surprised as he was.

"Arthur?" she said. Her hand seemed to lift of its own accord. She reached out toward the man tremulously.

The man ignored the overture. Instead he looked Miss Ellie in the eye, gave his leash a sharp tug, and spun away. Within seconds, both he and the Newf had disappeared into the crowd. Miss Ellie remained rooted to the spot, staring after them.

"Who was that?" I asked.

"Arthur," she repeated, sounding bemused.

"Who is he?"

Miss Ellie gave her head a small shake and began to walk once more. "An old friend."

"If you don't mind my saying so, he didn't look particularly friendly."

"Oh please," Miss Ellie snapped. "I thought you said you showed dogs."

"I do."

"Then surely you know how things work. Half this room is filled with disgruntled former *friends*. This is a competition, not a playground. And the big winner is never everybody's favorite person. I should hope you've figured that out by now."

Well, sure, I thought. I wasn't an idiot.

"But it's been years since you've competed against any of these people." Not just Newf-guy, I thought, but also the other exhibitors who'd stared and whispered. "How can animosity that old still matter now?"

"Welcome to the South," Miss Ellie said.

"Excuse me?"

"People have long memories in Kentucky. And we hold grudges even longer." Absurdly she sounded almost proud of that fact. "It's the way we're brought up. It's what we know how to do."

"Like the Hatfields and the McCoys?"

I was mostly kidding in my reference to that famous Kentucky feud but Miss Ellie nodded anyway.

"Now you're catching on," she told me.

As if that was a good thing.

It was definitely time to head to friendlier surroundings. Thank goodness we were on our way to Poodle territory.

Miss Ellie and I had missed the beginning of the Mini judging. By the time we arrived at ringside, Puppy Bitches were already in. I started to look around for a couple of seats, but abandoned that plan when I realized that Miss Ellie had no intention of sitting still.

Instead she started by staking out a prime spot by the rail. Standing with her feet braced slightly apart and her fists propped on her hips, Miss Ellie stared at the puppy entry in the ring. There were three for her to look at, including the black bitch whose topknot I'd watched Terry set earlier.

Midcompetition with Crawford, the puppy looked perfect now. No one would ever suspect that he and his assistant had been rushing around earlier trying to get everything done. But that was part of Crawford's genius. He always made it look easy.

"You're trimming them differently now than in my day," Miss Ellie commented.

"Yes," I agreed.

"It's a more stylized look. I like it."

As well she should, I thought. Poodle presentation had come a long way.

"Crawford has the puppy in the middle," I told her.

The judge had completed his individual examinations. Now he'd stepped back to take one last look at the line of puppies before pinning the class.

"So I see," Miss Ellie replied. "He won't win this one."

"No?" I said, surprised.

Where I came from, Crawford almost always won everything. Even so, expecting him to do so here was a knee-jerk reaction on my part. But since we'd just arrived at ringside, I hadn't yet had time to form an actual opinion about the Minis in front of us.

Apparently Miss Ellie was like Aunt Peg, however. When it came to sorting out Poodles, it didn't take her any time at all to know what was what.

"Not if that judge has any sense," she said, keeping her voice low as ringside etiquette dictated. "The puppy at the back of the line is a much better Mini."

Aldous Connor, the day's judge, agreed with her. He wasted no time in reversing the order of his line and pinning the class that way. Less than a minute passed before Crawford had stepped out of the ring, handed off the puppy and its red ribbon to Terry, then reentered with his Open Bitch. This time, Bertie and a cream bitch were in the ring with him, as well as six other assorted Mini bitches.

"Nice entry," Miss Ellie said, running a practiced eye down the line. "There's plenty of quality to choose from in there."

"There are majors in all three varieties," I told her. "The entire weekend has great Poodle judges so they drew entries from all over. Aunt Peg is judging Poodles on Sunday. I know she can't wait."

"I may have to come back for that." Miss Ellie smiled.

Now that we were surrounded by her own breed, she seemed to have relaxed. "That will be well worth watching."

Just as it had in the other parts of the room we'd visited, awareness of Miss Ellie's presence spread quickly around the perimeter of the ring. In no time at all, there was a crush of exhibitors and spectators flocking to her side to pay court. Once again, I found myself shunted aside in favor of my vastly more interesting companion.

Not that that was a hardship. While Miss Ellie was busy greeting long-lost friends and talked about old times, I got to relax and enjoy watching the judging.

Crawford won the Open Class and then went Winners Bitch. Bertie's bitch who was behind him in second, was Reserve Winners. She would get no points for that, but I knew that Bertie would be pleased anyway. It was a nice placement in a big entry. Not only that, but today's win would finish Crawford's bitch, so for the rest of the weekend she would be out of Bertie's way.

A Midwest handler won the Variety with a gorgeous Mini Poodle whom I'd only seen previously in magazine and online pictures. Crawford's class bitch was Best of Opposite Sex. Then the Minis were finished and the first Toy Poodle class filed into the ring. By the time Toy judging was halfway done, I had found an empty chair near the in-gate and taken a seat. Still surrounded by well-wishers, Miss Ellie didn't even notice that I was gone.

"So that's the famous Ellie Gates Wanamaker," Terry said, coming up behind me. He nodded toward the side of the ring. "Has she been running you ragged all morning?"

While Crawford was in the ring with one Toy Poodle, Terry was in charge of minding the rest of the handler's entry. He also held armbands and hairspray, and kept the dogs ring-ready so that Crawford could hand off one Poodle and grab another with minimal turnaround time.

Terry was holding two Toy Poodles, one cradled gently

under each arm. The silver was Crawford's specials dog. He would compete later for Best of Variety. The other was a black puppy who had already lost in his class. Since it didn't matter anymore if his coat got mussed, I held out my hands.

Terry passed the puppy over gratefully. The little dog was a charmer. He licked my face, then lay down and settled happily in my lap.

"It's been a whirlwind," I told him. "I think Miss Ellie knows half the people here."

"I'm not surprised," Terry replied. "I Googled her after you left. The Gatewood name came up in the same context as Standard Poodle kennels like Ale Kai and Rimskittle. Her dogs really must have been something special."

"I'm sure they were," I agreed. "And Miss Ellie herself is quite a character. It's been interesting walking around with her. Not everybody is happy to see her here."

Terry grinned wickedly. "She sounds like my kind of woman. Now I can't wait to meet her."

"Your kind of woman," I scoffed. "What kind is that?"

"The kind with secrets, of course. I know all about these old Southern families. They all have skeletons in their attics."

"If Miss Ellie does have any secrets," I said, "I doubt that she'll be divulging them to you."

"That's only because you underestimate the full extent of my charms."

"I've seen your charms," I said with a laugh. "But I've also seen Miss Ellie in action. She is one tough lady. You may have met your match."

"Oooh," Terry trilled. "I hope so!"

He set the silver Toy down on a nearby table and got out his comb and his can of spray. Terry smoothed down the Poodle's long, luxurious ear hair and made a few quick repairs to its topknot. When Crawford exited the ring a minute later, handler and assistant switched dogs and armbands with the efficiency of a much-practiced maneuver.

Then Crawford was gone again, and Terry was back at my side.

"Brace yourself," he said happily. "Here she comes!"

Once again I witnessed the indefatigable power of Miss Ellie's stature. People watched her as she approached. They stepped back to remove themselves from her path. Then their eyes followed her after she'd passed.

Terry was grinning like an idiot. As I got to my feet beside him, he leaned in close and said, "Oh my God, I love her already. She's like Scarlett O'Hara, only all grown up. You must introduce me! And for heaven's sake, make me sound debonair and interesting."

It wasn't difficult. Indeed all I had to do was perform minimal introductions, then get out of the way and let Terry handle the rest. By the time Crawford came out of the ring and joined us, Terry and Miss Ellie were already halfway to being best friends.

Belatedly I realized that Crawford was holding not only the silver Toy but also the purple and gold Best of Variety ribbon. He'd won the whole thing and none of us had even noticed. Crawford juggled the Toy Poodle to one side, wrapped an arm around Miss Ellie's shoulders, and pulled her in close for a warm hug.

"How many years has it been?" he asked. "We've missed you on the East Coast."

"Too many," Miss Ellie replied. "I see that now. I shouldn't have stayed away for so long."

"What about your Standard Poodles?" Crawford wanted to know. "Do you have any left?"

"I'm afraid not," Miss Ellie told him. "I lost the last one ten years ago."

"No problem," Terry said. "Crawford can set you up and get you started again anytime you want."

"My, you do move fast." Miss Ellie arched a brow in Terry's direction. "I can see I'm going to have to keep my eye on you."

Terry inclined his head in a small bow. "The feeling is entirely mutual."

"I'd love to have the chance to catch up properly," said Crawford. "But we have Standards right after lunch, so we're a little pressed for time. Maybe when the judging is finished for the day?"

"Of course, you're busy," Miss Ellie acknowledged. "And I wouldn't dream of getting in the way. Go tend to your Standards. I'll come and find you later. In the meantime, I think I'm going to let Melanie feed me lunch."

Terry held out his free hand and I gave him back the Toy puppy. Handler and assistant left for their setup. Miss Ellie watched the two men go. Her expression looked almost wistful.

"I've been away for so many years," she said. "And yet in some ways it feels like no time at all."

"Were you and Crawford close?" I asked as we made our way to the food concession.

"No, not close exactly." Miss Ellie seemed to be considering her words with care. "Crawford and I were *competitors,* not friends. We had a relationship built on mutual respect. And mutual esteem. I never underestimated Crawford, not even for a single minute. And I believe he felt the same way about me."

The two of them must have had a *Clash of the Titans* thing going on, I thought. Too bad I'd come along a dozen years too late. That would have been fun to watch.

"And that young man with Crawford?"

"Terry," I supplied.

"He's a bit of a hot pistol."

"You could say that," I agreed with a laugh.

Terry would adore hearing himself described that way. I'd have to make sure to tell him about it later.

Dog shows aren't known for their good food. Limp hamburgers, flat soda, and soggy prepackaged sandwiches are usually the order of the day. Savvy exhibitors pack a cooler but Miss Ellie and I were at the mercy of the Expo Center's culinary offerings.

She opted for a wilted, overdressed salad. I made do with a soft pretzel and a glass of sweet tea. We found a quiet place to sit down and sank into our seats gratefully.

"Peg was a dear to encourage me to come today," Miss Ellie said. "I hadn't realized how much I'd missed all this."

"It's too bad she couldn't join us for lunch."

Miss Ellie waved the thought away. "Peg will be eating with the judges, as she should be. I'm sure she and I will have another chance to see each other over the weekend. Now tell me, did you enjoy your visit to Six Oaks?"

I took a sip of tea and nodded. "It was wonderful. The Thoroughbreds we saw there were beautiful and the scenery was spectacular."

"It must be very different from what you're used to in Connecticut."

"Absolutely," I agreed. "I live in the suburbs. My house is surrounded by streets and neighbors. A family farm on a thousand acres of land sounds like heaven to me."

"It can be," Miss Ellie said tartly. "If your family knows how to behave themselves and get along."

"Is that why you no longer live on Green Gates Farm? Because you don't get along with your family?"

Miss Ellie didn't answer right away. Instead she stared downward and picked at her salad, seemingly lost in her own thoughts. I watched as she pushed a limp cucumber aside and ate all the tomatoes first.

I'd probably asked another question that was outside the bounds of Southern etiquette, I realized. But I had no intention of withdrawing the query. Instead I sat and waited her out.

Miss Ellie finally looked up. "I no longer live on the farm," she said, "because I no longer have a claim to the land that my great-grandfather settled more than a century ago."

Not the answer I'd expected. "Ouch," I blurted, without thinking. Quickly I moved to moderate my response. "What a shame that must be."

"It's more than a shame, it's a travesty," Miss Ellie retorted. "My grandfather, Bentley Gates, had three sons: James, William, and my father, Walker. Granddaddy loved that land. He worked his whole life to build Green Gates Farm into the showplace you see today. What he wanted more than anything else was for his three sons to work together, sharing both the property and the responsibilities that came with it.

"While Granddaddy was alive, the three boys got along. The horse industry was booming and there was plenty of business to go around. Nobody had to worry about protecting his own piece of the pie. But then it seemed like everything fell apart at once."

"What happened?" I asked curiously.

"The tax codes relating to horse ownership were changed and the Thoroughbred industry went into a huge slump. Suddenly a lot of people who'd been living high on the hog were scrambling to make ends meet. And in the middle of all that, Granddaddy dropped dead of a massive stroke. My daddy, bless his heart, he was a great horseman but he wasn't as business-minded as some."

"Like his brothers?" I guessed.

"You got it. Maybe Granddaddy should have broken up the farm in his will and left a piece to each son. But he couldn't bring himself to do it. Instead he thought his boys would be able to work as partners to protect his legacy."

"I gather that didn't happen," I said.

"Not even close. Next thing Daddy knew, he was being pushed aside. Every time he opened his mouth, he got outvoted. I was married then and off living my own life, but even I could see how that kind of treatment affected him.

It affected all of us. My family had grown up thinking of Green Gates Farm as our home. That land was part of us, something we knew we'd always be indelibly tied to."

Miss Ellie drew in a deep breath and sighed. "Daddy began to drink a little, and then a little more. Pretty soon he was drinking a lot. He made some poor decisions and he ended up having to sign away everything, including the land that should have been my inheritance. When he died five years later, there was nothing left. In the next generation, the farm passed to James's and William's sons, Sheldon and Billy. My two cousins own Green Gates Farm now."

While she was speaking, I'd finished my pretzel and tea. Now Miss Ellie pushed the remains of her salad away. Clearly she had lost her appetite. Having heard her story, I couldn't blame her.

"The only thing I have left is the Gates name," Miss Ellie told me. "And knowing the way Daddy was treated by his own family, sometimes I wish I didn't even have that."

Chapter 10

I felt like an idiot.

Miss Ellie had begun the meal by talking about how much she was enjoying her day at the dog show. And thanks to me, she had ended it in morose silence after I'd all but forced her to rehash her family's unsavory history.

Well done, Melanie.

I gathered up our rubbish, carried it to the nearest garbage bin, and dumped it in. The Standard Poodle judging would be starting soon, but I was well aware that Faith had been waiting patiently in her crate for several hours. Next on my agenda was retrieving her from Bertie's setup and taking her outside for a long walk.

I asked Miss Ellie if she wanted to accompany me.

"I think I'd rather wander around by myself for a while," she said. "You've made a wonderful guide and I appreciate your efforts, but when it comes to dog shows I'm not without resources of my own."

That was putting it mildly. No doubt Miss Ellie had many more resources than I did. Or maybe she wanted to escape my dismal company and was just being polite. Either way, there was nothing I could do but agree.

"I'm sorry if I upset you," I said. "I always seem to ask too many questions."

"Don't you worry about that." Miss Ellie reached over and patted my arm. "That story I told you is ancient history. It was a bitter pill to swallow at the time, but I've had many years to come to terms with it. Years that I devoted to breeding wonderful Standard Poodles. Indeed you might say that Daddy's loss became my gain because it forced me to strike out in a new direction. And by doing so I was able to create something important that came from me and not just my family connections."

The more I got to know Miss Ellie, I thought, the more I admired her. I hoped we'd be able to stay in touch after the trip was over.

"Besides," she continued, "it isn't as though Green Gates Farm has been entirely lost to me. For one thing, my son is there every day, working on the land whose history is in his blood."

I nodded. She had mentioned Gates the day before.

"And for another, I still take my dogs and visit the farm. Jack Russells need *lots* of exercise. Without it, those little devils would drive me right around the bend. I've walked that land since I was a child and I know every inch of it. As long as we steer clear of the horses, nobody even notices we're there. And with a thousand acres to explore, eventually you can wear out even a Jack Russell."

Miss Ellie headed off in one direction and I went in the other. I figured we would reconnect later, if not ringside for the Standard Poodle judging, then afterward in the grooming area when she came to see Crawford. In the meantime I hurried back to Bertie's setup.

"I was wondering where you'd disappeared to," she said. "I was looking forward to meeting Miss Ellie. I thought you were going to bring her around."

"That was the original plan," I told her. "But Crawford was right. I spent most of the morning just trying to keep up with her."

"And apparently not doing a very good job of it." Terry joined our conversation from the next setup. "Because it appears that you've lost her."

"Impossible," I said. "Everywhere we went people noticed Miss Ellie. Even in crowds like these, she stands out."

"It's no different than walking a really good dog into the ring," Crawford said as he hopped his first Standard down off its tabletop. "Everybody knows class when they see it."

"I'm sure she'll turn up shortly," I said. "In the meantime, I'm going to take Faith outside for a walk."

"You'd better do it fast," said Bertie. "Or you'll miss the start of the judging. We're almost ready to head up to the ring."

Having heard my voice, Faith was already standing up in her crate. As I twisted the latch, she nudged the door open with her nose and came flying out into the narrow aisle. I started to bend down to say hello but my dog was way ahead of me. Faith knows better than to jump up but, manners be damned, she was barely out of the crate before she was already dancing happily on her hind legs.

I wrapped my arms around the big Poodle's body and gave her a hug. "I know," I said. "I missed you, too."

I looped a leash around Faith's head and tightened the collar under her throat. Head up, tail up, Faith was good to go.

We had barely reached the parking lot when my cell phone rang. To my delight, I saw that it was Sam. I was already smiling as I lifted the phone to my ear.

"So how's the South treating you?" he asked.

"Funny you should ask. I thought Kentucky was a Midwestern state but now that I'm here, everyone tells me differently. We've been sipping sweet tea and debating who actually won the Civil War."

"Yup." Sam chuckled. "You're in the South, all right. How's Peg's horse?"

"She's beautiful. And the farm she lives on looks like something from *Lifestyles of the Rich and Famous*."

"I believe it. Years ago, there was a terrific Standard Poodle breeder who came from Kentucky. I think she lived on a plantation. Give me a minute and I'll come up with her name."

"Ellie Gates Wanamaker," I said.

"Good guess!" Sam sounded surprised. "That's exactly who I was thinking of."

"It turns out that Aunt Peg and Miss Ellie are old friends. We visited her yesterday so that Peg could learn about Thoroughbred horses, and Miss Ellie is here at the dog show today."

"Ellie Wanamaker stopped breeding and showing a long time ago," Sam said thoughtfully.

I spied a small patch of grass at the other end of the parking lot and steered Faith in that direction. "That's right, she did."

"Something happened back then. . . ."

I could hear the frown in his voice. Sam had lived in Michigan before moving to Connecticut. From that geographical vantage point, he'd probably been more attuned to what was happening in the Kentucky dog show scene than East Coast exhibitors were.

"I remember that there were rumors floating around at the time . . . Of course who even knows if they were true. But there was some kind of scandal . . . or maybe an accident?"

"There was a car accident," I said. "Miss Ellie told me about it this morning. She wasn't injured but her best dog was killed in the crash."

"That must be what I was thinking of." Sam sounded relieved to be able to put the topic aside. "So how's everything else going? Are you taking good care of Bertie?"

"About that," I said.

"Yes?"

"It turns out that she doesn't need my help."

"Oh."

Oh indeed. Or to put it another way . . . busted.

On the other hand, there are worse things than a husband who would arrange a surprise trip for his wife because he thought she needed a little time off. Especially when that meant that he'd be assuming full care of five Standard Poodles and an active three-year-old child.

"Bertie and I are doing just fine," I told him. "How are you managing with Kev?"

"I'm not sure *managing* is the right word," Sam said with a laugh. "That child thinks he rules the world."

I laughed with him. "Kev's three. At his age, the thing he's best at is pushing people's buttons. You just have to reward the good and try not to let the bad get to you."

"At least he's outgrown his naked stage. That's something to be thankful for."

Kevin had spent the previous winter removing all his clothes every time we took our eyes off of him. We were *all* thankful that stage had passed.

"I'm going to give Davey a call later," I said. "I want to find out how the hike is going."

"Good thing I caught you then. Bob called this morning to say that because they're in the mountains, he and Davey will be moving in and out of cell phone range over the next few days. He wanted us to know that everything is fine and that we shouldn't worry if we can't reach them."

Davey's father, my ex-husband, wasn't generally known for his thoughtfulness. But over Christmas he'd gotten remarried to a wonderful woman named Claire. It sounded as though some of her consideration for others was rubbing off on him.

"Good to know," I replied.

After much sniffing around, Faith had finally found a sandy area to her liking. She squatted and peed, then looked up at me, ready to resume our walk.

"I have to go," I told Sam. "Faith is giving me a dirty look."

"That must be your imagination. Faith is an angel. She doesn't know any dirty looks."

He had that right. Suddenly I found myself missing Sam's physical presence with a sharp, penetrating ache. There's nothing better in the whole world than a man you can share laughter and dogs with.

"All right, you caught me," I admitted. "I'm the one who's feeling guilty because I'm supposed to be paying attention to her and instead I'm talking to you. I love you. Give Kevin a kiss for me."

"Will do. Stay out of trouble. I love you, too."

I rung off, shoved the phone in my pocket, and looked down at Faith. "Now it's your turn," I told her. "Let's get some exercise in before you have to go back in your crate."

Luckily the entry was large in Standard Poodles because by the time I'd returned Faith to Bertie's setup and made it to the ring, twenty more minutes had passed. The dog classes were finished but Bertie quickly filled me in. As neither she nor Crawford had won, the report didn't take long.

Now puppy bitches filled the ring. There were five in the class. Three were black and two were white. And Aldous Connor was taking his time deciding what he wanted to do with them.

Before finding a seat, I looked around for Miss Ellie. Standard Poodles always draw a crowd, and spectators were tightly packed on all sides of the ring.

It took me a minute to search through the throng of people. I didn't see Miss Ellie anywhere.

The Puppy class finished. A single Bred-by bitch came and went. The Open class entered the ring. Eight Standard Poodle bitches took up the entire length of the long mat. As the dogs and handlers got themselves situated, I had another look around. This was Miss Ellie's breed. If she didn't show up soon, she was going to miss the whole thing.

Then the judge sent the class around the ring for the first time and I forgot all about Miss Ellie. The sight of that many lovely Standard Poodle bitches gaiting together in unison was a study of beauty in motion. Crawford was at the head of the line. Bertie was toward the back. My gaze focused on the ring as I devoted myself to watching the competition.

Mr. Connor performed his individual examinations—pulling out each Poodle by itself and using his hands to feel for correct conformation, then moving the bitch down and back across the matted floor to assess soundness—and I found myself judging the class along with him. Many other spectators were doing the same. The fact that we weren't able to put our hands on the dogs to verify what we *thought* we saw from ringside, didn't deter us in the slightest. We all formed firm opinions anyway, about which bitches we favored and which we would send to the end of the line.

As Mr. Connor made his cut and then his final decision and gaited the bitches one last time around the ring, I heard both mutterings of disapproval and a scattering of applause. Imperturbable, the judge ignored both reactions. No doubt he was well aware that no judge ever succeeds in pleasing everybody. He pinned his class, then chose his Winners Bitch and Reserve.

Best of Variety was another nail-biter. In a ring filled with quality, Mr. Connor had more than one deserving option and he gave each Standard Poodle every chance to show what it could do. In the end, Crawford who had won Toys and lost in Minis, was again victorious with his Standard. Bertie, whose class entries hadn't made it as far as the BOV ring, ended up with nothing more to show for her efforts than a couple of colored ribbons.

Everybody gathered up their dogs and headed back to

the setups. I trailed along behind. There'd still been no sign of Miss Ellie. I hoped she would come and meet us in the grooming area.

But an hour later, Miss Ellie still hadn't put in an appearance. The Poodles who weren't needed for further judging had had their hairspray and tight show ring topknots removed. Their hair was brushed out, rebanded and wrapped, and they'd been returned to their crates. Only Crawford's two Variety winners remained out on their tabletops to await the start of the group judging.

"I guess I did lose Miss Ellie," I said finally. "She told me she wanted to see the show on her own for a while, but I thought she intended to catch up with us later."

"I'm sorry I missed her," said Crawford. "If I'd known that was the only chance I'd get, I would have *made* time earlier to talk to her."

"Maybe she got tired and went home," said Bertie.

The rest of us nodded. Even when you weren't exhibiting, dog shows could be a long day.

"Miss Ellie said she might come back on Sunday to watch Aunt Peg judge Poodles," I said. "Hopefully you can get together with her then."

Crawford's Standard Poodle made the cut in the Non-Sporting Group but didn't get a ribbon. He was too much of a professional to visibly show his dissatisfaction with the outcome, but I could tell by the set of his jaw and the way he exited the ring almost before the judge had even finished pointing at her winners, that he was not happy. Fortunately the Toy Group went better and the day ended on a high note.

Over dinner that evening, Bertie, Aunt Peg, and I rehashed the day's events. I related the highlights of my morning with Miss Ellie and Aunt Peg told a story about an exhibitor in an adjoining ring who'd tripped over the edge of a mat and lost hold of her leash. The woman's Basenji had bounced several times around its own ring before hopping over the barrier into Aunt Peg's domain. Its unexpected appearance had set her class of Shiba Inus to leaping and spinning.

"Nothing like a little levity to liven up the proceedings," Aunt Peg said, recounting the tale with relish. She had snagged the dangling leash and returned the errant hound to its embarrassed owner. Their reunion had been accompanied by a large round of applause from the spectators.

Having judged Non-Sporting breeds on Thursday, Aunt Peg had a full slate of Toys to judge on Friday. Faith's and my morning routine was the same as it had been the previous day. She and I arrived at the show and went straight to Bertie's setup.

As we drew near, I saw a cluster of colorful cardboard boxes arrayed on an empty tabletop in Bertie's setup: Ritz Crackers, saltines, Stoned Wheat Crackers, Wheat Thins, water biscuits. There were enough crackers on the table to host an impromptu cheese tasting.

I looked over at my sister-in-law and lifted a brow.

"Crawford brought them for me this morning," she said sweetly. "Wasn't that nice of him?"

"Crackers," Crawford said from the next row over where he had a Bichon Frise out on a grooming table. "They're supposed to settle her stomach. I didn't know which kind she liked so I figured I'd better bring a selection."

I might have stopped and stared. Even Faith looked a bit flummoxed by the handler's explanation. Even after all the time I've known him, Crawford can still manage to surprise me.

"*What?*" he said, grinning at the look on my face. "You think I don't know how to use the Internet?"

The handler returned to his Bichon. Terry, for once, wisely remained silent. I slipped Faith into her crate. Bertie sidled over next to me.

"I might have been a little annoyed that Crawford's still trying to boss me around," she muttered under her breath as she reached for another saltine. "Except the damn things seem to be working. I feel better than I have all week."

After that auspicious beginning, the rest of the day went swimmingly. Bertie put points on both her Mini bitch and a Bearded Collie. Crawford repeated his Variety wins in both Standards and Toys. I spent much of the day watching Aunt Peg judge. She ruled her ring with authority and sorted through her entry with such deft precision that even the exhibitors who didn't win knew that their dogs had been given every consideration.

Aunt Peg joined Bertie and me late that afternoon when she was finished judging. The three of us made our way over to the center of the pavilion where the group judging was due to begin shortly. Two side-by-side rings had been opened up and joined together to form one large space. The mats were repositioned and group markers situated in the middle of the ring. More than two dozen Sporting dogs—spaniels, setters, retrievers—all clustered near the in-gate.

Everything appeared to be ready, but some invisible hand stayed the dogs and handlers from entering the ring. Standing in front of the gate were several people I didn't recognize. The group was engaged in a heated discussion.

As we watched, one of the participants stepped away from the others. He hesitated briefly as if gathering his thoughts—or perhaps his courage—and then strode out to the middle of the ring.

"Who is that?" I whispered to Aunt Peg. I knew it wasn't the Sporting Group judge. That man had remained beside the gate.

"Ken Dolby, the show chairman," she replied in a low tone. "I wonder what's going on."

Mr. Dolby reached the center of the expanse and paused,

as if he was waiting for silence. He needn't have bothered. The stillness around the ring was palpable. Even the dogs quieted.

"I'm afraid I have some sad news." Mr. Dolby's voice sounded loud in the hushed room. "Today we have lost one of our own. A dedicated dog woman, a longtime breeder and exhibitor, Miss Ellie Gates Wanamaker was a friend to many of us here. She died today on her family farm in Midway. Godspeed, Miss Ellie. We know your Standard Poodles are waiting for you at the Rainbow Bridge."

Chapter 11

"I called the front desk and extended our stay," said Aunt Peg. "I'm sure there will be a service in Miss Ellie's honor and I wouldn't want to miss it."

She and I were back in our hotel room. Ninety minutes had passed since Ken Dolby's announcement had cast a pall over the remainder of the dog show. The Sporting Group began as soon as Mr. Dolby left the ring but almost nobody appeared to be watching the dogs compete for the coveted prize. Instead, most people were standing in small clusters talking among themselves

Aunt Peg had left Bertie and me and gone to see what she could find out. She'd returned fifteen minutes later looking grim, and unfortunately none the wiser. Everyone she'd spoken to was as shocked by the dire news as we were. But no one had had any further details to share.

The Toy Group followed the Sporting dogs and we all made a pretense of directing our attention back to the ring. Non-Sporting was after that. When the Poodles were defeated in both groups and thereby eliminated from further competition, we decided we'd seen enough. Bertie went to tend to her dogs and Aunt Peg and I slipped out and went back to the hotel.

"What could possibly have happened?" I asked yet again. I was sitting on the bed in Aunt Peg's room, cradling Faith in my lap. In times of stress, hug a dog. That credo has always worked for me.

Aunt Peg hadn't had an answer the first several times I'd voiced the question and she still didn't now. "Nobody knew anything about the circumstances of Miss Ellie's death," she said. "I'm not even sure how the news made its way to the showground so quickly."

"That's the least of my concerns." I ran one hand down the length of Faith's body. "Miss Ellie was *fine* yesterday. How can she be dead today?"

"Maybe she wasn't fine." Aunt Peg sank into a chair near the room's wide window. "Didn't you tell me that she disappeared yesterday afternoon?"

"Well . . . yes. But not in an ominous way. Miss Ellie just said that she wanted to be by herself for a while."

"Maybe she didn't feel well," Aunt Peg mused. "I wonder if she had a weak heart or some kind of chronic illness."

I'd been set down once for bringing up Miss Ellie's age. I certainly wasn't about to do so again.

"She must have made it back home though," I pointed out instead, "because Mr. Dolby said that she died in Midway."

"Not just in Midway, but on the family farm. I wonder what she was doing there."

Yet another question for which I had no answer.

Aunt Peg looked over at me. Her expression was thoughtful. "You spent the entire morning with Miss Ellie yesterday."

I nodded.

"I imagine you must have spent at least part of that time talking."

"We did. We had a long conversation over lunch."

"Did she mention anything about her family's rather contentious history?"

"I asked Miss Ellie about Green Gates Farm," I admitted. "I wanted to know why she no longer lived there. She talked about some of the problems her father had had and told me that he'd lost his share of the property to his two brothers."

Never one to sit still for long, Aunt Peg stood up and began to pace back and forth across the small room. She appeared to be deep in thought. Faith lifted her head and watched Peg's movements with interest. That made two of us.

Several minutes passed. Abruptly Aunt Peg stopped pacing. She turned to face us. "Did Miss Ellie say anything to you about a plan to get that land back?"

"No," I replied, surprised. "Not a thing. Why?"

"I'm just wondering about a comment she made the other night when she and I were talking on the phone about Lucky Luna. Remember I called her to tell her how the visit to Six Oaks went?"

"Sure. That was when you convinced her to come to the show."

"Precisely. But before that she wanted to know everything about Lucky Luna. So I tried to oblige her but seriously, how much could I possibly have to say about a *horse?* Especially one that I'd just met."

If it was even one tenth of what she might have to say about a dog she'd just met it could have been a long conversation, I thought. The question must have been rhetorical, however, because Aunt Peg didn't wait for my reply.

"I was trying to think of things I could add and I happened to remember that comment Erin Sayre made about Miss Ellie. You know, when she was wondering whether Ellie had recommended that I move Lucky Luna to Green Gates?"

I nodded.

"Well, Miss Ellie gave an odd laugh when I told her about that. And then she said, 'I wouldn't dream of doing such a thing now, but in the future, who knows? Even things that people think are set in stone can change.'"

"Wow," I said, sitting up straight. "That's interesting. Did you ask her what she meant?"

"Of course I did. But Miss Ellie just muttered something about old wrongs being made right again, and that I would find out soon enough and we would talk about Lucky Luna again. Before I could ask any more questions, she changed the subject. Next thing I knew we were talking about Poodles and the upcoming dog shows and you know how that goes."

Everybody knew how that went. Aunt Peg could wax poetic about her two favorite subjects for hours.

Aunt Peg frowned in annoyance. "It didn't seem worth pursuing at the time. Now I wish that I had forced her to elaborate."

"As if anyone could force Miss Ellie to do anything," I muttered. Faith flicked her tail up and down in agreement.

"I was *so* looking forward to this trip," Aunt Peg said quietly. "Lucky Luna provided a convenient excuse for Miss Ellie and me to renew our friendship, but I'd intended to make sure that happened regardless. I hate not knowing what went wrong."

Faith slipped out of my lap and down off the bed. She padded softly across the room and leaned her body against Aunt Peg's legs. Automatically Peg's hand reached out. Her fingers cradled Faith's muzzle. Her thumb stroked the Poodle's cheek. Aunt Peg exhaled a deep sigh. Faith closed her eyes and silently pressed closer.

"You're not judging tomorrow," I said.

Approved for the Toy and Non-Sporting breeds, Aunt Peg had been hired to judge at three out of the four cluster shows. Saturday, she had off. We'd been intending to explore Louisville but now I suspected that we'd be heading back to the Lexington area.

The comment might have sounded extraneous but Aunt Peg immediately knew what I was thinking.

"You're right," she agreed. "We ought to call on Miss

Ellie's son and pay our condolences. It would be the polite thing to do. As I recall, he works at Green Gates Farm."

"Along with the rest of Miss Ellie's family," I mentioned. "Including that man you antagonized the last time we were there."

"Perfect." Aunt Peg blithely ignored my cautionary tone. "Everyone all in one place. Surely someone will be able to tell us how this terrible thing happened."

Six Oaks Farm had been a showplace. Green Gates had the look and feel of a working farm, albeit a very large one. As we'd come to expect, the front gate swung open upon our approach. And once again the first structure we came to was the farm's office, this time a plain clapboard building beside an old maple tree.

I'd suspected this was going to be a long day, so rather than making Faith spend another chunk of time waiting for us in the minivan, I'd left her in Louisville with Bertie. The Poodle would be comfortable there and I wouldn't have to worry about her. From force of habit, Aunt Peg parked in a shady spot beside the building anyway.

The single-storey structure consisted of just three rooms. Two offices with cluttered desks and worn furniture opened off the narrow reception room. Both offices were empty. A receptionist, seated behind a low counter, took a minute to finish what she was doing before looking up from her computer screen.

"Can I help you?" she asked.

"My name is Margaret Turnbull," Aunt Peg said with authority. Her impeccable posture and air of total assurance gain her access to all sorts of places that mere mortals—like me—would be denied. "We're here to see Gates Wanamaker."

The woman glanced down at a sheet on her desk. "Is he expecting you?"

"No, but we are old friends of his mother," Peg replied

imperturbably. "Here in Kentucky for only a few days. I know he won't want to miss us."

I wasn't even slightly surprised to see the woman pick up her phone and make a call. Dogs and humans both tend to jump to do Aunt Peg's bidding. I've been known to do the same thing myself.

The receptionist spoke for a moment, then replaced the receiver. "Gates is on his way," she told us. "If you would go back outside and wait next to the fence on the right, he will be with you shortly."

The day was warm and sunny for late March. In Connecticut, we'd have been wading through slush and hoping that winter's storms were over for the year. But in Kentucky, spring was already on the horizon. The grass was turning green and trees were beginning to bud. From the spot where we'd been told to wait, I could gaze out over a large open field where a group of mares and foals was grazing contentedly.

At Six Oaks, Erin had come to get us in a pickup truck. Gates Wanamaker arrived on foot. A long dirt driveway led from the other side of the fence where we were standing to a big center-aisle barn that was painted white with green trim. As I watched, a man exited the barn and hurried in our direction.

Gates looked to be in his mid-twenties and had the strong build of a person who worked outdoors for a living. His brown hair glinted with red highlights in the sun and he walked toward us with a slight limp. As he drew near, I saw that he shared his mother's sharp features and direct gaze.

"I'm sorry to keep you waiting," he said as he approached. He unsnapped the latch on a nearby gate and motioned us through the opening. "I wasn't expecting visitors today."

"No, I imagine you weren't," Aunt Peg replied. She quickly made introductions. "I can't tell you how sorry I was to hear of your mother's loss. She was a remarkable woman."

"Thank you." Gates looked away from us as he carefully reclosed the gate. "It was kind of you to come. Shall we walk for a few minutes? I find I always feel better when I'm moving."

He started back down the driveway that led to the barn. The farm road was narrow and rutted. I watched where I placed my feet as Aunt Peg and I fell in beside him.

"I knew you when you were a child," Aunt Peg said to Gates. "It was many years ago. You probably don't remember that."

Unexpectedly Miss Ellie's son smiled. "We met at a Poodle show in Pennsylvania. Dog shows were my mother's thing, not mine. But when she went away on long trips, I got dragged along anyway. I remember sitting under a big tent on a hillside and being bored stiff. All anyone wanted to talk about was Poodles."

That sounded like our national specialty all right.

"You took pity on me," Gates said to Aunt Peg. "You dug up a book of crossword puzzles from somewhere and found me a pencil. Over the next three days, I think I finished nearly every puzzle in that book."

"You're right." Aunt Peg sounded pleased. "I'd forgotten that part."

"Your kindness made quite an impression on me." Gates paused, then added, "As did the fact that you were one of the few people I'd ever seen who didn't let my mother push them around."

I tried to smother a burst of laughter. Unfortunately I wasn't fast enough. Gates didn't seem to mind, however.

"Did you know my mother, too?" he asked.

"I knew who she was," I told him. "In Poodle circles, Miss Ellie and the Gatewood Standard Poodles were famous. But we just met for the first time the other day."

"I heard about your visit." Gates turned back to Aunt Peg. "Mother was so pleased to hear from you and to know that you were coming to see her. My mother didn't have the easiest life." He paused, swallowing heavily before speaking again. "I'm happy she got the chance to reconnect with an old friend. That morning you spent together was a wonderful bright spot for her."

"And for me, too," Aunt Peg said.

"Miss Ellie also joined us at the dog show in Louisville on Thursday," I told him. "I know she enjoyed herself there."

"And that made what followed seem all the more incomprehensible," said Aunt Peg. "Miss Ellie was so very full of life that it's difficult for me to come to grips with the fact that she's gone. Do you mind telling us what happened?"

Gates's steps slowed. He stopped and gazed out over the verdant pasture beside the road. I saw his fingers clench, then he shoved his hands deep into the pockets of his jeans and sighed.

"It was an accident," he said slowly. "A stupid, senseless accident."

"We heard that she died here," I said. "On your family's farm."

"That's right." His gaze shifted back to us. "Since you visited the house, I guess you met her dogs."

It didn't seem to be a question, but Aunt Peg and I both nodded anyway.

" 'The little terrorists,' she called them." Gates smiled ruefully. "They're a yappy, scrappy bunch. She liked to bring them over here a couple times a week to run around and let off steam."

Miss Ellie had mentioned that to me, I thought. I'd forgotten all about it.

"To tell you the truth," Gates continued, "that was probably just an excuse to come to the farm. Mother always loved this land. She grew up here. I guess you already know that?"

"We do," Aunt Peg affirmed.

"The farm is owned by two of my mother's cousins now, Sheldon and Billy Gates. In Kentucky we believe in keeping good land in the family. In due time, this farm will pass to my generation. Although not, of course, to me."

Gates's tone was matter-of-fact, betraying none of the bitterness Miss Ellie had when she'd spoken about the forfeiture of her heritage. Perhaps because he'd never had ownership in the land himself, he didn't feel its loss as keenly as his mother had.

"An accident?" Aunt Peg prodded gently.

Abruptly Gates started walking again. "It was those damn dogs," he said. "Or maybe it wasn't, and I'm just looking for something to blame. But they're the reason Mother was here yesterday morning. As usual I didn't see her. I didn't even know she was here until much later. Nobody did."

"As usual?" Aunt Peg sounded surprised.

"It's a big farm," said Gates. "And the horses we have here are worth a significant sum of money. So we do everything we can to keep them safe. But unfortunately you can't wrap them up in bubble wrap. The best way to keep horses happy and healthy is by letting them live outside as naturally as possible. But giving them that freedom also increases the chances that something can go wrong. An astute horseman once said that all Thoroughbreds get up every morning trying to figure out how to commit suicide. And that the more valuable they are, the more likely they are to succeed."

Aunt Peg and I shared an amused look.

"We have to let horses be horses," Gates continued, "and that means there's only so much we can do to protect them from themselves."

"And horses and loose dogs are not a good combination," Aunt Peg guessed.

Gates nodded. "The last thing anyone wants is a dog chasing the horses and making them run."

"I thought racehorses liked to run," I said.

"They do. But it's one thing for horses to race around their pasture for the sheer joy of it. And quite another for a perceived predator—or in this case a pack of noisy terriers—to panic them into a mad scramble for escape. That's how accidents and injuries happen."

"So Miss Ellie confined her walks to the more remote areas of the farm because she didn't want to disturb anyone," Aunt Peg said.

"That was one reason. But I also think that she enjoyed being on her own. Green Gates Farm has changed quite a bit over the last several decades. We've added new barns, an updated breeding shed, and the training track. I think Mother preferred visiting the outlying parts of the property that still look the same way she remembered from her childhood."

The big white broodmare barn was right in front of us now. The dirt road ended at the foot of its wide center aisle.

"Mother had a fall," Gates said quietly. "I'm sure she thought she knew every path, every hill, every hollow on this farm. And maybe she did. But somehow she must have stumbled or maybe lost her balance. We found her at the bottom of a ravine. She had broken her neck and was already gone before help arrived."

"How awful." Aunt Peg exhaled a soft breath. "I can only imagine what a shock that must have been for you."

"It was the last thing I ever expected," said Gates. "I always thought Mother would outlive us all. It seems crazy that something so trivial would take her from us."

There was a minute of silence before anyone spoke again.

"One of the farm workers found her," Gates said then. "Her dogs were howling and making an awful racket. Finally somebody went to investigate. He immediately called Sheldon who called for an ambulance."

"The police must have responded, too," I said.

"They did," Gates confirmed. "Sheldon and Billy were both there by then. They walked around the scene with the deputies and together they figured out what must have happened."

"Will they be investigating your mother's death?" Aunt Peg asked.

"No, ma'am. This is a working farm in an agricultural community and everybody is aware that accidents happen. Besides, this is Gates land. The sheriff said he was satisfied that there didn't appear to be anything that needed looking into."

Aunt Peg pursed her lips. I could see that she wasn't happy.

"Were *you* satisfied?" she asked gently.

Gates didn't answer right away. "My mother was getting on in years," he said finally. "So she could have taken a bad step. If the sheriff was satisfied with what he saw, it's not my place to argue with that. It's not like I know anything different, and going against the family would cost me my job. And that's the *last* thing my mother would have wanted."

I tipped my head around and glared at Aunt Peg. *Back off.*

She still didn't look happy but she did change the subject. "I wasn't sure if we'd find you here today," she said to Gates. "I thought you might be taking some time off."

"The cousins offered. They told me to take as long as I needed. But I'd rather work. I feel better when I keep busy. Besides, it's foaling season."

Aunt Peg looked every bit as baffled by that last remark as I was.

Gates managed a small smile. "You both have dogs, right? So I'm sure you understand what it's like to be a caretaker for animals. You can't just take a day off because you don't feel well or there's something you'd rather do. And spring is our busiest season. Mares are foaling and being bred back. There are matings to plan and new babies to take care of."

Gates turned away. His gaze slowly scanned the land around us.

"This farm is the place my mother loved best," he said softly. "And I'll tell you what. If there is a Heaven on earth, it's right here. And if I know Mother, she put her foot down when she met Saint Peter and said she wasn't leaving. So I'm just as happy to be here keeping her company."

Chapter 12

I was so caught up in the conversation that I didn't even notice the battered pickup truck that had come around the side of the barn until its driver changed course, headed our way, and tooted the horn softly. We stepped off the uneven road onto the grassy verge as the truck pulled up beside us.

The driver rolled down his window and stuck out his head. He was wearing a faded baseball cap with the Green Gates Farm logo embroidered above the brim. Then I saw the man's face and realized that he was Miss Ellie's cousin Billy.

"I been looking for you," he said to Gates. "They told me in the barn they didn't know where you'd gone off to."

"I'm on my way back there now," Gates replied. "I was just talking to a couple of my mother's friends."

Though he'd interrupted our conversation, Billy hadn't bothered to acknowledge Aunt Peg or me. Now he turned and had a look at us. His gaze narrowed at what he saw.

"I know you," he said to Aunt Peg.

"I'm Margaret Turnbull," she told him. "We met the other day at Six Oaks Farm. I'm sorry for your loss, Mr. Gates."

Billy dipped his head in a short, sharp nod. "What happened to Miss Ellie was a terrible thing. You say you were a friend of hers?"

"She and I showed Poodles together for many years."

"That explains it."

His tone was so dismissive that I didn't need to ask for clarification. Apparently Billy Gates recalled his prior meeting with Aunt Peg quite clearly.

"I was just about to tell them that the funeral is on Monday," Gates said. He turned back to Aunt Peg and me. "I'll make sure you get the details before you leave. We'd be happy to have you join us if you're still here."

"Oh?" Billy asked with interest. "Where are you going?"

"Aunt Peg and I live in Connecticut," I told him. "We came to Kentucky for dog shows and so that Peg could visit her new broodmare at Six Oaks. Fortunately we were able to spend some time with Miss Ellie during the first two days of our visit."

I shifted my gaze away from Billy's weathered face, looking past him at the picturesque all around us. "You have a beautiful farm. Miss Ellie told us how much she loved this place."

"That she did," Billy agreed. "And she never let anyone forget it. Miss Ellie could be like a bad rash, always itching away at you until she finally got what she wanted. At her age, maybe it wasn't so safe for her to be walking around these hills. But who could stop her? Miss Ellie never wanted to hear a damn thing that wasn't her own idea first."

Billy fell silent. He wiped a hand across his face. All of us pretended not to notice that he'd brushed away a tear. "I'm supposed to be the guardian of this land. You take care of the land and it takes care of you; that's what I was always taught. But that's not what happened, is it?"

Gates reached in through the opening and placed a hand on Billy's shoulder. I saw him give a firm squeeze. "Nobody blames you for what happened. It was an accident, that's all."

Billy didn't reply. I heard a grinding noise as he shoved

the truck back into gear. "Ma'am." He tipped the brim of his hat to Aunt Peg, then turned to Gates. "Y'all call me when you're done here." He rolled his window back up and the truck rattled away down the drive.

"We've kept you long enough," said Aunt Peg. "We had better be going, too."

Gates walked us back to the office. Once there, he ducked inside the building to write down the information about Miss Ellie's funeral. When he reappeared, Aunt Peg drew him aside. They chatted only briefly. I couldn't hear what they were saying but I saw Gates shake his head twice. Then the two of them walked back to the minivan where I was waiting.

"Thank you for taking the time to come and see me," he said. "It's gratifying to know that my mother had such wonderful friends. I expect there will be a big turnout on Monday. I hope you'll be able to come."

"We will be there," Aunt Peg said with certainty.

I waited until we'd reached the end of the driveway and were back out on the road before turning to Aunt Peg. "What was that about?" I asked.

"What?" She spared me a glance across the front seat of the van.

As if she didn't know. This was clearly payback for my interference in her earlier interrogation of Miss Ellie's son.

"That private chat with Gates?"

"Oh that."

I turned in her direction so she couldn't miss the gesture and rolled my eyes with a bit of theatrical flair. Aunt Peg's lips twitched.

"I simply asked Gates quite casually whether his mother had ever said anything to him about trying to regain her inheritance."

So much for backing off, I thought. On the other hand, I wasn't about to complain. I was curious, too.

"And what did he say?"

"He told me that as far as he knew the thought had never crossed her mind. Indeed he seemed quite taken aback by the question."

"So maybe the comment Miss Ellie made to you was about something else entirely."

"That's one explanation," Aunt Peg said, but she didn't sound convinced. "But it's also possible that since Gates is employed by her cousins, if Miss Ellie made such a plan she didn't let him in on it."

At least Aunt Peg is consistent. You can always trust her to bypass the easy answer in favor of a difficult one.

I was delighted to be reunited with Faith when we got back to the hotel later that afternoon. Bertie met us there as she'd already finished up at the dog show. She would need to return to the Expo Center later to feed and exercise her string, but in the meantime the three of us could have an early dinner.

While I waited for the others to get ready, I took a few minutes to call Sam. I wanted to bring him up to date on recent events and also to make sure that he didn't mind if I stayed in Kentucky a bit longer than originally planned.

I started with the news about Miss Ellie. Not surprisingly, Sam was shocked to hear of her sudden demise. "What a terrible turn of events," he said. "Peg must be crestfallen. I know she was hoping to spend more time with Miss Ellie today when she wasn't judging."

"How do you know that?" I asked with a small frown.

"Peg and I talk. You guys have been away for five days. You've called me twice. She's called me three times."

"Really?" I gulped. *He'd actually been keeping count?*

"Sure. Mostly we just talk about her judging assignment and the dogs she's seen."

"And Miss Ellie too, apparently." I might have sounded a bit snippy. It turns out guilt can do that. I couldn't believe that Aunt Peg was calling home—to *my* home—more often than I was.

"And Miss Ellie," Sam agreed easily. "Although I hadn't heard from Peg since early yesterday. I guess now I know why."

"Aunt Peg wants to stay a few extra days to attend the funeral," I said.

"Is that the only reason?"

"What do you mean?"

The question just slipped out. I was pretty sure I knew what Sam meant.

"Peg wants to know what happened, doesn't she? A random, accidental death with no witnesses? I'm not a suspicious kind of guy and even I have to wonder about that. Stay as long as you want. Kev and I are doing great."

The mere mention of my son's name brought a smile to my face. "Put him on for a minute, will you?"

"Sure thing."

"Mom-meee!" Kevin shrieked into the receiver a moment later.

I laughed and held the phone away from my ear. It was great to hear his voice.

"Hey, Kev," I said. "I miss you."

"Miss you, too," he replied solemnly.

"Are you having a good time with Daddy?"

"Good time," he said. "Tar ate Davey's ear buds."

"*What?*"

"Tar—"

Abruptly Kevin's voice disappeared and Sam was back.

"It was just one," he told me. "And I made him throw it right back up. And we've been to the vet. No harm done."

Except to the ear bud presumably.

"You know Tar," said Sam.

Well, yes, I surely did. I adored Tar but he was a leap-first kind of dog. The thought of consequences simply never crossed his mind.

Come to think of it, he and Aunt Peg had more than a little in common.

"Is everything else good at home?" I asked.

"Couldn't be better," Sam replied. He put Kev back on the phone long enough to say good-bye and then we ended the call.

Faith watched me slide the phone back in my pocket regretfully. Sitting beside me, she had listened in while I'd chatted with Sam. When Kevin had shrieked into the phone she'd stood up and wagged her tail. Too late, it occurred to me that I probably should have held the phone to her ear and let her hear a few words from the rest of her family. Faith would have liked that.

"Next time," I promised her.

Since Bertie still needed to return to the Expo Center to care for her dogs, we opted for an easy dinner in the hotel's café. Aunt Peg ordered salmon. I had a Caesar salad with chicken. Bertie ordered a Hot Brown.

"Oh my." Aunt Peg peered at Bertie's dish when our entrées arrived. A hodgepodge of ingredients were layered on a large plate and the whole thing appeared to be smothered in white sauce. "What *is* that?"

"A Hot Brown is a traditional Kentucky dish," Bertie told us. She had read the description on the menu. "It originated right here in Louisville. It's got bread, and turkey, and tomatoes, and cheese."

"Bacon, too," I said somewhat enviously. My Caesar salad suddenly looked Spartan by comparison.

"Not just bread," the waiter informed us. "It's Texas toast. And Mornay sauce. You'll love it. Everybody does."

Aunt Peg leaned in for a closer look. "It looks like a heart attack on a plate," she decided. A weight gain over the winter had had no effect on her sweet tooth, but it had convinced her to start watching other elements of her diet.

Bertie just grinned. "You know you wish you'd ordered one, too."

"I could make a substitution," the waiter offered.

He started to reach for Aunt Peg's plate. She slapped his hand away.

"Don't you dare. My salmon looks delicious."

"So does your broccoli," I told her archly. "And that tiny little dab of couscous." I slid my bread plate in Bertie's direction. "That thing is too big for one person. Cut me off a sliver so I can taste it."

"Keep your hands to yourself," Aunt Peg chided me. "Bertie is eating for two."

"The sad thing is, I could easily finish this whole dish," Bertie said. "And possibly have seconds. When I'm not throwing up, I'm starving. I wasn't like this the first time around. Do you suppose that means I'm having a boy?"

"I thought you didn't want to know the sex ahead of time," I said.

"I don't. But that doesn't mean I'm not going to spend the next six months guessing which it is."

The waiter refilled our drinks, then left us to our meal. We all dug in to our entrées, some of us with more enthusiasm than others. Surreptitiously watching Aunt Peg pick at her salmon and broccoli, I suspected that we'd be having something filled with sugar for dessert.

"So tell me about your trip to Lexington," Bertie said as we ate. "Did you find out what happened to Miss Ellie?"

"She had a fall," I said.

Aunt Peg snorted.

"Into a ravine," I added. "She broke her neck."

"How awful," said Bertie.

"If that's the way it happened," Aunt Peg muttered.

As usual, Sam's guess had been right on the money.

"You were right there with me earlier," I said to Aunt Peg. "You heard what Gates and Billy had to say. Neither one of them was suspicious about what happened."

"Maybe they lack imagination," Peg retorted.

Certainly no one had ever accused Aunt Peg of *that*.

"Ellie Gates Wanamaker was not a stupid woman," she said.

"I don't believe anyone said that she was," I replied.

"Gates told us that Miss Ellie had been walking that land since she was a child. That she knew every nook and cranny on the farm. So why did she fall in a hole?"

"Maybe she slipped," I said.

"Maybe somebody pushed her," Aunt Peg uttered darkly.

Bertie looked up from her plate. "Who?"

"If I knew that," Aunt Peg said, "I wouldn't be sitting here."

Bertie shook her head. "No, what I mean is . . . who would want to? What would anybody have to gain from Miss Ellie's death?"

Aunt Peg didn't reply. Despite the agile workings of her always devious mind, she had no more idea of the answer to that than I did.

"There is one thing," I mentioned.

"Oh?" Aunt Peg beamed approvingly in my direction.

Interested in the conversation, she'd stopped eating. Bertie, on the other hand, was working her way through that gooey mass of carbohydrates as if she thought she might never see another meal.

"It was really interesting walking around the dog show with Miss Ellie on Thursday," I said. "Tons of people recognized her. It was almost like escorting a celebrity."

Aunt Peg flapped a hand impatiently, motioning me to get to the point.

"But not everyone's reaction was positive. In fact, I got the impression that some people weren't at all happy to see her."

"You must have been mistaken," said Aunt Peg.

"I don't think so. I mean, we were together for several hours. So it's not like it only happened once."

"Like *what* happened?" Bertie wanted to know and Aunt Peg nodded.

"Some people were delighted to see Miss Ellie, of course.

But others looked really surprised—they were pointing and whispering as we passed by. There were even a few exhibitors who deliberately snubbed her."

Aunt Peg frowned. "That doesn't sound right. Did Miss Ellie say anything about it?"

"Not a thing. It was as if the unfavorable attention was beneath her notice. Finally I asked her about it. Miss Ellie just said that she'd enjoyed a great deal of success in the show ring and that the people who weren't happy to see her were those who'd lost to her."

"That's nuts," said Bertie. "Anyone who shows dogs gets used to taking their lumps. Nobody wins all the time, no matter who they are. Besides, didn't she stop showing dogs a long time ago?"

"Indeed," Aunt Peg concurred.

"Miss Ellie told me it's a Southern thing. Apparently people around here hold grudges forever. Remember the Hatfields and McCoys?"

"Those guys were *real people?*" Bertie laughed. "I thought that crazy feud was a made-up story like *The Dukes of Hazzard*."

"No, it really took place," I said. "And the feud lasted for more than two decades."

"Please tell me that those guys weren't feuding over a dog."

That made us all laugh. Not because the thought was inconceivable, but sadly because it wasn't.

I polished off the least piece of chicken in my salad and said, "We ran into a couple of people at the show who were almost hostile. One was a man named Arthur who bumped into Miss Ellie and then stood there staring at her like he was looking at a ghost. She greeted him by name but he didn't say a single word to her. He just turned around and left."

"How very strange," said Aunt Peg. "What breed?"

Nobody was surprised by that question. Aunt Peg characterizes people by their dog affiliation. Not only that, but her designations often have merit.

"Newfoundlands," I said.

Bertie shook her head. "I don't think I know him."

"Nor I," Aunt Peg agreed. She had finished her salmon and was now casting a covetous gaze at a hot fudge sundae that had been delivered to a nearby table.

"The other incident was even more odd. A woman with a Bedlington"—I figured I might as well lead with that information and forestall the inevitable question—"came sidling over to Miss Ellie and said, 'I just want you to know that I never believed those nasty rumors I heard about you.' "

"Curiouser and curiouser," said Aunt Peg. "And what was Miss Ellie's reply to that?"

"Bless your heart."

"Excuse me?" Bertie lifted a brow.

"Bless your heart," I said again. "Judging by the context when she used it on me, I'm pretty sure that it's the Southern equivalent of *go jump in a lake.*"

Bertie grinned. Aunt Peg looked seriously disgruntled.

"That is *not* helpful," she said. "And why am I just hearing about these things now?"

I shrugged. "Because when they happened, Miss Ellie was alive and well and none of it seemed like a big deal."

"Well, in light of subsequent events, perhaps you might want to rethink that opinion," Aunt Peg told me. "Do you have a name for the woman with the Bedlington?"

"Miss Ellie called her Mandy Jo."

"That's a good start," said Aunt Peg. "I'd imagine we can get the rest from a catalog."

"The same is true for Arthur, the Newfoundland man," Bertie pointed out. "And if he's not in the catalog, maybe you can locate him at ringside during the judging."

As if my need to identify these people was a foregone conclusion.

Just to make sure that there weren't any misunderstandings, I said, "That assumes I'll be looking."

"Oh pish," Aunt Peg replied. "Of course you'll be looking. How else are we supposed to find out what happened to Miss Ellie if you don't ask questions?"

"You asked Gates plenty of questions," I pointed out. "And you didn't like his answers."

Peg was unruffled by my complaint. "His answers were fine. But there also seems to be a distinct possibility that there are *better* answers to be had. It never hurts to do a little checking around. If I'm wrong, you may feel free to tell me so."

Like that was ever going to happen in my lifetime.

"Cheer up," said Bertie. "It will be more fun than helping me prep dogs."

"And a better use of your talents." Aunt Peg never misses an opportunity to point out that my grooming technique could still use some improvement.

When the two of them both ordered hot fudge sundaes to finish the meal, I didn't even try to fight the impulse to follow suit. Calories be damned. It looked as though I was going to need to keep my strength up.

Chapter 13

Sunday morning started out much the same way as the previous dog show days had. Bertie was out of bed and over at the show site before the sun rose. Faith and I slept another hour. Then the Poodle and I enjoyed a luxuriously long walk before meeting up with Aunt Peg so that we could go over to the Expo Center together.

Aunt Peg had been looking forward to Sunday's assignment all week as she would finally be given the opportunity to judge all three varieties of her favorite breed. Having studiously avoided asking Bertie and me which Poodles we'd seen on previous days and which had fared well under earlier judges, I knew she couldn't wait to get her hands on them.

Entries usually drop on the last day of a long, tiring cluster of shows. But Aunt Peg's numbers not only held steady, they even rose slightly. That was a sure testament to her popularity as a judge because in order to avoid the appearance of favoritism, neither Bertie nor Crawford would be showing under her. I'd been watching Aunt Peg judge for several years now and I knew there were many good reasons for the approval she'd earned from exhibitors.

Aunt Peg's judging was as insightful as it was decisive. She had a thorough understanding of the Poodle breed and a very firm opinion about what kind of Poodle she wanted to see in front of her. She wasn't swayed by a dog's previous show record, nor by who was holding the end of its lead. She ignored prejudicial ringside chatter entirely. Everyone who showed under Aunt Peg—professionals and owner-handlers alike—knew that they would each be given the same fair and equal opportunity to succeed.

That morning, Aunt Peg wasn't the only one who was eager to get started. Sunday's dog show was the final event of the Kentuckiana Cluster. So that last day would be my only opportunity to seek out answers about Miss Ellie before the competition ended and all the other exhibitors packed up and went home.

I had checked the judging schedule the previous evening. Newfoundlands weren't due to be judged until noon. I had also learned from the catalog that the name *Arthur* wasn't listed among that breed's owners or handlers.

Bedlington Terriers, on the other hand, would be in the show ring midmorning. Not only that, but there was an Open Bitch entry named Bluefield's Caprice who was owned by Amanda Jo Proctor. With luck, the Bedlington would still be in attendance this late in the weekend and I could locate Mandy Jo during the judging.

Just as we'd done the other mornings when we reached the show site, Faith and I went directly to Bertie's setup in the grooming area. She, along with Crawford and Terry next door, were all hard at work getting dogs ready, but there wasn't a single Poodle in sight. It looked very odd to see all the tabletops at those two setups utterly devoid of my favorite breed. Bertie was brushing a Bearded Collie. Terry and Crawford were prepping an assortment of Toys.

I dropped Faith's leash and let the Standard trot on ahead for the last few feet. Faith went directly to Terry. Stepping in beside him, she lifted her nose to check out the pocket in his pants where bait for the ring would be stored later.

Feeling her light touch, Terry swiveled around and looked down. One hand remained beneath a Maltese's chin, the other flicked gently in Faith's direction.

"Mind your manners there, missy," he said. "Before you go any farther, you'll need to at least buy me coffee."

"Faith!" I snapped my fingers and the Standard Poodle scampered happily back to my side.

"Sorry about that," I said.

"Don't be." Terry waggled his eyebrows like Groucho Marx. "That's the closest I've come to a good time all day."

Crawford cleared his throat. "Day's young," he said.

Behind me, Bertie snorted out a laugh. After a moment, I joined in. Even Terry looked nonplussed. Crawford was usually the soul of decorum. A comment like that was *very* unlike him.

"What's so funny?" Crawford looked up innocently.

"You," I told him. "You always listen to us goofing around at dog shows but you never join in."

Crawford just shrugged. "Light day today. No Poodles to do up. Plus"—he lowered his head and went back to work—"I guess I've been thinking a bit about Miss Ellie."

"What about her?" I asked.

"Just that you never know what life is going to throw at you. Something happening out of the blue like that makes me want to try harder to appreciate every single day."

I knew just how he felt. I scooted Faith into her floor-level crate, then walked over to Crawford's setup and leaned against the rim of an empty table.

"You never really got a chance to talk to her, did you?"

"No, I didn't," Crawford said. "And now I'm sorry that I brushed her off the way I did. I was sure she'd come and find us later when everything was over. I thought we'd take some time then to sit down and have a nice chat."

"We all thought Miss Ellie would be around at the end of the show," said Bertie. "I never even got to meet her."

"I wonder why she disappeared," Terry mused aloud.

"So does Aunt Peg," I said.

"No surprise there." Crawford shook his head. "I'm guessing you've been deputized to find out."

"Well . . ."

"Oh, goody!" cried Terry.

Crawford shot him a dark look.

"But aren't you curious, too?" I asked.

Before he could reply, Terry stepped in. "We don't have to be curious," he said happily. "All we have to do is stay here and get our work done while we wait for you to bring back answers. Easy peasy. So what's first on your agenda?"

"Bedlingtons." I looked back and forth between him and Crawford. "Do either of you know a woman named Mandy Jo Proctor?"

If we had been in the Northeast, it would be a pretty sure bet that one of the two handlers could help me out. But dog shows in Kentucky drew from an entirely different pool of local exhibitors. I wasn't surprised when nobody spoke up.

"How about a guy named Arthur with Newfoundlands?"

Again no response.

"Are they suspects?" Terry's eyes lit up with interest.

"No," I said lightly. "Just people I want to talk to."

"Suspects for what?" asked Crawford. "I heard that Miss Ellie's death was an accident."

"That's what Aunt Peg and I were told as well," I admitted.

"That woman." Crawford snorted. Coming from him, the epithet sounded almost affectionate. "She can find trouble on a clear blue day."

"Or make it," Bertie mentioned.

I assumed we were talking about Aunt Peg.

"Don't knock it," said Terry. "More often than not, Peg's suspicions are right." He lifted a hand and shooed me away. "So go take a walk. We'll keep an eye on the lovely

Faith while you snoop around to your heart's content. Just be sure to come back later and tell us what you find out."

There was a supported entry in Bedlington Terriers, and the numbers were fairly sizable for the breed. I had gotten a good look at Mandy Jo when she'd bumped into me on Thursday so I was pretty sure that I'd recognize her when I saw her. That hunch turned out be right.

Mandy Jo appeared at ringside shortly after the Bedlington judging began. She was younger than Miss Ellie but not by much. Probably in her late fifties, I guessed. Mandy Jo's blond hair was styled into a rigid helmet around a face whose skin appeared—even at a distance—to be too tight for its age. She wasn't smiling when I caught sight of her. Judging by the amount of work she'd had done, I wondered if she could.

Mandy Jo was carrying her Open Bitch cupped beneath her arm and she had a Greyhound comb tucked inside her belt. She paused to survey the spectators watching the judging, then strode around the ring to a spot across from where I was standing. I watched as she nudged herself in beside another exhibitor. Immediately the two of them tipped their heads together and began to talk. Even from afar I could tell that they were discussing the dogs in the ring.

It took me only a minute to work my way around to where the two women were standing. Neither one paid any attention when I sidled over close to them, choosing a location that was well within earshot. Considering the scathing nature of the comments they were making about the Open Dogs, I would have expected the two women to observe basic dog show etiquette by either lowering their voices or at least making sure that no one related to those dogs was nearby.

Mandy Jo and her companion did neither of those things. During the course of the class, I listened to them complain about one dog's straight shoulder and another's weak rear.

There was a muttered reference to epilepsy and another to possible deafness. When the judge did find his winner, Mandy Jo and her friend didn't agree with that choice either.

Listening to their conversation, I suddenly found myself wondering whether the comment I'd heard Mandy Jo make to Miss Ellie had been intended ironically. Because this Bedlington breeder appeared to deal in nasty innuendo like it was her stock in trade. No wonder Miss Ellie had been in such a hurry to escape Mandy Jo's company. Upon further exposure, I was feeling much the same way myself.

Mandy Jo's friend slipped past me and entered the ring with her Puppy Bitch. She won that class but Mandy Jo wasn't as lucky when her turn came. In a medium-sized group of Open Bitches, Bluefield's Caprice didn't even manage to place. That had to have been a low blow.

Watching the judging, I'd been hoping for a good outcome for Mandy Jo's bitch. In my experience, people are always excited and eager to talk after a victory—even to someone they don't know. But after a moment I realized that I could make the loss work to my advantage, too. In fact, it might even provide me with a better opening for insinuating myself into Mandy Jo's confidences.

Mandy Jo didn't wait around to watch the remainder of the Bedlington judging. Instead, as soon as she and Caprice exited the ring, she swept the bitch up into her arms and headed back to the grooming area. Casually I trailed along behind.

Reaching her setup, Mandy Jo briefly placed the Bedlington on a tabletop to remove her collar. Then she leaned down and slipped the terrier inside a wooden crate. A small cooler was nearby. Mandy Jo fished around inside and pulled out a plastic water bottle. I waited until she'd tipped back her head for a long, cold drink before making my approach.

"That was too bad," I said. "Your bitch is very pretty. I guess the judge was looking for something else today."

"Who knows what that man was looking for? Not the best bitch in the ring, that's for sure." Mandy Jo slowly lowered the bottle and peered at me above its rim. "Do I know you?"

"I'm a friend of Ellie Wanamaker's. Melanie Travis? We met briefly on Thursday."

Okay, so that was stretching things a bit. Mandy Jo didn't seem to notice. Either that or she didn't want to admit that she'd forgotten me.

"Right," she said. "I thought you looked familiar."

"It's terrible what happened, isn't it?"

"You mean in the ring"—Mandy Jo nodded in the direction of the arena where the Bedlington judging had just taken place—"or to Miss Ellie?"

Like the two things were even remotely comparable.

"I was talking about Miss Ellie." I leaned back against a grooming table behind me, making myself comfortable as if I intended to stay a while. "I guess you just never know what's going to happen next."

"I heard it was an accident," said Mandy Jo. "Is that right? She had some kind of fall?"

"I heard the same thing." I lowered my tone to a confidential whisper. "But that sounds crazy to me. I'm not sure if I believe it. Do you?"

"Why not?" Mandy Jo shrugged. "It wouldn't be the first time Miss Ellie screwed up her life on account of an accident."

I thought back to my conversation with Miss Ellie. "You mean the car crash years ago where her good dog was killed."

"That's right. Dunaway. He was a hell of a Standard Poodle."

"I know," I said. "I have Standards myself."

"Are you showing today?" Mandy Jo asked. "If you

are, good luck with that. Your judge is Margaret Turnbull from the East Coast. I've heard she's a bit of a drill sergeant."

"Good description," I said with a laugh. "And no, I'm not showing today. Peg Turnbull is my aunt."

"Well, then."

I watched as Mandy Jo lifted her water bottle and enjoyed another long swallow and wondered, *Well, then . . . what?*

She answered my question when she finished drinking. "I guess that's how you know Miss Ellie," Mandy Jo said. She paused to wipe her mouth on the back of her hand.

"I was just getting to know her," I admitted. "But I saw the two of you together the other day. It looked like you were old friends."

"Once upon a time, I guess we were. Dog show friends, you know?"

I did.

"When Miss Ellie stopped coming to shows, we lost touch." Mandy Jo walked two steps and lobbed the empty bottle into a nearby trash can. "Even so, I didn't enjoy hearing those things that were being said at the time."

"Oh?" My tone was deliberately light. "Like what?"

Mandy Jo turned back to face me and I could see that my casual demeanor hadn't fooled her one bit. She was deliberating how much to say.

"You're not from around here, are you?" she said finally.

"No."

"I didn't think so."

"Miss Ellie told me about the car accident," I said. "And about Dunaway."

"That was a horrible thing." Mandy Jo frowned. "And it wasn't just about Dunaway."

I was itching to ask her what else it had been about. More than anything, I wanted her to keep talking. But

Mandy Jo seemed like the kind of person who'd be just perverse enough to do the opposite of what I wanted. So instead I remained silent and attempted to look indifferent, waiting her out with a slightly blurred gaze and a vague half smile on my face.

I'm no actress, but luckily it didn't matter. As I'd suspected, Mandy Jo was eager to dish some dirt.

After a minute spent gathering up grooming supplies and packing them in her tack box, she turned back to me and said, "There were people hurt in that crash, too. Hurt bad. A woman in the other car was mangled pretty badly. And Miss Ellie's son's leg was crushed. He was only a child then. He nearly lost his foot."

So that's where Gates's limp had come from, I thought. I wondered why Miss Ellie hadn't mentioned that part when she'd told me about the accident.

"I had no idea about any of that," I said.

"Most people don't. The Gates name carries a lot of weight in central Kentucky. And that family keeps its private business to itself. Stuff they don't want outsiders to know doesn't get out. And that's just the way they like it."

Mandy Jo returned to packing up. She swept up the monogrammed towel that had covered her tabletop, folded it into a neat square, and shoved it into a carryall. I was running out of time.

"I was with Miss Ellie last Thursday morning," I said. "But I lost track of her after that. Would you happen to know where she was that afternoon?"

"No idea," Mandy Jo replied. "Bedlingtons were judged after lunch on Thursday. I wasn't thinking about Miss Ellie at all. I was busy with my own stuff."

"Did you win?" I asked.

"Reserve," she said with a grimace.

I understood the sentiment. Reserve was like honorable mention. *So* close, but just not good enough. It came with no points and was the most frustrating award of all, especially in a decent entry.

"How about the next day?" I asked. "I hope you did one better."

"That was the day Miss Ellie died," said Mandy Jo.

She was no dummy. She knew I was wondering if her time had been accounted for on Friday.

"I wasn't entered," Mandy Jo told me. "I didn't like the judge. I knew Caprice would never stand a chance under him. There was no point in even coming to the show."

"It sounds like it hasn't been your week," I said.

"Nor Miss Ellie's," Mandy Jo replied.

Chapter 14

I still had an hour to wait before the start of the Newfoundland judging.

Though I hadn't seen Arthur's name in the catalog, I was hopeful that I might be able to spot him at ringside just as I'd done with Mandy Jo. Possibly his dogs were bred and entered under a kennel name that I didn't recognize. Or maybe Arthur was a handler who'd picked up a handling job too late to be listed in the book. Worst case, I figured I could talk to a couple of Newf people and see if anyone could tell me who he was.

In the meantime I took a leisurely stroll around the pavilion. Three days earlier when I'd walked the same path with Miss Ellie I'd often felt as though all eyes were upon us. Now I deliberately thought back to that day, trying to recreate images in my mind of the numerous faces I'd seen. Unfortunately, seventy-two hours later my impressions were little more than a hazy jumble of color and shape. Nor did any of the people I saw around me jog a useful memory.

I reached the Poodle ring shortly before judging was due to begin. Aunt Peg was already there, surveying her domain and adjusting it to her satisfaction. I watched her lay out her things on the steward's table, then take a minute to decide where to place the grooming table on which Minis and Toys would be examined. Running a practiced eye over the rubber mats that had been laid around the perimeter and across the diagonal of the arena, Aunt Peg carefully smoothed a wrinkle down into place with the toe of her shoe.

Then she nodded to her steward who called the first class into the ring. As four Toy Puppy Dogs—one silver, one black, one white, one apricot—came prancing through the gate, I snagged an empty chair and settled down to watch.

Some judges use their eyes to evaluate a dog's conformation. Others rely on touch to tell them what they need to know. Their hands check the angle of a dog's shoulder and feel for depth of chest. They skim over the topline and down the slope of the hind legs. Dog show judges are required to touch a dog in just two places: the mouth to check for a correct bite, and the rear to determine whether or not a dog has two testicles.

It's not unusual to see judges who seem to think that the Poodle's big hair and intricate trim should not be mussed by questing hands. They place their fingers on a dog tentatively, or only in the areas where the hair has been clipped away. And by doing so, they miss a lot—skipping over both good points and bad—as a competent Poodle groomer can use the dog's profuse coat to create a variety of illusions.

Necks can be made longer, and backs shorter. A low tail set can be raised. A front assembly set too far forward can magically appear to be back underneath the dog where it belongs. So a judge who relies solely on his eyes to scrutinize a dog's structure can definitely find himself at a disadvantage in the Poodle ring.

Aunt Peg, however, suffered no such impediment to her judging technique. She had decades of experience in putting her hands on Poodles. She not only knew all the grooming tricks she might encounter, she had invented some of them. A pretty trim was no deterrent to her curious fingers. Now I watched as she sorted through her Puppy class with deft proficiency and a happy smile on her face.

As the judging progressed, I made sure to keep an eye on the ringside as well. Here at the Poodle ring, where she'd been surrounded by a lively coterie of old friends, was the place that Miss Ellie had been the happiest and most relaxed on Thursday. If anyone might know where she had disappeared to that afternoon, I was betting it would be a fellow Poodle enthusiast.

When the Bred-by-Exhibitor Bitches entered the ring, a woman with a dainty silver Toy caught my eye. Upon reflection, I was quite certain she'd been one of the exhibitors who had shared a delighted hug with Miss Ellie. The woman's small silver Poodle won her class, so I knew that she would be required for further judging. I stayed in my seat as the Open Bitches were called to the ring.

Ten minutes later, Aunt Peg put up a pretty black bitch who'd been shown to perfection by her Midwestern handler. The handler accepted his blue ribbon and hustled his Toy bitch back into place at the head of the mat as the previous class winners filed in behind him. Attuned to Aunt Peg's subtle body language as she assessed the four Toy Poodles in front of her, I was pretty sure she already knew who her Winners Bitch would be. Nevertheless, she didn't hurry through the process. Instead she offered each of the remaining competitors every opportunity to change her mind.

In the end Aunt Peg went with her Open Bitch, just as I had guessed she would. The woman with the silver Bred-by bitch was Reserve. I was standing just outside the gate when the pair exited the ring with their striped ribbon. Toy Poodle nestled in the crook of her arm, the woman walked around the corner and found a spot from which to watch the Best of Variety judging.

Luckily there was room right beside her. "That's a lovely Toy," I said.

The woman's eyes skimmed my way briefly, then slid right back to the action in the ring. I couldn't blame her for that. I didn't want to miss a thing either.

"Thank you." She lifted her free hand to scratch beneath the Poodle's chin. "I think so. That was tough company. I was happy to go Reserve, especially under that judge. It's nice to have the chance to show to someone whose opinion really means something."

"I'm Melanie Travis," I said.

"Shirley Drake." The woman stuck out her hand and I shook it. "Do you have Poodles?"

"Yes, Standards. But I live in Connecticut. I've never shown in Kentucky."

"Just here to watch then?"

"Mostly." I gestured toward the ring. "Margaret Turnbull is my aunt."

Shirley choked on a laugh. "Thanks for the warning—even if it came a little late. I guess it's a good thing I didn't say anything terrible about the judging."

"Actually you were quite complimentary," I said. "Aunt Peg would be delighted to hear comments like those. Do you mind if ask you a couple of questions?"

"Feel free. As long as you don't mind if we talk and watch at the same time."

"Ellie Gates Wanamaker," I said.

Shirley's gaze flicked in my direction. "What about her?"

"I saw the two of you together the other day. You seemed very pleased to see her."

"Oh Miss Ellie." Shirley sighed. "Of course I was pleased. She's kept herself away from the show scene for years. I've missed competing against her and I've missed talking Poodles with her. Her reappearance on Thursday was a delightful surprise. And I certainly wasn't the only one who felt that way."

In the ring, Aunt Peg was making her final cut. A white Toy dog with a Japanese handler was moved to the head of the line. The bitch who had beaten Shirley's puppy for Winners was positioned second behind the dog, making her the likely Best of Winners and Best of Opposite Sex. We would see in a moment when Aunt Peg pointed for her placings. She was about to send the line of Toys around the ring for the last time.

"I wish we'd had more time to catch up," Shirley said unhappily. "But it was right in the middle of judging and I was busy. So now I feel doubly bad about what happened. Miss Ellie wasn't just a friend; she was an absolute treasure in this breed. When I think of the wealth of knowledge that that woman possessed. . . ."

"I know," I agreed quietly. "Miss Ellie's death was a huge loss. My aunt is very upset about it, too."

"Have you heard about the funeral?" asked Shirley. "It's tomorrow in Lexington and I'm sure that the dog show community will turn out in force to pay their respects. I can get you directions if you need them."

"Thank you. We already have the address," I said. "One last thing?"

Eyes still focused on the ring, Shirley nodded.

"Last Thursday when Miss Ellie was here, did you happen to see her in the afternoon?"

"No, I don't think so. Why?"

"She and I were supposed to spend the whole day together but she disappeared after lunch. I was just curious if anyone knew where she'd gotten to."

"Not I," Shirley told me. "I only saw Miss Ellie that one time. But stay here for a minute. I'll ask around and see if anyone else knows."

The Toy judging was just ending. As the line of Poodles circled the ring one last time, Aunt Peg indicated the placings. The white specials dog was Best of Variety. The Winners Bitch was Best of Winners and Best Opposite. Shirley paused to observe the outcome, then hurried away.

I watched as she moved around the exterior of the ring, pausing here and there to have a word with the other Poodle exhibitors. Time and again, I saw people shrug or shake their heads. No one seemed to have the information I was seeking.

"Sorry," Shirley said, when she returned a few minutes later. "Nobody knows any more than I do. But now that Miss Ellie is gone . . . does it really matter?"

"I don't know," I told her. "I hope not."

Shirley frowned. "What does that mean?"

"Just that I would hate to think that somebody here might have had something to do with Miss Ellie's accident."

Shirley must have tightened her hold on the Toy Poodle in her arms because abruptly I saw the small dog stiffen. "Is that a possibility?"

"It's a dog show," I said. "It's always a possibility."

I left the Poodle ring as the first class of Minis was being called and hurried down the length of the pavilion. It was almost time for the Newfoundland judging. The entry wasn't large and it wouldn't take long. I didn't want to miss my chance to see if Arthur would put in an appearance.

By the time I reached the other end of the room, the first of the Newfoundland classes was already in progress. A single Twelve-to-Eighteen-Month dog gaited around the ring. Fewer than a dozen other Newfs were standing in the area with their handlers, waiting their turns to be shown.

I'd only seen Arthur once and then just briefly, but Miss Ellie's startled reaction when she'd happened upon the man had made me take a closer look. Now, however, a thorough inspection of the people who were standing at ringside didn't prove to be productive. I didn't see anyone who even resembled the older man that I remembered.

The Twelve-to-Eighteen-Month Class was pinned. Two Open Dogs filed into the ring. The judge quickly decided between them. A minute later, the two dogs from the Open Class were awarded Winners and Reserve. At this rate, the breed judging would be over in no time.

Still there was no sign of Arthur. I'd clung to a small hope that he might be exhibiting a bitch or a special, and could possibly appear at ringside midway through the judging. But so far, no such luck.

The catalog for the cluster of events—four dogs shows and a dozen specialties, plus obedience and rally trials—was big and cumbersome and I hadn't brought one with me when I'd set out earlier. Now I found myself itching to take another look at the Newf entry on the off chance that I might have missed something.

A woman seated not far from where I was standing had a catalog open in her lap. Though she glanced down and referred to the book occasionally, for the most part she was concentrating on the dogs and the judging. I stepped over next to her.

"Excuse me," I said. "Would you mind if I had a look at your catalog?"

She didn't even look up. Instead, eyes still fastened on the ring, she simply lifted the heavy tome and passed it up to me.

The book was already open to the Newfoundland page. A brief scan revealed nothing that I hadn't already seen. Sticking my finger in the page to hold it, I thumbed back quickly to the previous three shows and checked through their Newfoundland entries yet again. Still nothing.

I flipped the book back to the correct page and blew out a frustrated breath.

The woman looked up. She held out her hands. I passed the catalog back into them.

In the ring, the Bred-by bitch class had just finished. There was a brief pause in activity while the Open bitches got themselves assembled in the correct order on the mat.

"What are you looking for?" the woman asked. "Maybe I can help."

"That would be great," I said.

I grabbed a free chair and slid it over. As I sat down next to the woman, the class began. She didn't shift her eyes away from the ring but she did nod slightly to acknowledge my presence.

"Last Thursday, there was an older man here showing a Newfoundland. Medium height, poor posture, dark hair mixed with gray? A friend of mine spoke with him. She called him Arthur. Would you happen to know who he is?"

"I might," the woman replied. "Why do you want to know?"

"I'd like to speak with him about something important. I was hoping to find him here today."

"In that case, I'm afraid you're out of luck." The woman paused to watch the judge complete his examination of the last bitch in line. She paid close attention as the Newf gaited back and forth across the diagonal mat. "If I'm guessing correctly who you're talking about, Arthur's dog is entered but he isn't here. He hasn't shown up since that very first day."

In the ring, the judge motioned the bitch at the head of the line up to the front. The woman beside me clapped her hands together and jumped slightly in her seat. I reached over and grabbed the catalog before it could slide off her lap and fall to the floor. She didn't even appear to notice.

"I'll take them just that way," the judge said, pointing. "One, two, three, four."

The bitch the woman was rooting for took the blue. Prudently I remained silent as the two other bitch class winners returned to the ring. Together we watched the outcome. It happened quickly. The Puppy and Bred-by bitches were barely even settled in place before the judge motioned the Open bitch over to the Winners marker.

"Well done!" the woman cried. Then she glanced back my way. "My friend's been trying to finish that bitch for ages. Now then, where were we?"

"Arthur," I said. "I was hoping you could tell me how I can get in touch with him?"

"Yes, of course."

She flipped to the back of her catalog, tore out a blank page, and scribbled down some information. "I believe Arthur Ludwig is the man you're looking for. He lives in Frankfort. It's Sea Haven Kennel and I'm sure there's a Web site. You'll be able to find Arthur's phone number there."

"Thanks so much," I said. "That's great."

"Happy to help," she told me. "If you're looking for a puppy, Arthur will do right by you. He and his wife started Sea Haven many years ago, and after her death he devoted himself to his dogs with a passion. Arthur has bred some very, very good Newfoundlands."

"Thank you," I said again. "You've been a great help. And congratulations to your friend."

Best of Breed was just wrapping up in the ring. The man with the Winners Bitch exited the ring and came trotting in our direction. He held the Newf with one hand; in the other were the ribbons he'd just won. He raised them in the air and shook them gleefully.

I left those two to their celebration and headed back down the long room to the Poodle ring. Aunt Peg would probably be halfway through her Minis by now. But at least I'd be able to see all of the Standard judging.

I threaded my way quickly through the Sunday crowd, dodging past everything from wayward children to dog crates on wheels. Harried exhibitors rushed to and from their rings. Spectators stood two and three deep at the more popular breeds, clogging access to the aisles.

At one point, confronted by a knot of people who were simply not moving, I came to a precipitous halt. Waiting for the confusion in front of me to sort itself out, I let my gaze wander over the nearby rings. Bull Terriers were in one, Bloodhounds in another. A third was filled with Springer Spaniels.

Then, suddenly, I went still. My eyes slid back to the Bloodhound ring. A faint memory tickled the edge of my subconscious.

I seemed to recall that there was something Miss Ellie had said . . . or done. . . .

I took a closer look at the Bloodhounds that were in the ring. One was being shown by a tall man with bushy dark eyebrows and a mustache to match. He wore a tweed jacket and corduroy pants and he looked vaguely familiar.

And then all at once I remembered.

When we'd passed the Bloodhound ring on Thursday, Miss Ellie had paused momentarily. She had blown a kiss to a man standing ringside with a dog. To *that* man who was now in the ring. He had smiled and waved in return.

The Bloodhound judging was wrapping up. Best of Breed was in the ring. There wasn't time now to go see Poodles. If I wanted to find out more about Miss Ellie, I had to grab this chance in front of me before it was gone.

I adjusted my course and veered in that direction.

Chapter 15

I reached the Bloodhound ring just in time to see the man with the tweed jacket lose in Best of Breed. He didn't appear to be unduly upset by his dog's defeat. Instead he shrugged philosophically and shook the winner's hand on his way out of the ring.

I waited a short distance away while he accepted commiserations from several bystanders, then stopped to chat with another group of onlookers. They appeared to be engrossed in the favorite pastime of dog show exhibitors everywhere: engaging in a postmortem of their breed's judging.

By the time Mr. Tweed Jacket finally left his friends and strode away from ringside, Wirehaired Dachshunds had already taken over his ring and their judging was halfway finished. I caught up to him just as he walked through the wide doorway that connected the main pavilion to the grooming area.

"Excuse me," I said. "Do you have a minute?"

"Just about." He glanced down at his watch. "But if you're looking for a puppy, I should tell you that this dog isn't mine. I just handle him for his owner. I can give you the owner's name though."

"No, that won't be necessary," I said. "You're the one I want to talk to."

"Okay then." He kept moving, his long strides covering the ground quickly. We appeared to be heading toward a setup in the back of the room near the windows. "Who are you?"

"Melanie Travis." Automatically I stuck out my hand. Of course he didn't take it. He didn't even look. "And your name is . . . ?"

"Liam Dailey. What's this about?"

"I wanted to talk to you about Ellie Gates Wanamaker."

Abruptly he came to a halt. The Bloodhound skidded to a stop beside him. Now Liam was finally looking at me. He was also frowning.

"No comment," he said.

"What?" I asked, surprised.

"No comment." He looked annoyed. "You're a reporter, right?"

"No, I'm a friend."

"Not a friend of mine, you're not." Liam took off again.

At least this time, we didn't have far to go. Twenty feet later, we'd nearly reached the other side of the room—and apparently Liam's setup. He slid nimbly between two grooming tables, then slipped the collar off over the Bloodhound's head and guided the big dog into an empty crate. A moment later, I heard the sound of water being lapped up noisily.

"I was a friend of Miss Ellie's," I said as Liam latched the crate shut and straightened.

He turned around and looked at me. "Are you still here?"

"Yes." It seemed obvious to point that out but . . . *he'd asked.*

"Why?"

"I was hoping we could talk."

"I'm pretty sure I already said no."

"That was when you thought I was a reporter," I pointed out.

"I'm still not convinced that you're not."

"I don't get it. Why do you think a reporter would be chasing you?"

"Because Ellie Wanamaker died two days ago. And that's news."

"In the dog show world, sure." I was still perplexed. That made me sarcastic. "Who do you think I write for, *Dogs in Review*?"

"Not just in the dog show world." Liam stopped and peered at me across the top of the grooming table. "So you really knew Miss Ellie?"

I nodded. "We met for the first time early in the week."

"Bad timing for you."

"You could say that." This conversation was going nowhere fast. It was time to play the *I've Got Connections* card.

"My aunt and Miss Ellie were old friends," I told him.

Liam didn't look impressed. "Who's your aunt?"

"Margaret Turnbull."

"Standard Poodles?"

"The very same."

Usually the mere mention of Aunt Peg's name is all it takes to make people sit up and pay attention. Not Liam Dailey. He didn't look even slightly impressed by this new information. All at once, Kentucky began to feel like it was a very long way from Connecticut.

"I don't do Poodles," Liam said with a shrug. Like that settled that.

I braced both hands on the top of the table between us and leaned in, stiff-armed, toward him. "I don't do Bloodhounds," I snapped. "What's your point?"

"My God, you're an annoying woman. Has anyone ever told you that?"

"You're not the first," I admitted. "Now are we going to talk about Miss Ellie or not?"

Liam grimaced. But he was weakening. I could tell.

"Let's get this over with," he said. "Five minutes. That's all I'm giving you."

"I thought you said you only had a minute."

"Sure, I *said* that. I was trying to blow you off. For all the good it did."

"I'll take the five," I told him. "And you'd better be prepared to talk fast."

Five minutes later, Liam Dailey and I were on our way to becoming the best of friends. We were also sipping Kentucky bourbon. His was coming from a flask, mine out of a paper cup.

Drinking in the middle of the day isn't my style. Especially not something like bourbon that rolled over my tongue as smooth as velvet, then raced down my throat like liquid fire. Three small sips and I was already feeling a bit light-headed.

I suspected that was precisely what Liam Dailey had had in mind.

"Miss Ellie blew you a kiss," I said.

I'd already clarified my relationship with Ellie Gates Wanamaker yet again, and then explained how I'd come to be escorting her around the show earlier in the week. I'd told Liam how shocked I'd been to hear of Miss Ellie's death and confessed that I was talking to some of her friends in an attempt to make sense of what had happened.

"Of course she blew me a kiss," he replied. "I'm that kind of guy."

"What kind?" I inquired.

"Friendly."

You couldn't prove that by me. At least not until the bourbon had come out. But obviously he and Miss Ellie had shared an entirely different kind of relationship.

I lifted my cup, tipped it to him, and took a companionable sip. "Are you that friendly with all the women exhibitors?" I asked him. "Or was there something special about Miss Ellie?"

Liam matched my drink with one of his own. As he swallowed, he pursed his lips, savoring the burn. "It sounds to me like maybe you're implying something untoward."

"I don't think so," I said. I blinked and thought about it. Heck, maybe I was. Liam's bourbon definitely packed a punch. "But if I was . . . would it be true?"

"Miss Ellie and I were buddies," said Liam. "Mates, that's all. We got along. We understood each other. We shared the same interests."

"Dogs?" I said.

Liam nodded.

"Horses?"

"That, too."

"Bourbon?"

"The lady liked a taste now and again," Liam said. "Dog shows are my workplace. Sometimes the days drag on a bit. It never hurts to liven up the proceedings. Miss Ellie made very convivial company."

Liam held up his hand and extended the flask in my direction. "More for you?"

"No." I shook my head for emphasis. "Thank you."

Convivial indeed. The man was a pro at recruiting *mates* and creating a sociable atmosphere. But if I got any more convivial I might find myself lying flat out on the floor beneath the grooming table.

"Not everyone found Miss Ellie's company as congenial as you did," I said as Liam wiped his palm across the mouth of the flask to dry it, then screwed the cap back into place. He reached over and slid the slim container into his tack box.

Liam looked back with a laugh. "Oh, Miss Ellie was no saint. I don't believe I said that, did I?"

"No," I replied slowly. "You didn't." I waited a beat, then added, "Would you care to elaborate?"

"It's not as though I'm telling tales out of school," Liam said. "Miss Ellie was a fierce competitor. Everybody knows that. She liked to win. But even more than she liked to win, Ellie Gates Wanamaker absolutely *hated* to lose."

"It sounds as though she might have made herself some enemies," I mentioned.

"I don't doubt she did." Liam reached around me and opened a midsize crate. He slid in a hand and withdrew a Beagle. The dog's tail was already wagging happily as the handler placed it on the next grooming table down the line. "It's the nature of the game, isn't it?"

"Are we talking about anyone in particular?" I asked.

"If you don't mind my saying," said Liam, glancing my way. "That seems like a funny question. Especially now that the lady is gone and it wouldn't appear to be important anymore."

"Or maybe that's exactly why it *is* important," I said.

That was definitely the bourbon talking. I really hadn't meant to blurt that out.

"Oh? Then I'm thinking you must know things I don't."

"I sincerely doubt that."

I burped slightly. My hand flew up to cover my mouth. Bourbon again.

Deliberately I set my cup down on the edge of a nearby crate. To my surprise, I realized that the cup was empty. Maybe I was a more convivial person than I thought.

Liam unfurled a show lead and slipped it over the Beagle's head. Then he grabbed an armband out of his tack box and slid it beneath the rubber band that encircled his upper arm.

"Then we make quite a pair." He looked at me, his eyes hardening. "You know nothing. And I don't either. Excuse me. I have to be getting up to the ring."

"One more thing," I said. "Were you here on Friday, showing dogs?"

"Of course." Liam picked up the small hound and tucked him beneath his arm. "I've been here every day this week. Like I said, this is my job. So I put in my time. Just like I'm supposed to do."

He brushed past me and started back across the room toward the main pavilion.

"Good luck!" I called after him.

Liam just kept walking.

I left Liam's grooming area and made my way to the other end of the large room where Bertie's and Crawford's setups were.

Bertie was my *best friend*, I thought happily. And now it occurred to me that I hadn't spent nearly enough time with her this week. She was probably down at her setup right now, *missing me*. Of course she was. What else would she be doing?

Though my legs had felt perfectly steady when I was leaning against Liam's grooming table, now they seemed to have developed a definite wobble. For some reason, I didn't find that worrisome. In fact, quite the opposite.

Striding down the long room past hordes of exhibitors all hard at work preparing their dogs for the ring, I couldn't seem to stop smiling. No, make that grinning. In fact, my goofy grin was so wide that it made my ears hurt.

But here's the funny thing. As I hurried past them, people kept smiling back at me. People I didn't even know. They all seemed delighted to see me. What a friendly place Kentucky was!

Liam was right, I realized suddenly. Convivial was the way to go!

By the time I arrived at my friends' setups, I was slightly breathless. That didn't stop me from singing out cheerfully, "Good morning, everyone!"

Bertie was brushing through a Sheltie. Terry was setting the topknot on a Shih Tzu. Crawford was probably in a ring showing something. Anyway, he was nowhere to be seen.

Which meant that only two pairs of startled eyes turned in my direction.

"Afternoon," said Bertie. "Don't you mean afternoon?"

"Whatever." I waved a hand airily.

"I thought you were going to watch Peg judge Standards," said Terry. "What are you doing here? They're in the ring now."

"Oh. Right." My happy mood deflated slightly. "I forgot."

"You *forgot?*" Bertie said with a frown.

I nodded guiltily.

Her eyes narrowed. "What's the matter with you? You don't look right."

I leaned in closer so that I could lower my voice. "I might have been drinking bourbon," I said confidentially.

The leaning in was a bad idea. Only a moment earlier, I'd been so steady on my feet. Now the wobble was suddenly back.

As I started to tip over, Terry grabbed my arm and hauled me upright. I sagged against him gratefully. Since I was already pressed up against him, I figured I might as well give him a hug, too.

"Thank you," I said on an exhale. I straightened, attempting to retrieve my lost dignity. I was pretty sure that didn't happen.

Definitely not, if the look on Terry's face was any indication. "*Might* have?" he repeated incredulously. "Your breath smells like a distillery."

"Oh please." His tone of voice made me giggle. I couldn't believe I was meant to listen to censure from *Terry* of all people. He wouldn't know what good behavior was if it came up and bit him in the rear. I fluttered my eyebrows at him suggestively. "You say that as if it's a bad thing."

Terry laughed at that. So I joined in. Why not? We were one big happy family, weren't we?

"Oh my." Bertie left the Sheltie on the table and crossed through the setup to join us. "How much bourbon did you have?"

"I'm not entirely clear on that," I admitted. "It was probably more than a little."

"You have *no* head for alcohol," said Terry. He was grinning delightedly.

"Again . . ." I held up my hands innocently. "Not a bad thing, right?"

"Not at all," Bertie said. "As long as you're not drinking."

She was the only one of us who didn't look happy. When had my *best friend* turned into a party pooper? I wondered.

"Then that's just perfect," I told her. "Because I'm not drinking."

For some reason, my hands seemed to be up in the air. So I waved them around and opened and closed my fingers so Bertie could see how empty they were. *Look, Ma, no drinks!*

"I think you need some coffee," said Bertie.

"No drinks!"

This time I said it aloud. You know, just in case Bertie wasn't paying attention. Because hadn't she just told me that I shouldn't be drinking?

Terry slipped his hand in his pocket. It emerged a moment later holding his phone. "I've got to get this on video," he said,

"Don't you dare," Bertie snarled.

A real snarl! Just like an angry dog. It was great.

"Don't you dare," I echoed happily. I had no idea what we were forbidding Terry to do, but if Bertie cared enough to snap at him like that, I figured she probably deserved some backup.

"Nobody will believe it," said Terry.

"*I* don't believe it." Bertie looked at me and shook her head.

"Don't worry," I told her solemnly. "I don't believe it either."

The three of us were all in accord. Wasn't that wonderful? We were *such* good friends.

"I love you guys," I said.

I tried to gather them both close to me for a hug. My two best friends were oddly resistant. That was probably a good thing because unexpectedly I burped again. And then another time.

"Uh-oh," I said.

Suddenly it felt as though all the bourbon-induced happiness was draining from my head. Now, somehow, it seemed to be rolling around in my stomach, causing turmoil. And threatening to come back up.

Bertie took one look at the expression on my face and grabbed my hand. Terry jumped back out of the way.

"Follow me!" cried Bertie. "Sad to say, I know just where to go for that."

Chapter 16

"That was pathetic," said Aunt Peg. "I cannot believe that you missed the Standard Poodle judging on the last day of the Kentuckiana Cluster because you were drunk."

"Tipsy," I said, from the backseat of Aunt Peg's minivan. "I was only tipsy."

It was late Monday morning and Aunt Peg, Bertie, and I were on our way to Lexington for Miss Ellie's funeral. Due to my transgressions the previous day, I had found myself unceremoniously demoted from front seat status. Instead, Bertie—who'd delayed her departure from Kentucky by a day in order to attend the service with us—was now sitting beside Aunt Peg.

"You were way past tipsy." Bertie corrected me with annoying conviction. "But don't worry. Apparently you're a happy drunk. Terry and Crawford were thoroughly entertained."

"Wonderful," I muttered.

I didn't even remember seeing Crawford. He must have come by the setup after my precipitous run to the ladies' room. Drinking bourbon on an empty stomach at barely past noon? Seriously, what had I been thinking? I barely had a head for alcohol at the best of times. And I'd never been much of a drinker. Obviously this was one of the reasons why.

After throwing up in the restroom, I'd been slightly more sober but no less miserable. Bertie had given me a ride back to the hotel where I'd intended to spend the remainder of the day sleeping it off. Instead, the next time I opened my eyes it was Monday morning and Faith was staring at me from the other side of the bed with a worried look on her face.

"Oh no!" I moaned and flopped back on the pillow, drawing a hand over my eyes to block out the sun. "I'm so sorry. I forgot all about you."

Faith's expression cleared and she swished her tail from side to side. She was just happy to see that I was finally awake. Unlike her faithless owner, that wonderful dog never forgets about me. Not even for a second.

Of course that only made me feel worse. I spent the next ninety minutes making it up to her, an effort that was especially necessary because my Standard Poodle was going to have to be left behind once again while we attended Miss Ellie's funeral.

When I'd finally approached Aunt Peg's minivan two hours later—showered, appropriately dressed, and ready to go—Aunt Peg had pointed wordlessly to the backseat. Bertie looked sympathetic but that hadn't stopped her from hopping up front and settling in. For the few minutes it took us to get under way, nobody said a thing.

I'd even begun to harbor the small hope that Aunt Peg wouldn't feel obliged to discuss my lapse in judgment with her usual excruciating attention to detail. I should have known better. We'd barely made it onto Interstate 64, heading east toward Lexington, before she ended the uncomfortable silence.

"I should certainly hope," Aunt Peg said, glancing back at me in the rearview mirror, "that since you couldn't be bothered to watch your own breed be judged, at the very least you managed to gather some useful information for us?"

"I did," I told her. If Aunt Peg was ready to move past the topic of my transgressions to something more interesting, I was right there with her. "I tracked down several of the people Miss Ellie spoke with when she was at the show on Thursday."

"Was your mysterious Arthur among them?"

"I'm afraid not. He wasn't there. But I did find out who he is: Arthur Ludwig of Sea Haven Kennel in Frankfort. And Mandy Jo Proctor—the woman with the Bedlington—told me more about the car accident that killed Dunaway. It turns out that Miss Ellie's son, Gates, was very badly injured in the crash, too."

"Poor woman," Aunt Peg said sympathetically. "That must have been horrifying for her. No wonder she stepped away from the dog show world. Her son's health and recovery would certainly have taken top priority."

"Did anybody know where Miss Ellie disappeared to on Thursday afternoon?" asked Bertie.

"No. No one I spoke to saw her after lunch. So that remains a mystery." I paused and thought back. "Except . . ."

"What?" Aunt Peg took her eyes off the road to look back at me again. It would serve her right if she came to regret exiling me to the rear of the van.

"It occurs to me that I forgot to ask Liam Dailey about that."

"Who's Liam Dailey? I don't think I know that name."

"He's a local handler. I found him yesterday in the Bloodhound ring. On Thursday Miss Ellie blew him a kiss. It turns out that the two of them were pretty chummy."

"Liam Dailey is the person who gave Melanie bourbon," Bertie said. She must have wormed that information out of me when I wasn't paying attention.

"Indeed?" Aunt Peg was not amused. "Then one can

only hope that your midday tippling was in aid of a good cause?"

"We were socializing," I said. "It was all very civilized. Well, except for the fact that I was drinking from a Dixie cup. Liam thought that a drink from his flask would liven up his day. And I hoped that humoring him and joining in would loosen his tongue."

"Did you get your wish?" Aunt Peg inquired archly.

"Liam got his," Bertie said with a laugh.

I kicked the back of her seat hard enough to make her jump. Bertie was unrepentant. I could still hear her chuckling under her breath.

"Liam told me that Miss Ellie was no saint," I said.

"Pish," Aunt Peg scoffed. "I could have told you that."

"And that she hated to lose."

"Really, Melanie." Heedless of oncoming traffic, Aunt Peg now turned entirely around in her seat. "Does anybody *like* to lose?"

"Not me," Bertie grumbled. Though she'd picked up two majors and a bunch of minor points, she hadn't managed to finish a single dog at the four-day cluster of shows. The topic was a bit of a sore spot.

"So maybe Miss Ellie had enemies," I said.

Aunt Peg was right, I thought. I *was* pathetic. I was grasping at straws, trying to make it sound as though I hadn't squandered my last dog show opportunity by having learned nothing useful at all.

"*Of course* she had enemies," Aunt Peg snapped. "We're on our way to her funeral, aren't we?"

There was that. I sat back in my seat with a sigh.

The first thing I thought of when we arrived at the funeral home on the outskirts of Lexington was the movie *Gone with the Wind*. The big white building in front of us was adorned with a wide front porch and a stately row of ionic columns. It looked as though it should have been surrounded by countless acres of plantation farmland rather than a small plot of well-tended lawn, an extensive parking lot, and a nearby strip mall.

In the past when I've attended the funerals of people who'd died under questionable circumstances, the police had shown up at the service as part of their investigation. Here, they were directing traffic.

Gates had told us that the family was expecting a sizable turnout. Even so, I hadn't been prepared for the mob scene that greeted us. There was still three quarters of an hour before the service was scheduled to begin but the parking lot was already jammed. We were lucky to find an empty sliver of space in a far corner. Aunt Peg tucked the minivan into it adroitly.

Though the building's double front door was open wide so that arriving mourners could enter without delay, the entrance was still clogged with people who were waiting to move inside. When we finally passed through the entrance, I saw the reason for the holdup. In the wide front hall, two men stood side by side greeting each arrival and accepting condolences.

Both men wore black suits adorned with somber boutonnieres. Both had graying hair, strong jaws, and blunt features. I recognized the shorter and stockier man as Miss Ellie's cousin, Billy Gates; and the resemblance between the two was strong enough for me to guess that the second man must be Miss Ellie's other cousin and the second co-owner of Green Gates Farm.

As the line moved slowly forward, I tried unsuccessfully to remember the name Miss Ellie had mentioned when she'd related her family's story to me at the dog show. Had that only been four days ago? It felt like eons longer than that.

Aunt Peg was at the front of our small party. When our

turn came, she shook Billy Gates's hand and reminded him of her connection with Miss Ellie. He nodded as if he remembered who she was and he pumped Aunt Peg's hand heartily enough. But throughout the exchange his expression remained slack and when his eyes slid past her and came to rest on me, I saw that they were watery and slightly unfocused. Cousin Billy was doing his familial duty but he wasn't having an easy time of it.

I took only a few seconds of Billy's time before moving on to the man beside him. Thankfully he introduced himself as Sheldon Gates, thereby saving me the embarrassment of admitting my ignorance. While Billy appeared pale and weary, Sheldon was sharp as a tack. His handshake was firm, and even under the somber circumstances he managed to greet me with a small smile. When he asked if I had come from Connecticut with Aunt Peg whom he'd just met, Sheldon's attentive demeanor made him appear genuinely interested in hearing my reply.

"We came here last week for dog shows in Louisville," I told him. "And because my aunt unexpectedly found herself the owner of a Thoroughbred broodmare."

"Really? How did that come about?"

Of course he would ask. I should have seen that coming.

"It was an inheritance," I mumbled. Cheeks warmed by my lack of tact, I quickly changed the subject. "Miss Ellie was kind enough to offer Aunt Peg some valuable pointers about Thoroughbred ownership."

"Miss Ellie would have done a fine job of that," Sheldon said with a nod. "As I'm sure you know, she grew up in the business. And of course her son, Gates, is currently an important member of our team on the farm. Is your aunt's mare boarded nearby?"

"She lives in Midway at Six Oaks Farm."

"Ah, with our neighbors. Then I'm sure she's in good hands. But should you ever wish to make any changes, we at Green Gates would be happy to discuss alternative options with you."

"Thank you," I stammered.

I hoped I didn't sound as surprised by the overture as I felt. Miss Ellie hadn't even been buried yet and one of her closest family members was eager to discuss business at her funeral? Man, that was cold.

The crush of people was now behind us and the area ahead had freed up. Aunt Peg moved on, making her way into a large reception room. I quickly followed her. After a minute, Bertie joined us.

"Some grieving family," she muttered under her breath. "Those guys were kind of creepy, don't you think?"

"Did Sheldon try to talk business to you, too?" I asked.

"No." Bertie grimaced. "But he did hold on to my hand for *way* too long and try to look down my dress. I thought Southern men were supposed to have good manners."

"Not this crew," I said. "Miss Ellie's family has a pretty contentious history. I gather they don't even treat each other well, much less outsiders like us."

Aunt Peg was gazing around the room. "I hardly see any familiar faces," she said on a note of complaint. "I'd have expected there to be more dog people here."

"Whatever else Miss Ellie might have done"—Bertie stepped forward suddenly as she was jostled from behind—"she certainly knew how to fill a room. This place is packed. If they're not from the dog community, who *are* all these people?"

"It's Kentucky," I said in a low tone. "I think everybody here is related to everyone else. Maybe these are just the members of Miss Ellie's extended family?"

"Speaking of family," said Aunt Peg. "There's Ellie's son, Gates."

Gates entered the room through an arched entrance in the far wall and strode through the crowd with confidence.

He hadn't joined his elder relatives in greeting guests at the door, but he was making up for that omission now. Gates stopped and had a few words with nearly everyone he passed. I watched him shakes hands and trade hugs and condolences with each new group of mourners he came to.

I'd been following Gates's progress across the room for nearly a minute before I realized that there was a slender young woman in a slim-fitting black sheath trailing along several steps behind him. Then the crowd shifted and I got a better look at her. It was Erin, the girl who'd shown Aunt Peg and me around at Six Oaks Farm.

I nudged Aunt Peg and pointed. "Look, there's Erin."

"So it is."

Aunt Peg lifted a hand and waved. Erin smiled in reply. She waited until Gates was ready to move on again, then leaned over and whispered something in his ear. He glanced our way and nodded. The pair angled their path in our direction.

"Who's Erin?" Bertie asked me.

"She works at the farm where Lucky Luna lives. She's the one who showed us around last week."

"Oh," Bertie replied with a notable lack of enthusiasm. "Someone else I don't know. Listen, I think I saw Crawford and Terry coming in when we were talking to Miss Ellie's cousins. I'm going to head back that way and see if I can find them."

"Good idea," I said. "Aunt Peg and I will catch up with you later."

Bertie slipped away into the crowd as Gates and Erin approached.

"Thank you for coming," Gates said when the pair had finally reached us. "I know it was an imposition, having to tack on extra days to your trip. I'm sure you must be eager to get home to Connecticut."

"It wasn't an imposition at all," Aunt Peg said smoothly.

"It was important to us to be here. Melanie and I certainly weren't going to leave Kentucky without paying our last respects to your mother."

Gates nodded in acknowledgment.

As she'd done with their previous encounters, Erin had hung back and let Gates take the lead in the conversation. Now, however, he turned and slid an arm around her shoulder, then drew her forward into the group.

"Have you met Erin Sayre?" he asked.

"We met Erin last week," I told him. "Aunt Peg has a broodmare at Six Oaks Farm and Erin gave us a wonderful tour." I turned to Erin and asked, "Were you and Miss Ellie good friends?"

"I've known Miss Ellie since I was a little girl," she replied. "I'm not sure if we were friends exactly as she was more my mother's generation than mine, but Miss Ellie always had my utmost respect. She was good at educating people. And she never let me forget, even for a minute, that when it came to horses I still had a lot to learn."

"She never let any of us forget that," Gates said with a smile. "Mother was a tough taskmaster. She was raised with a strong belief in the value of good breeding and high standards and she applied those principles to all of us: horses, dogs, and people alike. Anyone who dared to step out of line around her would immediately discover their mistake. Mother had no qualms about putting people in their place no matter who they were."

It was too bad Miss Ellie wasn't on hand to have a word with her cousin Sheldon, I thought. Maybe she could slap some better manners into him.

"Excuse me. I hope I'm not interrupting?"

The older man who'd approached us looked vaguely familiar. Gates turned to see who it was and then stepped to one side creating an opening for him to join our circle. The newcomer was tall and well dressed. He had a decisive manner and sharp gray eyes that flickered from face to face as he looked around the group.

Our gazes met briefly. Abruptly I remembered where I'd seen him before. He was the client Aunt Peg and I had seen at the training center the previous week. He and Billy Gates had been evaluating two-year-old colts.

"You're not interrupting, Mr. Nash. Please join us. And thank you for coming today." Gates quickly introduced Daniel Nash around.

When that was done, Nash turned back to Miss Ellie's son. "Gates, I'm so very sorry for your loss. Billy introduced me to your mother last week. She seemed like a wonderful woman. Even though I didn't know her long, I felt it was only right to come and offer my most sincere condolences."

"That's very kind of you," Gates replied. "This is a tough day for everyone in the family, but you can rest assured that Billy is nevertheless keeping your interests at the forefront of his thoughts."

"I'm not worried about that in the slightest," Daniel Nash replied. "There'll be plenty of time to talk about horses on another day." He paused to let his gaze travel around the vast hall. "I'm from Boston myself. I'm afraid we Puritans don't put on this much of a show. I was told that your family held a position of some eminence in Kentucky, but I never expected to see such a crush of people here."

I had to agree. This Southern funeral was very different than I was used to as well. It appeared to me that there were as many people in the room who had attended the event to be seen as there were who'd come to mourn the family's loss.

"Funny thing is," Nash continued, "I've been in Kentucky more than a week and I don't think I've met more than three people all together before today."

I saw Gates grimace slightly. "That's the way cousin

Billy does things. He likes to play his hand close to his vest. Billy never introduces his clients around. He prefers to keep them all to himself."

"Why is that?" I asked.

"Billy just figures that there's no point in letting someone else come along and horn in on a contact he's already developed."

I wondered if that was business as usual for the horse industry. Based on my introduction to Sheldon and how quick he'd been to offer me other options for Lucky Luna—even as he presided over his cousin's funeral—it sounded as though Billy was right to be cautious.

"You mean he's afraid that someone else might steal away his clients?" Aunt Peg sounded affronted by the very idea.

"It happens all the time," said Erin. "People change farms, they change trainers, they change bloodstock agents. Everybody's always looking for a better deal, or an inside tip, or a way to get a leg up on the next guy. There are aspects of this industry that can be pretty cutthroat."

"You can tell your cousin that he needn't have any worries on that score," Nash said to Gates. "Billy and I are getting along splendidly and I'm sure his advice will prove invaluable, both during the sales process and afterward. This is my first foray into Thoroughbreds so I did my homework ahead of time. I wanted to make sure that I started out right, with someone whose opinion I could trust."

"That's very wise of you, sir," said Gates. "The horse industry has a well-deserved reputation for separating newcomers from their money. So it's good that you're taking things slowly and starting out with the best connections you can get."

Nash accepted the compliment with a satisfied nod. "Gates, I know this is a busy day for you so I won't take up any more of your time. Ladies? It was a pleasure making your acquaintance. I hope we have the opportunity to meet again under more agreeable circumstances."

As Daniel Nash walked away, Erin's gaze followed him. She mumbled something under her breath. I was standing right next to her and I barely caught the words, so I was pretty sure that no one else heard.

"That poor man," she said.

Chapter 17

"Gates, I think your cousin is looking for you," said Aunt Peg.

She gestured toward the arched doorway where Sheldon stood with his head lifted so that he could see over the crowd as he scanned the room. When his gaze came to rest on Gates, Sheldon lifted a hand and beckoned with an impatient motion.

"I think you're right," said Gates. "If you'll excuse me for a minute?"

"Of course," we all agreed.

As he hurried away, I turned to Erin. "What did you mean by that?" I asked.

"Nothing," she replied quickly.

"What's nothing?" asked Aunt Peg. She hates it when she misses anything.

"When Daniel Nash was walking away," I told her, "Erin called him a poor man."

Aunt Peg turned and nailed Erin with a quizzical gaze.

"I shouldn't have said anything," Erin insisted. "It's not my place to have an opinion."

"Your place indeed." Aunt Peg sniffed. "Where would you even get such an idea? Everyone is entitled to an opinion."

And some people felt more entitled than others, I thought.

"Go on," Aunt Peg prompted. "Tell us why you think you shouldn't have said anything."

"It's none of my business," Erin replied.

"What isn't?"

"Daniel Nash," I guessed when the young woman didn't answer right away. "And his dealings with Billy Gates."

"Can't we change the subject?" asked Erin. "Talking about the Gates cousins behind their backs could get me fired."

"You don't work for Billy," I said.

"No, but that wouldn't matter if I said something I shouldn't and it got back to him."

"Nothing you say to us here will be repeated," Aunt Peg told her firmly. "I can assure you of that."

When Erin still remained stubbornly silent, I tried a different tack. "What if we speak hypothetically instead? Let's not talk about Billy Gates at all. Tell us about newcomers getting involved in the Thoroughbred industry and wanting to buy racehorses. How does that work?"

"There are several different ways that could happen," Erin said. She sounded relieved that we were no longer pressing her to discuss Billy's business affairs. "Some people start with a trainer who claims a horse for them at the track. Others prefer to buy young horses that haven't raced yet and bring them along themselves."

"Or they start with a broodmare," said Aunt Peg.

"Not very often." Erin shook her head. "Actually your situation is pretty unusual. Nobody ever wants to start with a mare."

"Why not?" I asked.

"Because it's too slow. People who get involved in horseracing like speed, and high turnover, and fast results. From the time you breed a mare until you have something ready to send to the track, nearly three years will have passed. Very few people want to wait that long."

"Pish," said Aunt Peg. She'd devoted decades to lovingly creating her superb line of Standard Poodles. "The breeding is the fun part."

"No," Erin corrected. She was warming to her subject now. "The *winning* is the fun part. In fact, if you took a poll in this room right now I bet most people would tell you that it's the only thing that matters."

"Say I wanted to go to a sale and buy a horse that can win races." I made a subtle attempt to steer the conversation back to Daniel Nash. "How would I do that?"

"The first thing you'd need is a team of advisors," said Erin.

"Why do I need so many people?"

"Actually you don't. But important people are happier when they're surrounded by a team. It makes them feel like they're getting all the best opinions that money can buy. And though they may be newcomers here, the people who invest a lot of money in horses are already important somewhere else. They might run corporations or hedge funds. They could be celebrity chefs or quarterbacks. So your first step is to assemble your team."

"Excellent!" Aunt Peg sounded inordinately pleased by the prospect. She loves to be in charge. "Tell us more."

"You'll start with a bloodstock agent. He's like a team captain. He'll analyze pedigrees and evaluate the conformation of horses you're interested in. Then he'll hire a vet to read each horse's X-rays and to scope their throats to make sure that their airways are functioning properly. Another man will do heart scans. And you might have a guy to take the horse's measurements and create a symmetry profile."

"That's a lot of stuff to worry about," I said. "How is someone who doesn't know anything about horses supposed to figure all that out?"

"That's the beauty of the system," Erin told me. "The buyer doesn't have to worry about any of it. Because everyone reports back to the bloodstock agent. He's the one who collates all that information and decides which horses should be rejected and which should remain on the client's shortlist."

"So the bloodstock agent is the Big Cheese," I said.

"That's right."

Aunt Peg frowned. "I would have thought that the person whose money was being spent was the important one," she said.

"That would make sense," Erin agreed. "But it's not how things work. Because everyone knows that if they want to do business with the moneyman, they have to go through his agent."

We'd circled right back around to Billy Gates, I realized. The man who was keeping his clients from meeting other people who might expose them to different opinions.

"Lots of buyers don't want to get that involved in the process," Erin continued. "They figure they hired a top advisor, so it only makes sense to defer to his expert opinion. It's not unheard of for an agent to sign for a horse he thinks his client ought to have and then tell the guy afterward what he bought."

"What happens if an agent buys someone the wrong horse?" Aunt Peg asked.

"Good question," Erin said. "But who gets to decide that a horse is the wrong horse? Much of what goes into making these decisions is totally subjective. Lots of times a group of good horsemen won't agree on which horse is the best one."

"It sounds much like judging dogs," Aunt Peg said thoughtfully. "It all depends on how you define breed type, and what virtues are most important to you. Then you decide which faults you can live with and which you consider to be deal breakers. It's not unusual for two judges to see the same class of dogs entirely differently."

"But racehorses *do* have an objective measurement

system," I pointed out. "Because when the horses run in races some of them win and go on to fame and glory and others finish up the track. So ultimately there is a way to determine who made the right buying decisions and who didn't."

"Yes, but don't forget there can be months or even years between the time when a horse is bought and when it gets to the races. And all sorts of things can go wrong or change in the meantime. Poor performance can be blamed on the training center that broke the horse, or the trainer who has him at the track. There are plenty of ways to dodge responsibility when problems arise."

"I should have known you'd be talking about horses," Gates said as he came back to rejoin us. He looked at Aunt Peg and me apologetically. "As you've probably guessed, Thoroughbreds are Erin's favorite subject. She treats every event like it's a Farm Managers meeting. I hope she hasn't been boring you."

"Not at all," I replied. "In fact, I was the one who got her started by asking questions. I guess it seems only natural to talk about horses when you're in Kentucky."

"Not only that," Aunt Peg chimed in, "but as the new owner of a Thoroughbred myself, I've found it slightly alarming to discover just how much there is to learn. In fact, I've made another appointment with Ben Burrell for tomorrow afternoon. I'm determined to educate myself on the topic of racehorses as thoroughly as I can before we have to go back to Connecticut."

"I'd be interested in hearing more, too," I said, turning back to Erin. "Is there any chance you might be free for a short time while Aunt Peg is busy with Mr. Burrell?"

"I think I can probably manage that. Call me when you get to the farm and I'll come up to the office and get you."

"What a lovely young girl," Aunt Peg remarked when the couple had left us and gone to greet more new arrivals.

"She seems to have a great deal of knowledge about how things work in the Thoroughbred industry," I said.

"Not to mention a wonderful ability to change the subject. I assume you noticed that Erin never did tell us why she made that odd comment about Daniel Nash?"

I nodded. I had indeed.

"There's always tomorrow," I said brightly.

Aunt Peg glanced my way with fresh appreciation. "I do love a relative who knows how to make herself useful."

Like that was news.

The funeral service began shortly after that. Sheldon, Billy, and Gates all took seats in the front row. They were surrounded by what appeared to be numerous other family members. Erin remained standing in the back of the room. Bertie had saved some space for us in a middle pew and I found myself sitting between Aunt Peg and Terry.

The service was presided over by a Baptist minister who began by reading several passages from the scriptures. He then devoted nearly thirty minutes to expounding upon Miss Ellie's excellent character and the numerous good qualities she had displayed during her long and virtuous life.

Miss Ellie must have been an ardent churchgoer to merit an homage like that, I thought. I was pretty sure that anyone asked to chronicle my virtues would find himself on and off the podium rather hastily.

By the end of the minister's long address I wasn't the only person who was squirming on the pew's hard seat. Beside me, Terry had long since stopped listening to what the pastor had to say. Instead he was shifting from side to side and spinning his head around like a swivel to check out the other congregants.

"What are you doing?" I whispered, nudging him none too gently with my elbow.

"Looking for Colonel Sanders. He must be here somewhere. Everybody else seems to be."

A laugh bubbled deep in my throat and I quickly clamped my lips shut to stifle it. Apparently I wasn't entirely successful because Aunt Peg turned in her seat and glared daggers at me.

Sure, I thought. Like she was a model of decorum.

Finally the minister stepped away from the podium and Sheldon Gates took his place. Miss Ellie's cousin delivered a heartfelt eulogy that seemed to be more about the venerable history and local consequence of the Gates family than about Miss Ellie herself. When he was finished, Gates Wanamaker read a poem by Ralph Emerson that left many in the congregation sniffling and wiping their eyes. After that, several of Miss Ellie's friends got up to tell stories and to talk about how much they would miss her.

Terry tried and failed to stifle a yawn. Once I'd noticed what he was doing, I found it impossible not to yawn, too.

"I barely knew the woman," he said in a low voice, "but I can tell you for sure that she was a whole lot more interesting when she was around than this place is after her death. Is there going to be a parade after this?"

"A parade?" I said, frowning.

"That's New Orleans," Aunt Peg snapped, leaning across in front of me. "You're not that far south."

"Too bad," Terry muttered, unrepentant. "A little singing and dancing would be an improvement."

Another interminable half hour passed before the service finally ended. The Gates family left first. Presumably they were on their way to the private graveside ceremony. When they were gone, the rest of us filed slowly out of the building.

Aunt Peg and I were halfway across the parking lot when she stopped and looked back at the white columned building. "The Ellie Gates Wanamaker I used to know would have hated that whole display," she said with a contemptuous snort. "Virtuous indeed. I'm not sure those people even knew who she was."

"Maybe they only wanted to remember the good things about her."

"The boring things, you mean. When I die, you be sure to let Terry plan my funeral. He'll come up with something good. I want a proper send-off, starting with that parade he was talking about. And maybe some fireworks to cap things off. I intend to go out with a bang."

I'd never doubted that for a moment.

Back in Louisville later that afternoon, Faith and I had another reunion. Once again I gathered the big Poodle into my arms and issued an apology.

"I wish things were different," I said, hugging her close. "This trip isn't turning out the way either one of us thought it would, is it?"

Inside the hotel room I quickly changed my clothes. I pulled off my funeral dress and heels and replaced them with jeans, a sweater, and a pair of sneakers. Eyeing the leather leash that was lying on the dresser, Faith waited impatiently for me to be ready to go. As I was tying my second shoe, she swept her lead off the dresser, brought it over, and dropped it at my feet.

But you know . . . take your time, Mom. No pressure here.

Laughing, I slipped the looped collar over Faith's head. If only she had thumbs, she could have done that for herself, too. Faith hates elevators so she and I ran down the stairs together. We were both eager to get outside.

Late afternoon in March, the air was just beginning to turn chilly, and I was glad I'd opted for the sweater. At the other end of the parking lot, I could see Bertie tending to her own string of dogs. Now that the shows were finished, the Expo Center was closed. As a result, Bertie's dogs were kenneled in her truck. That was close quarters for all of them and she would be heading back to Connecticut in the morning.

Faith and I spent an hour running around to blow off steam, attending to necessary business, cleaning up after that necessary business, and then exploring the surrounding area. When the Poodle's energy finally began to flag, I found a small patch of grass and a bench where we could sit down for a few minutes. I gave Faith a drink of water from the bottle I'd brought with me, then waited while she got settled at my feet with a stick to chew on. Once she was happy, I pulled out my phone and called home.

To my surprise, Davey answered.

"Hey," I said. "What are you doing home? I thought you were camping with your father."

"I was," Davey replied with the exaggerated patience of a preteen. "But I'm back now. You've been gone almost a week."

Oh, I thought. Right. Time flies when you're on vacation.

"How was the trip?" I asked.

"Awesome! We went hiking and fishing, and we even scaled a couple of cliffs. Dad was great. He and I lived off the land."

I bit back the first retort that came to mind. My ex-husband is no Nature Boy. Bob's idea of *living off the land* probably meant grilling a fish on his camping stove to eat along with all the other prepackaged supplies he'd brought from home.

"I would like to have seen that," I said finally.

"Yeah, but you don't like to go camping. That's what Dad said."

"He's right about that," I admitted. "If God had meant us to sleep in tents, he wouldn't have invented beds."

I heard Sam's voice in the background. "That must be your mother."

"Yup. She's still in Kentucky."

"Let me talk to her, okay? You can finish telling her about your trip when she gets back."

"Bye, Mom! Love you!" Davey sang out. "Here's Sam."

There was a few seconds pause as the receiver passed from one hand to the next, then Sam's voice came on the line. "I'm glad you called," he said. "I was about to call you."

"Oh?" I sat up. "Is everything all right?"

"Everything's great. Davey's back; you obviously already know that. He's in good shape aside from a mild case of sunburn. Kev misses you, but I'm letting him sleep in the bed with me at night so that makes up for it."

"I'm glad I'm so easy to replace," I muttered unhappily.

"Never." Sam laughed. "I just figured I shouldn't pass up a chance to make you feel guilty for staying away for so long."

"Aunt Peg's the one driving the minivan," I said in my own defense. "Faith and I only go where she takes us."

Could be that neither one of us was fooled by that statement.

"So Miss Ellie's funeral was today," Sam said, changing the subject.

"That's right. We just got back. You should have seen the place. Half of Kentucky must have been there, including an ex-governor or two."

"I'm not surprised, considering Miss Ellie's family connections. And actually, that's what I wanted to talk to you about. Give me a minute; I'm going to take the phone in my office. Hang on."

I listened as Sam asked Davey to keep an eye on his little brother. There was the sound of muffled footsteps and I pictured him walking down the hallway. Thirty seconds later, I heard a door close behind him.

"Still there?" Sam asked.

"Right here," I said. "What's going on? What don't you want the boys to hear? Now you're worrying me."

"Nothing's wrong," Sam assured me. "I just wanted a little privacy for the rest of our conversation. Remember when you called last week and I said that I had a vague recollection of some rumors years ago concerning Ellie Wanamaker?"

"Sure, I remember. Didn't we decide that they must have been about the car accident she was involved in? The one where Dunaway was killed?"

"That's right, we did. And at the time I didn't think anything more about it. Then Miss Ellie died and I started to wonder whether it might be worthwhile to do a little digging around."

"I love you," I said.

I heard Sam grin. Don't ask me how. I just did.

"So I made a few calls. Checked back in with some friends from that part of the country. It took me a couple of days to hear anything back, but earlier this afternoon I got more information about that car crash. It wasn't just Miss Ellie's dog who was killed."

"I know," I said. "There were other injuries as well, including a very serious one to her son."

"Not just injuries," Sam told me. "It was worse than that . . . A woman died. She was the wife of another exhibitor who'd been at the show. I wasn't able to find out who was to blame for the accident. Nobody seemed to have the full story. I gather that some Gates family influence was brought to bear at the time and the whole thing was hushed up pretty quickly."

"Wow," I said, "I didn't hear anything like that. Did you get the name of the other exhibitor? The one whose wife was killed?"

"You bet I did. He's a local Newfoundland breeder. His name is Arthur Ludwig."

Chapter 18

Holy crap, I thought. *That* would explain a few things.

"Melanie? Are you there?"

I exhaled so suddenly that Faith sat up and cocked her head. I reached out and gave her a reassuring pat.

"Yes, I'm here," I said. "Are you sure about that?"

"Pretty sure. Like I said, there was some kind of cover-up at the time. So it's not like you can go searching around on the Internet to verify. Because actually I've already tried that and I didn't turn up a thing. But that's what people who were showing dogs in the area at the time have to say."

"Arthur Ludwig," I said. "Sea Haven Kennel."

"You know him?"

"No, not exactly. But I saw him last week when Miss Ellie and I were at the dog show together. Arthur Ludwig looked absolutely horrified when he saw Miss Ellie there. She started to speak to him but he hurried away without saying a word. I've been looking for him ever since she died."

"Of course you have," said Sam. "Why doesn't that surprise me?"

"Ludwig lives in Frankfort," I told him.

"That's nearby, right?"

"It's near Midway, the town where Six Oaks Farm is.

Aunt Peg has an appointment there tomorrow afternoon. Maybe we can kill two birds with one stone."

"I hope you're not thinking of leaving Peg at the farm and going to talk to Arthur Ludwig by yourself."

I didn't like the sound of that idea either. "No," I told him. "I'll take Aunt Peg with me."

"Great," Sam muttered. "In that scenario, which one of you is supposed to be taking care of the other?"

"Both of us." I would never admit it out loud but I actually liked the fact that Sam cared enough to worry about me. "And we'll have Faith with us, too."

"I guess that makes me feel a little better. I know you'd never let any harm come to her."

He had that right.

"We'll be fine," I told him.

"I hope so," Sam said. "I love you."

"I love you, too. I'll give Faith a pat for you."

"Tell her to hurry home. Things are too quiet around here with the two of you gone."

I ended the connection and put the phone away.

"Sam sends his love," I told Faith.

"Woof!" she said in reply.

While I'd been exercising Faith and talking to Sam, Aunt Peg had made a phone call of her own.

"Vurr-sales," she said with a frown when we went back inside and stopped by her room.

"What about it?" I asked. The word meant nothing to me.

"That's how you pronounce Versailles if you live in Kentucky," she informed me. "And since Midway doesn't have a police department of its own, that's where you call if you want to talk to the local sheriff. Vurr-sales."

"Well done!" I said. It was about time that someone encouraged the authorities to get involved.

"Not really," Aunt Peg replied. She sat down and patted

her lap. Faith trotted across the room and hopped up obligingly. "I miss my Poodles. Maybe Faith would like to sleep in here with me tonight?"

"I doubt it." I grinned. "But you can ask her. So what did the Sheriff of Versailles have to say?"

"He said that what happened to Ellie Gates Wanamaker was a terrible tragedy and that his department had no intention of making things worse for the family by pursuing an investigation into something that was clearly a random accident."

Oh. That was disappointing.

I sank down onto the bed. "Then I guess they're not going to want to hear what I just learned about Arthur Ludwig."

Aunt Peg perked up. "Something interesting, I hope?"

"You might say so."

I related the contents of my conversation with Sam and asked if she thought we ought to stop in Frankfort on our way to Six Oaks the next day.

I might as well have asked a Border Collie if he wanted to chase a ball.

"So now all we have to do is come up with a good excuse for showing up at Arthur Ludwig's house," I said. "Since we can't exactly call ahead and ask if he'd like to discuss Miss Ellie's suspicious death."

"Melanie, why must you *always* make things so complicated?" Aunt Peg reached around Faith and picked up her large handbag. After a full minute of searching around inside, she pulled out a phone. "Newfs, right?"

"Right. Sea Haven Kennel."

While I sat and watched, Aunt Peg made calls. Three, to be precise. That's all it took.

No need to inveigle an invitation when Aunt Peg was around. She just *fixed it.*

"Done," she said with satisfaction. "Arthur is expecting us at ten-thirty tomorrow morning."

"How did you do that?" I wanted to know.

"I have connections."

In Poodles, sure. And also among the other Non-Sporting breeds. You could add in Toy breeds too, since Aunt Peg judged those as well. But Newfoundlands were in the Working Group. That was a whole different collection of people.

"In *Newfoundlands?*"

"They're dogs, aren't they?"

Game, set, match, Aunt Peg.

"What do we know about Frankfort, Kentucky?" I asked the next morning as Aunt Peg, Faith, and I were once again speeding eastward on I-64.

Bertie had gotten up early and was already on her way back to Connecticut. Motivated by her departure, Aunt Peg and I had packed our own bags and checked out of the hotel as well. The Kentuckiana Cluster—our reason for being in Louisville—was over. If we were going to be spending the next day or two in the Lexington area, it only made sense for us to move there.

Since Bertie was no longer with us, by default I'd been restored to the minivan's front seat. It wasn't an automatic upgrade. Aunt Peg might have chosen to bestow the honor on Faith.

But instead, when it was time for us to set out, she'd gestured the Standard Poodle onto the back bench. "Much safer for you back there," she told Faith.

So now we all knew where we stood in Aunt Peg's order of importance.

"Frankfort is the state capital," she said, "even though as cities go it's relatively small. And Daniel Boone is buried there. That's all I know. Maybe Miss Ellie's man, Arthur, will be able to tell us more."

"Is he expecting this visit to be a social call?" I asked.

"It *is* a social call. I don't know about you, but I'm a very sociable person. I expect that Arthur and I will find that we have quite a lot to talk about."

Dogs were Aunt Peg's universal common denominator. She could hold forth on the topic for hours. And had, numerous times.

"Then I'll let you take the lead," I said. "And after you get Arthur softened up with small talk, we can broach the tough questions."

As might be expected for a man who bred large dogs, Arthur Ludwig didn't live in downtown Frankfort. Instead, his small, shingled house sat on several acres of land on the outskirts of the capital itself. The entire perimeter of the property was fenced. I had to get out and open a gate to grant us access. I closed it behind us after Aunt Peg drove through.

Arthur's two-storey home had a covered front porch and three gabled windows evenly spaced along the roofline. At least a dozen dog runs extended outward from the back of the house. Though I didn't see any dogs, I could hear the deep-throated rumble of their barking as Aunt Peg parked the van.

Faith immediately hopped to her feet and peered out through the windshield. "You're going to have to wait again," I told her regretfully as Aunt Peg lowered the windows for her. "But this time I promise we won't be long."

Faith sighed and sat back down on the seat. Here's a tip: If you don't want a dog who's fully capable of indicating when your behavior isn't up to snuff, don't buy a Poodle. Much like Miss Ellie, Faith had her standards. And lately I wasn't coming anywhere near to living up to them.

Arthur Ludwig looked much as I remembered him: medium height, stoop shouldered, and slender bordering on frail. He had a smile, however, that lit up his whole face. That expression hadn't been anywhere in evidence when I'd seen him the previous week.

"You must be Margaret Turnbull," he said, welcoming us both inside. "I'm happy to make your acquaintance."

"It's Peg, please. And this is my niece, Melanie Travis."

"Nice to meet you, too," he said. Arthur's gaze rested on my face for an extra beat. "Have we met before?"

"No, I'm afraid not," I told him. No use starting things on the wrong foot by bringing up our shared connection to Miss Ellie.

"Funny," he said. "I'm usually very good with faces and you look familiar."

"Maybe you saw Melanie at the dog show in Louisville last week," Aunt Peg told him. "She was making the rounds with Ellie Gates Wanamaker. Perhaps you ran into them?"

Wonderful. *That* was her idea of small talk?

"I saw Miss Ellie briefly." Arthur's smile faded. "First time I'd seen that woman at a dog show in more than a decade. Briefly was plenty."

"We heard that the two of you had some trouble in the past," Aunt Peg said.

I might as well have waited in the minivan with Faith, I thought, because there was no point in my even opening my mouth. So much for their shared dog connections and Aunt Peg's social call. We were barely even inside the door and Peg was already launching an interrogation.

" 'Trouble' is putting it mildly," said Arthur. "And now that woman is dead. Is that why you came today? You think I might want to talk about that?"

Aunt Peg nodded.

Arthur grimaced.

Since I was apparently superfluous, I just stood there and waited to see what would happen next.

After a minute Arthur reached around us and closed the front door. "I figured somebody would show up sooner or later to ask questions," he muttered unhappily. "You'd better come in and sit down."

We followed him into a cozy living room, whose wide

windows looked out over the rolling countryside. A rustic brick fireplace held the charred remains of its latest blaze, testament to that fact that even though spring had arrived, nights in the Bluegrass could still be chilly. Tabletops around the room displayed a collection of Newfoundland sculptures and figurines. I also saw a Newfoundland lamp, a set of Newfoundland bookends, and several win photos featuring Arthur and his big black dogs.

Aunt Peg took a seat in a straight-backed chair. I perched on one end of a love seat. Arthur sat down across from us. His gaze traveled back and forth between us as if he was wondering which direction he'd have to defend himself from first.

Since I hadn't had much to say thus far, I figured I might as well jump in. "Why were you expecting someone to come and question you?"

"Isn't it obvious? Ellie Gates Wanamaker killed my wife. And now that she's fallen off a cliff, I figured somebody might wonder about that. Actually I was thinking it would be more along the lines of the police who'd come by. I wasn't expecting it to be you two."

"The police think Miss Ellie's death was an accident," Aunt Peg told him.

Arthur snorted. "Do you believe that?"

"No." Aunt Peg and I both shook our heads.

"Me either. That woman was pure genius at making enemies. I'm just glad that one of them finally gave her the ending she deserved."

"You must have really hated her," I said.

"Maisie and I were married for thirty happy years. And we'd have been together for thirty more if not for Miss Ellie's negligence. I suppose that's reason enough for me to hate her."

"The three of you were involved in a car accident," said Aunt Peg.

"We understand that it happened on a rainy night, at the end of a long day at a dog show," I added.

"Accident, hell!" Arthur swore. "Is that what Miss Ellie told you? I'm surprised she said anything at all. Far as I know, she never talks about that night. When everything was over and done with, she just put it out of her mind and went on with her life as if nothing had changed at all."

That wasn't strictly true, I thought. After that night, Miss Ellie had had to devote a considerable amount of time to nursing her son back to good health. She'd also abandoned an avocation that had formerly meant a great deal to her. Her loss that night certainly hadn't had the magnitude of Arthur's, but it had been a loss nonetheless.

Arthur bounced back up to his feet as if he was too agitated to sit still. "If all you heard was what Miss Ellie had to say, then I'm betting there are huge holes in what you know."

"That's why we're here," said Aunt Peg. "Please fill us in."

"Did she tell you that we were all at the showground late that night because both our dogs had won their respective groups?" Arthur demanded. "Or that Dunaway and Sampson had been butting heads in the show ring all year long but that night it was her Standard Poodle who won the Best in Show?"

Miss Ellie hadn't mentioned that, I thought. But neither was I sure why the information mattered.

Arthur strode over to stand between Aunt Peg and me. He leaned down until his face was so close to ours that I could see the spittle on his lips. "Miss Ellie thought that beating my dog was great cause for celebration. And she was one lady who sure knew how to celebrate. I'm guessing Miss Ellie didn't mention how drunk she was when she got into her car to drive home that night, did she?"

I sucked in a shocked breath. *That was new.*

Aunt Peg looked equally surprised. A minute passed before either one of us spoke.

"No," she said finally. "We hadn't heard about that."

"Of course not," Arthur snapped. He straightened and stepped away from us. "The Gates name and Gates money took care of that. When that family wants something buried, it gets done."

An unfortunate turn of phrase under the circumstances, I thought.

"It was a fatal accident," Aunt Peg said. "Surely there must have been a police report."

"I imagine there was, though I wouldn't know for sure. At the time, I had other things on my mind. I spent the next three days after the crash at the hospital with Maisie, praying that she would beat the odds and pull through. I wasn't worried about what the police were up to. That never even crossed my mind. It wasn't until after I'd lost her that I began to think about who was to blame."

"Did you talk to the authorities then?" I asked.

Arthur hung his head. Abruptly his body crumpled as if he'd suddenly lost the strength to remain standing. Fortunately there was a chair behind him. He sat down and buried his face in his hands.

Aunt Peg and I exchanged a look of concern. We gave Arthur some time to gather himself.

When he looked up again, I saw that there were tears in his eyes. "A representative of the Gates family visited me in the hospital right after Maisie died. *Minutes after*. Her body was still there when he came into the room. I didn't want to talk to him. I didn't want to see anybody right then, but he came marching right in anyway like he thought he owned the world."

I could picture the scene. All at once Arthur wasn't the only one with tears in his eyes. I was pretty sure I knew what was coming next.

"The attorney told me how sorry the whole Gates family was about what had happened and he asked me to sign some papers he'd brought with him. There was a statement describing the accident and attributing its cause to the late night, the storm, and the dark and slippery roads. It said that nobody was responsible for the terrible losses we'd all suffered. In signing it, I agreed not to hold any member of the Gates family liable nor to seek any judgment against them."

"I certainly hope you didn't sign that document," Aunt Peg said huffily.

Arthur didn't answer right away. I knew then that there was more to the story than he'd let on.

"The attorney offered you something for your signature, didn't he?" I asked. "Some kind of settlement? The Gates family must have given you money in exchange for your cooperation and your silence."

"They did," Arthur admitted in a ragged tone. "And so help me, I took it. It was too late to bring Maisie back. Nothing could change what had already happened. I figured the least I could do was make those people pay good money for what Miss Ellie had done."

"That's why there was never any talk about the accident," I said. "And why no one ever knew the details."

Arthur nodded. "By the time I walked out of that hospital three days later, it was as if the whole thing had never even happened. The Gates connections must have been working overtime to accomplish that, but they got it done all right."

"And you took the settlement and went on with your life," I said.

"It's not as if I had a choice," Arthur replied bitterly. "If I'd turned that attorney away and tried to pursue justice on my own, do you think anyone was ever going to listen to me? I wouldn't even have been able to find a decent lawyer who was willing to take that family to court. Believe me, I've thought about it a lot since then. No matter what I did, Ellie Gates Wanamaker would never have been held accountable."

"Unless, after all these years, you took matters into your own hands," Aunt Peg said quietly.

"You must be joking." Arthur snorted.

"You expected the police to come and talk to you," I pointed out. "So obviously the idea isn't as farfetched as you'd like us to think."

Arthur stood up once again. Without looking at either of us, he strode across the room toward the front door. Clearly we were being ushered out whether we were ready to leave or not. Aunt Peg and I got up and followed.

"I already told you that I put all that behind me. I wanted nothing to do with Miss Ellie or anyone else from the Gates family." Arthur grasped the knob and yanked the door open. "That woman had the nerve to track me down at the dog show last week. After all these years, she wanted to apologize. Can you imagine that? I told her to get lost and stay that way."

So that was where Miss Ellie had disappeared to, I thought. Years too late, she'd attempted to make amends for her terrible deed. And Arthur had thrown the apology back in her face. No wonder she'd fled from the showground.

"What happened to Miss Ellie was an accident," Arthur said shortly. "You told me that yourself. Besides, I was in Louisville all last week with my new specials dog, Ulysses. You can check the entries. You'll see that I'm telling the truth."

"What a thoroughly unpleasant man," Aunt Peg said when we were once more on the other side of his gate and driving away down the road. "It's a shame that he has an alibi."

"I'm not sure he does," I said.

"A dog named Ulysses sounds like he'd be hard to miss," Peg pointed out. "And apart from that, proof of his presence would be recorded in the judge's book."

"The woman I spoke to on Sunday—the one at the Newf ring who gave me Arthur's name—also told me that his dog had been entered for the whole cluster but that she hadn't seen him since Thursday."

"The day he ran into Miss Ellie."

"That's right."

"What was the woman's name?" asked Aunt Peg.

"Umm . . . I don't exactly know. We got started talking. We never bothered to introduce ourselves."

Aunt Peg slanted me a look. "So one person we know who surely has a motive may or may not also have an alibi—depending on whether we choose to believe him or a woman about whom we know next to nothing."

"That about sums it up," I told her.

She shifted her eyes back to the road. "I was afraid you'd say that."

Chapter 19

Aunt Peg and I stopped for lunch in Midway again. We ate in a quaint café at the end of East Main Street named Darlin' Jean's. It was warm enough for outdoor seating to be available and nobody objected when Faith accompanied us to our table. She lay down on the plank floor underneath it and made sure to position herself within easy reach. I took the hint and slipped her several good-sized bites of my very good bagel melt.

A breach of conduct like that usually merits a lecture from Aunt Peg. Now she just looked the other way and pretended not to notice. Apparently I wasn't the only one who was feeling guilty about all the downtime Faith had had to endure recently on our behalf.

"What do you have left to go over with Ben Burrell this afternoon?" I asked as we were settling the check.

"I initially made the appointment because Lucky Luna's breeding contract needed to be rewritten in my name and now that it's ready, it has to be signed. But I have to admit that the business Erin was talking about at Miss Ellie's funeral really made me stop and think."

"Me, too," I agreed. "And I don't even have a horse."

"Ben was great about discussing everything with me last week," Aunt Peg said. "But dipping a toe into the Thoroughbred industry is like any other new endeavor. Sometimes you don't even know what kinds of questions you should be asking about until you've had the opportunity to learn more about how things work."

Faith stood up and had a leisurely stretch. We hopped down the steps at the near end of the deck and crossed the parking lot. Aunt Peg unlocked the minivan and the three of us climbed in.

"I thought about it overnight," she continued, "and it occurred to me that I might be precisely the kind of naïve new owner Erin was talking about. What if Six Oaks Farm thinks that they are managing *me* in the same way Billy Gates is handling Daniel Nash's affairs? Perhaps they, too, are giving me only the information they wish me to have and counting on the fact that I will be too stupid to seek out the rest on my own?"

Aunt Peg is a decisive and forceful woman. Certainly I'd never had any luck in getting her to do things my way. So it was hard for me to imagine anyone successfully manipulating her. But this business with Lucky Luna was all uncharted territory, and I could understand her concerns.

"Especially as I'm an absentee owner, I feel the need to clarify my position," Aunt Peg said. "If Ben and I both take the time now to outline our specific duties and expectations, I'm hoping that will cut down on the possibility of misunderstandings in the future."

"That sounds like an excellent idea," I agreed. "And while you're putting Mr. Burrell through his paces, Faith and I will be having fun with Erin."

I called ahead to the farm when we were on our way. By the time we reached the office at Six Oaks, Erin was waiting for us in the small parking lot out front. Aunt Peg left us and went inside the building. I beckoned Erin over and slid open the minivan's side door. Faith stood in the opening and wagged her tail obligingly.

"Is it okay if she comes with us?" I asked. "She's very well-behaved and I have a leash."

Erin hesitated. "You're sure she won't get away from you?"

"Positive."

"And she won't bark at the horses, or jump around and spook them?"

"No way," I told her firmly.

"I guess it's all right then. Bring her along and let's go."

I hopped Faith up into the cab of the truck and climbed in beside her. "I thought we'd head back to the broodmare division," Erin told me as she put the vehicle in gear. "The mares and foals are outside now and I like to walk around the fields in the afternoon and make sure that everything is as it should be. It's such a pretty day, I was hoping that you wouldn't mind walking with me?"

"That would be perfect," I said. "And Faith will love it."

"That's a pretty name." Erin glanced over at us. "My family had a Poodle when I was a little girl. His name was Jacques. He wasn't anywhere near as big as Faith is though."

Poodles are the quintessential family dog. And it was amazing how many people I met who had fond memories of growing up with one.

"Faith's a Standard Poodle," I said. "That's the biggest of the three varieties. Jacques would have been a Mini or a Toy."

"He was about this big." Erin took her hands off the steering wheel and indicated a space slightly more than a foot apart. "What would that make him?"

"Probably a Miniature. All three sizes are great dogs."

"Jacques was the smartest dog in the world. He learned all sorts of silly tricks just like that." She snapped her fingers. "I'm pretty sure that dog understood every word I said."

"Faith does, too," I told her.

Erin laughed at that. "Thanks for the warning. I'll be sure to watch what I say around her."

The farm road we were on wound past several expansive fields, then took us through another gate. Finally we turned down a long driveway and parked beside another big, horseshoe-shaped barn.

"Your aunt . . . she's somebody important in dogs, right?" Erin asked as we all got out of the truck.

"She is indeed." I nudged Faith's ear aside and double-checked the clasp on her leash just to be sure.

"Does she know anything about Jack Russells?"

"Aunt Peg has an amazing gift for understanding all dogs. Terriers aren't her specialty, but if you need help, I'm sure she'd be happy to try."

"I'm not the one who needs help," Erin said. "It's Gates. He took over the care of his mother's dogs but he lives in an apartment where pets aren't allowed. So for the time being they're still at Miss Ellie's house. He stops by a couple times a day to feed the dogs and let them outside but that's not working out very well. They're driving him a little crazy."

"I can imagine," I said, frowning. "JRTs are a busy breed. And that doesn't sound like a great situation for them *or* Gates. I'm sure Aunt Peg will have some ideas. And she can probably help find homes for them if that's what he decides he wants."

"Thanks," said Erin. "That would be great."

Each of the pastures in front of us was enclosed by double fencing whose purpose, according to Erin, was to keep the occupants of one field from interacting with those in another. As a result, a grid of wide alleyways separated each pasture from the next. Erin headed toward the nearest wide, grassy lane and Faith and I followed.

"You said that you wanted to learn more about the horse business," she said when we'd passed through the first gate and Erin had closed it carefully behind us. "Is there anything in particular you're looking to find out?"

"That stuff you were telling us yesterday about the Thoroughbred sales was fascinating," I told her. "It's surprising to me that buyers are willing to give up so much control. It almost sounds like they don't make any decisions at all."

"Sometimes that's true," Erin conceded. "But look at it this way. Buyers aren't handing over control so much as they are hiring expert consultants who can help them make the best possible choices. That's no different than what a businessman in any other industry might do."

Faith stopped to sniff the base of a fence post. A small group of mares was grazing nearby. Most of their foals were asleep in the grass at their feet. I paused and leaned my arms on the top rail of the fence, gazing at the idyllic scene.

"Last week when you took us over to the training track, we saw some young horses galloping," I said.

"That's right. The ones who were here prepping for the sale. They're all over at Keeneland now. The sale is next Monday, but there's a preview day on Thursday when the two-year-olds will breeze on the track for prospective buyers."

"Those two colts that Daniel Nash was looking at—a bay and a chestnut—will they sell well?" I asked curiously.

Erin shrugged. "We'll have to see, won't we? They're both good-looking, well-bred colts. But a lot will depend on how well they perform on Thursday."

"Billy Gates appears to be quite an expert."

"He is," she agreed. "Billy knows as much about horses as Peg does about dogs. Maybe even more. Horses and that farm are his whole life."

"So was Aunt Peg wrong?"

Erin glanced my way. "Wrong about what?"

"She liked the bay horse better. But Billy was recommending the chestnut."

Erin hesitated. When a minute passed and she still hadn't answered, I said, "Here's the thing. Aunt Peg can be incredibly annoying and opinionated. But she never tries to appear more knowledgeable than she really is. And much as I hate to admit it, when Aunt Peg ventures an opinion she's almost always right. So that's why I'm curious."

"I get it," Erin said with a sly grin. "You're hoping your aunt was mistaken, aren't you?"

"Maybe," I admitted, and we laughed together. "Trust me, it would make a pleasant change."

"I wish I could help you but to tell the truth, I don't know. Billy sometimes sees things in horses that other people don't. He's kind of a genius that way. That's why people hire him to do what he does."

"Then I guess Daniel Nash is lucky to have him." That thought brought up another question. "How do people who are new to the industry find a skilled advisor like Billy?"

"If they're lucky, they get someone good through word of mouth. But sometimes newcomers just read the trades and hire the big-name people who get the most press." Erin straightened, pushing herself away from the fence. "Come on. Let's walk some more. We've got a lot of ground to cover, and Faith looks like she'd rather be moving."

I could have stood and watched the mares and foals all afternoon. But Erin was right, Faith was growing impatient. When the three of us continued down the lane, Faith bounced and played at the end of her leash.

"If you're staying through Monday, you should stop by the auction at Keeneland," Erin said when we'd reached the far end of the first pasture and turned the corner. "You and your aunt might find it interesting to watch."

"We probably would," I agreed. "Finally something around here that's easy for non-horsemen to figure out."

"Not necessarily," said Erin.

"Why not? An auction is a straightforward system for setting a fair price." I turned and looked at her. "Isn't it?"

"It can be. But it isn't always."

"Explain that to me," I said. "Because I don't get it."

"That's probably because you're assuming that all the bidders are interested in acquiring the horse they're bidding on."

"Well . . . yes. If someone doesn't want to buy a horse, why would they be bidding on it?"

"Could be that the owner of the horse is bidding against you and running up the price. Or maybe you've had the bad luck to hire the wrong advisor. If so, he might be doing the same thing."

Abruptly I stopped walking. Caught by surprise, Faith hit the end of the leash. She circled back and looked at me reproachfully.

"Sorry, sweetie," I said. Then I shifted my gaze back to Erin. "My agent is supposed to be helping me shop and protecting my interests. Isn't that why I hired him?"

"Sure. But like in any other business, there are good guys and bad guys. And if a newcomer makes the wrong choices about who to get involved with, he could end up with an agent who's looking to make some extra money on the side."

"I can see how running up a horse's price would benefit the seller. But how would it help my agent?"

"Let's back up for a minute," said Erin. She started walking again. "Say you're a guy from out of town who's been to the races a few times. You got a great buzz from the betting, and the winning, and the excitement of the racing. And you start thinking this might be a terrific hobby to have some fun with. Are you with me so far?"

"Yup." So far, it was easy.

"So you come to Kentucky because everybody knows that if you want Thoroughbreds, this is the place to be. You look around and meet some people. Maybe you join TOBA."

Erin saw my blank look and added, "Thoroughbred Owners and Breeders Association."

"Of course," I replied as if that was the only possible answer.

Faith looked up and gave me a doggy grin. She hadn't known either.

"So now there's a sale coming up. Let's make it the Keeneland September sale. That's the best place to shop if you're looking for a yearling. But with more than four thousand to choose from, you don't know where to begin. You're a smart guy and you want to get this right, so you hire a bloodstock agent to help you.

"Of course I do," I agreed. Aside from that TOBA blip, she hadn't lost me yet.

"You tell your new agent that you want to buy a nice colt to take to the races. Let's make your budget something reasonable . . . say, one hundred thousand dollars."

"That's *reasonable?*"

"Middling," Erin told me. "That kind of money won't put you at the top of anyone's list. The important agents, they're looking for the millionaires."

"I hate to break it to you," I said on a strangled laugh, "but if I'm spending *one hundred thousand dollars on a horse*, I *am* a millionaire."

"Okay," Erin said airily. "Then they're looking for billionaires."

"Yikes. That's some rarified company."

"It's where everyone wants to be."

Me, too, I thought. Who wouldn't?

"Now the first thing your bloodstock agent is probably going to do is try to get you to raise your budget."

"Like a real estate agent when you're buying a house," I said.

"Same idea." Erin nodded. "Because in both cases your agent will be working on commission. So the more you spend, the more they make. There may be other charges too, but basically the fee for your agent's services is going to be a percentage of the purchase price of your horse."

"Got it," I said.

"Before the sale even starts, your agent will be over at Keeneland, looking at horses and trying to find something that might suit you. Book one—the yearlings that sell first—have the best conformation and come from the best families. They're the most expensive horses in the sale. In book two, things get a little more affordable. Same in book three and so on down the line. With the money you want to spend, your agent might be targeting some nice yearlings in book two."

"Wait a minute," I said. "How do people know ahead of time what prices the horses are going to bring?"

"They don't always, but that's where your agent's expertise comes into play. He looks at each horse and makes an educated guess. Most of these guys have been in the industry for years. And in a stable market, their estimates are usually just about spot-on."

I supposed I could see that. It was probably no different than Aunt Peg's ability to look at a litter of eight-week-old Poodle puppies and know which ones would become future show ring stars.

"Now say you've had the misfortune to choose an unscrupulous agent," Erin continued. "Your guy looks around the sale and finds a colt he likes a lot. One whose value he appraises at around seventy-five thousand. He figures that's approximately the amount that other people bidding on the horse will be willing to pay. But that's not what he tells you the yearling is worth."

"It's not?"

We'd come upon another tranquil scene: mares grazing peacefully while three or four foals raced with obvious enjoyment in large, looping circles around them. Erin and I both stopped to watch. Faith found a sunny patch in the grass beside us and lay down.

"No," she confirmed, "it's not. The first thing your guy will do is get you all excited about your prospective purchase. He talks that colt up like he's the second coming of Secretariat. You'll hear all about nicks, and scans, and every good horse your agent has ever bought for a client. Your guy will tell you to picture the colt wearing a blanket of roses on the first Saturday in May."

"Derby day?" I hazarded a guess.

"Of course." She seemed surprised that I even had to ask. "Then, when your agent has you convinced that you absolutely *have* to have this colt, he tells you that if you're *very* lucky you just might be able to buy this superior specimen of horseflesh for a hundred thousand dollars."

"I don't understand," I said. "Isn't that going to make him look stupid when the horse sells for less at the auction?"

"That's just it; he isn't going to. Because once you've okayed the price, your agent will get a buddy of his to stand out back and bid against you when the colt is in the ring. You'll think that another legitimate buyer is willing to pay just as much for that yearling as you are. But in reality, everyone else has dropped out and the price is being driven up."

I was still confused. Too bad Faith wasn't better with math. I might have asked her to explain it to me.

"How does that help the agent?" I asked. "Wouldn't the extra money go to the seller of the colt?"

"Technically, yes. But all kinds of private deals can be made ahead of time between seller and agent if that's the way they choose to do business. Commissions, kickbacks, maybe a little sweetener for the agent who made the sale happen. And even without something like that, your guy would still profit because he'll be getting a commission from you. So if the colt sells for the higher price, his fee is suddenly a third higher than it would have been. Just for doing the exact same job."

"That's despicable," I said.

Erin just shrugged. "That's the horse business. Buyer beware."

"And the people spending the money have no idea what's going on?"

"Most of them figure it out eventually. But in the beginning, they don't have a clue. Remember, they're not horsemen. They've done their due diligence and hired the 'right' people to help them make good decisions. So they believe what they're told."

"That sounds like a good way to run new people out of the business," I muttered.

"But not until they catch on," said Erin. "And that doesn't happen right away. In fact, right now the buyer is really happy. Maybe even ecstatic. He's just won a bidding war and landed a colt his agent told him is full of potential. Maybe he spent some serious money to do it, but that's okay, too. Because the people who get involved in this game are gamblers. They get off on the thrill of the big race, the big win, the big score. And the bigger the risk, the bigger the rush—you know what I mean?"

Chapter 20

By the time Erin, Faith, and I returned to the farm's front office, more than an hour had passed. Aunt Peg was sitting outside the building waiting for us. She looked perfectly comfortable settled on a carved wooden bench that had been well positioned to catch the afternoon sun. Aunt Peg appeared to be engrossed in something she was doing on her phone.

"Updating your Facebook status?" I inquired as Faith and I climbed out of the truck together.

"Bite your tongue," she replied, tucking the device away in her purse. Aunt Peg considers social media to be the downfall of civil discourse. She rose to her feet and came over to join us. "How was your walk?"

"Superb," I told her. Faith wiggled back and forth to add her own confirmation. "How was your meeting?"

"Illuminating."

"I hope that's a good thing," Erin said brightly.

"As do I," Aunt Peg replied.

Well, that was an ambiguous answer. I'd have to explore that issue later, however. Now I had something more immediate on my mind.

"Erin was wondering if you would be willing to help Gates figure out a way to cope with Miss Ellie's dogs," I said to Aunt Peg.

"I'd be happy to," she replied. "I can see how four Jack Russells could be a bit of a challenge, especially if Gates isn't set up to handle that kind of exuberance. Where are the dogs now?"

Erin looked pained. "They're still living at Miss Ellie's house," she admitted. "Pretty much by themselves, which isn't great."

Aunt Peg's lips tamped together, no doubt to keep her from blurting out something she might regret. "Not *great* indeed," she said sternly. "Who decided upon that expediency?"

"Gates can't have dogs in his apartment," I told her.

"He lives above a shop in Midway," Erin added. "No pets allowed. And the landlord is very strict. So until he can figure out what to do next, he left the Jack Russells where they were. At least there they have a backyard to run around in."

"And they're alone *all* day?" Aunt Peg inquired.

Erin hung her head. "Most days, either Gates or I try to get away at lunchtime and we run over and make sure they're okay," she said in a small voice.

Aunt Peg didn't look appeased. "Terriers are diggers by nature. You're lucky nobody's managed to burrow out beneath the fence."

"Yes, ma'am."

Under other circumstances, I was quite sure Aunt Peg would have taken Erin to task over the JRTs' current living situation. But with less than a week having passed since Miss Ellie's death, she must have felt that allowances could be made, because instead she said, "Has anyone been to see to the dogs yet today?"

"I'm afraid not," said Erin.

"In that case, Melanie and I will go over there now."

Aunt Peg wasn't asking permission. She had issued a directive. Nothing spurred her to action more expeditiously than the discovery of a dog in need. Or in this case, four of them.

"Really?" Erin asked with evident relief. "You would do that?"

"Try and stop her," I muttered under my breath.

"That's so great of you! I know Gates will appreciate it. Those dogs were Miss Ellie's best friends and he's felt bad for ignoring them as much as he has." Erin pulled out her phone as she spoke. "You know where the house is, right? There's a spare key under a rock next to the mailbox. I'll call Gates now and tell him that you're going to stop by and take care of things."

"We can provide assistance today," said Aunt Peg. "But long term, Gates is going to have to make some difficult decisions about the welfare of those dogs. They can't continue on as they are indefinitely."

"He knows that," Erin agreed with a small sigh. "It's just that Miss Ellie's death is so recent. Gates doesn't even want to think about making any changes just yet."

Aunt Peg and I nodded sympathetically.

"He and I went back to Miss Ellie's house last night after the funeral. I know it was incredibly hard for him just to be there and see everything looking exactly the same as it did when his mother was alive. That's why I've been trying to help out as much as I can with the dogs. It's difficult for him to go back to that house at all. And that reminds me . . . watch out for the boxes."

The sudden change of subject caught me off guard. "Boxes?"

"While we were there last night I went up to the attic, brought down a few cartons, and started to pack up some of Miss Ellie's stuff. Gates doesn't even want to look at his mother's things, much less deal with them. So I'm trying to get some of her mementos tucked away out of sight. There's a bunch of boxes stacked in the living room. I hope they won't be in your way."

"Don't worry about us," I said. "We'll be fine."

Aunt Peg nodded. "I'm sure this is a difficult time for Gates. It's nice of you to help him like that."

"Yeah . . . well." Erin's cheeks grew pink. "Gates and I have known each other since we were little kids. And his family can be pretty tough. Now that Miss Ellie is gone, it's not like the rest of them are going to step in and worry about his welfare."

"At least he has a good job on the family farm," I said. "So they must care about him some."

"It doesn't always look that way to me," Erin said. "Listen, I've got to get back to work. I'll let Gates know what you're doing, and thank you so much for helping out!"

She jumped into the truck and left.

"Those poor Jack Russells," Aunt Peg said. "Not only missing their mistress, but also left almost to fend for themselves. I guess we know how we'll be spending our afternoon."

Before climbing into the minivan, I got a bottle of cold water out of the cooler, opened it up, and poured some in Faith's bowl. She lapped it up eagerly.

"Illuminating?" I said as Faith was drinking. "What was that about?"

"Perhaps I'm not cut out to be in the horse business."

I waggled my eyebrows up and down suggestively. "Maybe you'd like to adopt four Jack Russell Terriers instead."

"I'm too old for all that nonsense." Aunt Peg snorted. She slid in behind the steering wheel. "I'll stick with my Poodles, thank you very much."

As if anyone was surprised by that.

The key to Miss Ellie's house was just where Erin had said it would be, underneath a smooth rock beside the mailbox. Before we'd even pulled into the driveway, I could already hear the cacophonous chorus created by a troop of terriers barking in competition with one another. That noise was loud.

"The neighbors must love that," Aunt Peg muttered. "I'm surprised they haven't complained."

"Who would they complain to?" I asked. "There's nobody here but the JRTs."

"Who are probably bored to tears," Aunt Peg said as we crossed the yard and let ourselves into the house. "It's a good thing those four haven't tunneled their way to China by now. Let's start by letting them inside and getting everyone reacquainted. They should remember Faith from the last time we were here. Hopefully they'll be delighted to see all three of us."

Delighted was an understatement.

When Aunt Peg opened the back door and called the four terriers into the kitchen, they greeted us like we were long-lost relatives. Tails wagging so hard that their small, hard-packed bodies undulated with the effort, the dogs snuffled our clothes, whined with excitement, and scrambled en masse into our laps when Aunt Peg and I sank down onto the floor. Even with four eager hands between us, we could barely keep up with all the excitement.

"The poor things are starved for human companionship," Aunt Peg said. "And no wonder. Do we know any of their names?"

"There are nameplates on their collars." I nabbed one squirming body and lifted it up to eye level. As short legs swum in the air and a whiskered muzzle and determined pink tongue tried to find my face, I tipped the terrier to one side and read the Gothic print. "This one's Ringo."

Aunt Peg hefted a second dog. "Here's Paul."

"George," I announced with a laugh as I checked out the third nameplate. I looked over at the last Jack Russell who was now on the other side of the kitchen, touching noses with Faith. "You must be John."

The little dog cocked his tipped ears in my direction and yipped once before turning back to Faith. I was pleased to note that the bark sounded much more cheerful than the discordant racket we'd heard upon our arrival.

"Goodness," said Aunt Peg. "They're the Fab Four."

"The who?"

"The Fab Four. That's what The Beatles were called in their time." She peered at me with a frown. "Do you really not know that? My, you're young."

"Young and spry," I said as I set Ringo aside and rose to my feet. "Let's find some leashes for these guys and take them for a run." I extended a hand downward. "Do you need some help getting up?"

"Young and fresh," Aunt Peg muttered.

She ignored my outstretched hand and levered herself up with no assistance from me, thank you very much. And if anyone might have heard her knees crack, neither of us was inclined to mention it.

We exercised the five dogs from one end of Miss Ellie's two-mile-long road to the other. There weren't any sidewalks in the sparsely populated neighborhood but there wasn't much traffic to worry about either. The few cars we saw were considerate enough to slow down and pass with care. Aunt Peg walked three of the terriers and I handled John and Faith. The Standard Poodle and the Jack Russell were quickly becoming fast friends.

"Don't get any ideas," I told him when we returned to the house an hour later. John was one of the two rough-coated terriers. He had stubby legs, a tail that was always wagging, and an endearing tan-colored patch over one eye. "I don't care how cute you are. You are not coming home with me."

"They're *all* cute," Aunt Peg agreed. "And nicely behaved too, as long as someone's paying attention to them. Not that I had any doubts, mind you. Miss Ellie never would have tolerated a pack of undisciplined dogs in her house."

I'd noticed Aunt Peg observing the quartet and making her assessment as we'd traversed the neighborhood together. Juggling my two charges, I'd attempted to do the same. Not that my opinion made any difference. When it came to dogs, Aunt Peg's viewpoint was always the only one that mattered.

"If Gates decides he's not in the right place to take on the responsibility of their care, I'm sure I'll be able to find good situations for them," she said. "They may have to be broken up into pairs, however."

There weren't any crates on the first floor of Miss Ellie's home. I took that to mean that it was all right if we gave the JRTs the run of the house. Releasing John, I hung his leash on a hook near the back door. While Aunt Peg freed her three charges and put away their leads, I picked up the big water bowl that was sitting on a woven mat on the floor.

The dish was nearly empty. I rinsed it out in the sink, then refilled it with fresh, cool water. When I set it back down on the mat, three of the terriers immediately crowded around for a drink.

"Who's missing?" Aunt Peg looked around quickly.

"I think it's Ringo."

"He was just here a second ago. He can't have gone far."

Aunt Peg was right. The Jack Russell hadn't gone very far at all. As I walked through the living room, skirting between two columns of stacked boxes, I saw the little dog lying on the hardwood floor in the front hall. Head resting between his front paws, he was staring at the closed front door with an air of patient resignation. How sad was that?

"You're waiting for Miss Ellie to come back, aren't you?" I asked.

Ringo glanced up at me briefly, then resumed his quiet vigil.

I crossed my legs and sank down to the floor beside him. "I wish I could tell you that everything is going to be all right," I said softly. "But I have a firm rule about lying to dogs."

Ringo's tail made an abbreviated swish across the hardwood surface. The gesture wasn't an indication of happiness. Rather it was simply an acknowledgment that the small dog had heard what I was saying.

"I know you miss her. But you're going to find somebody else to love. Somebody *great*. Aunt Peg will make sure of it."

"What's this?" asked Aunt Peg, coming up behind me. "Did I hear my name?"

"Ringo is missing Miss Ellie," I said. "I was telling him how much he's going to like his new home."

"Poor bereft boy." Aunt Peg reached down and lifted the little terrier into her comforting arms. "I quite understand how he feels. I wonder if Miss Ellie made provisions for these dogs in her will. Most responsible dog owners do."

That stung just a little. I consider myself to be a responsible dog owner but when Faith was young and newly mine, the thought of making a provision for aftercare had never even crossed my mind. A year later the topic had come up in conversation and Aunt Peg had demanded that I remedy that deficiency immediately. She'd kept after me until I'd sat down with a lawyer and fixed things.

"Gates will know," I said. "We can find out from him later."

Aunt Peg turned and headed back toward the kitchen with Ringo in her arms. I stood up and followed.

"Take a look inside there," she said, nodding toward an open cardboard box as she walked by. "I see some interesting reading material on top. Fond memories for me," she added archly. "Prehistoric archives for you."

I paused and had a look. The big carton was filled nearly to the brim with dog show memorabilia from the 1970s and '80s. There were marked catalogs from the Poodle Club of America National and Regional Specialties, and half a dozen well-read copies of the annual *Poodle Review* stud dog edition. Stacked beneath those were numerous glossy issues of other decades-old canine magazines and periodicals.

"Wow." I pulled out a worn copy of *Poodle Variety* and began to flip through its pages. "Look at these old ads. The Poodles in here are amazing."

"Of course they are." Aunt Peg was in the kitchen with Ringo, making sure that he got a drink. "They're the ancestors of most of the good Poodles you see in the ring today."

"Puttencove, Eaton, Bel Tor . . ." The illustrious kennel names rolled off my tongue like those of long-lost friends. "How cool is this?"

I set the first magazine aside and reached for another. Then I stopped and glanced up. "Do you think it's all right if I look at these? I mean, it's not like I have Miss Ellie's permission to go through her things."

"I think Miss Ellie would be disappointed if you didn't look," Aunt Peg said. "She kept all those magazines for a reason, probably because she referred back to them herself. I'm sure she would have been happy to share them with you."

I spent the next half hour happily immersed in Poodle history. After Faith and the Fab Four had settled down to nap, Aunt Peg came over and joined me. Together we worked our way through Miss Ellie's incredible collection of twentieth-century Poodle media.

Reaching into the carton for another new magazine to peruse, I found my fingers closing over something that was the right size and shape but bound with a hard cover. The book was wedged in down near the bottom of the pile.

Curious, I shifted some other things aside and jiggled it free.

The tome gave off a musty smell as I lifted it up and out of the box. Its pebbled-leather back cover was dotted with mold. I flipped the book over and saw that it was an old yearbook. FOXCROFT SCHOOL 1974 was emblazoned across the front.

"Look at this." I held the volume out to Aunt Peg. "I found Miss Ellie's high school yearbook."

"Hmmm, 1974." She opened the cover carefully and began to flip slowly through the pages. "I'll bet that was her graduating year. Let's see if she had a senior picture."

I looked over Aunt Peg's shoulder as she thumbed through the section of the yearbook devoted to the school's graduating class. Some of the pages stuck to each other and needed to be separated gently. The names of the senior girls were listed in alphabetical order.

"Elizabeth Bernice Everley, Sarah Marjorie Framingham . . ." Aunt Peg read. Then she pointed to the next page and said with satisfaction, "Here she is, Eleanora Bentley Gates from Lexington, Kentucky."

I leaned in for a closer look. Like all the others, Miss Ellie's photograph was black and white. She was wearing a creamy off-the-shoulder dress and had a string of pearls around her neck. Her head was tilted up toward the light and she had a dreamy, faraway look on her face.

"Miss Ellie was beautiful," I said. "What does it say about her?"

Beneath the picture was a quote that Aunt Peg identified as coming from John Lennon's song "Imagine." It was followed by a paragraph of humorous quips relating to Miss Ellie's time at Foxcroft. Lastly, she had filled in the blanks left in some rather predictable phrases.

"Favorite food . . . rare steak," I read. "Always ready to . . . play hooky. I'd rather be . . . at the stable."

Then my eyes skimmed over the last item and I lifted my head abruptly.

"Look at that," I said.

"What?" Aunt Peg pushed my hand aside. "I can't see anything while you're in the way."

I pulled back and Aunt Peg read aloud the same words that I'd seen a moment earlier. "When she should be studying, often found . . . writing love letters to Danny Nash."

Chapter 21

"Maybe it's a coincidence," said Aunt Peg.

"Maybe it's not," I shot back.

"Daniel Nash . . . Danny Nash . . . they might not even be the same person. And so what if they are? Lots of single people are reconnecting with old beaus from high school. It's the thing to do these days."

"Miss Ellie didn't mention him," I pointed out.

"Why would she have done that when we had so many other, more interesting things to talk about? There was no reason for Miss Ellie to make us privy to the intimate details of her life."

"It is *not* a coincidence," I insisted stubbornly. "Unless you're asking me to believe that two different people named Daniel Nash both happened to have connections to members of the Gates family?"

"All right. Then suppose they are one and the same," Aunt Peg said, equally stubborn. "Maybe Miss Ellie's old friend Danny Nash decided to buy a racehorse. He remembered that she came from a prominent Kentucky family and he asked her to introduce him around."

"Nope. That's not the way it happened."

"How would you know?"

"Because that's not what Daniel said when we were talking to him at Miss Ellie's funeral."

"Oh?" Aunt Peg thought back, then shook her head. "I'm not sure I remember that part."

"We were standing with Gates and Erin when Daniel came over to pay his respects," I told her.

"That's right. Gates introduced him to us and Daniel said that he was a Puritan from Boston. That made an impression on me because he's from our area of the country, more or less. It occurred to me that he was a long way from home, too."

"Daniel also mentioned that he hadn't known Miss Ellie long. He said Billy had just introduced the two of them a week earlier."

"How very interesting," Aunt Peg said thoughtfully. "Clearly I should have been paying closer attention at the time. I would hate to think that we might have overlooked something like that."

It wasn't exactly high praise. But it was closer to an expression of approval than I usually get from Aunt Peg. So maybe I basked just a little.

She shut that down in a hurry.

"Obviously we ought to have a conversation with Mr. Nash," Aunt Peg said. "What kind of contact information do we possess for the man?"

"None that I'm aware of."

"Do something about that, would you?"

"Umm . . . like what?"

"You have a phone; I suggest you put it to good use. In the meantime, I'm going to return the boys to the backyard and make sure that they have access to shade and water out there."

I started with accommodations on the west side of Lexington, those closest to both Midway and Keeneland. It only took fifteen minutes to track down the hotel in Beaumont Centre where Daniel Nash was staying. The person manning the front desk offered to connect me to Mr. Nash's room but I declined. Instead I bookmarked the hotel's address and handed the information over to Aunt Peg.

"I hate leaving these dogs on their own again," she said, "but I suppose it can't be helped. Hopefully Gates will be by in a few hours to tend to them. In the meantime, isn't it lucky that we were planning to switch locations anyway?"

"I take it we're about to join Daniel Nash in Beaumont Centre?"

"Indeed," Aunt Peg replied cheerfully.

We locked the back door and took one last look around the house to make sure everything was in order before letting ourselves out the front. As we passed through the living room, Aunt Peg reached into the carton where I'd replaced Miss Ellie's yearbook. Without even breaking stride, she scooped the book back out and slipped it beneath her arm.

"All in aid of a good cause," she said. "I'm sure Miss Ellie won't mind if we borrow this for a day or two, in case Mr. Nash needs further persuasion to talk to us."

"But Gates—"

"Pffft." Aunt Peg waved a hand through the air, shutting down my objection with her usual disregard for criticism. "We'll have it back where it belongs before he even notices it's missing."

Our plan hit a small snag: the hotel in Beaumont Centre did not accept pets. Luckily the hotel's daytime manager was the second person Faith would meet that day who had grown up with a Poodle and still remembered that childhood companion as the best dog *ever*. Having been introduced to Faith—who was her usual charming and Poodlely self—the woman allowed Aunt Peg to persuade her to bend the rules on our behalf.

In return we agreed to take a room in the back of the hotel on the ground floor. We also promised to keep a low profile and that Faith wouldn't be exercised where the other guests could see her. That appropriate cleanup was our responsibility went without saying.

It wasn't until after we'd completed the check-in and unloaded our things from the minivan that Aunt Peg casually mentioned that she'd also persuaded the day manager to divulge Daniel Nash's room number.

"How?" I asked. "She's not supposed to do that."

"She's not supposed to do this either," Aunt Peg said, gesturing toward Faith who was lounging happily on the nearest bed. "But she did."

Honestly, I don't know why this stuff even surprises me anymore.

"So what's our plan?" I asked.

"I'm going to ring Daniel Nash's room and invite him to join us for dinner this evening. Gates has already introduced us, after all. So I'll present myself as another newcomer to the Thoroughbred industry and ask if he wants to get together and compare notes."

Aunt Peg always sounds so sure of herself. I wish I had even half of her confidence. Maybe it's a height thing. I've always wanted to be taller, too.

"What if Daniel says no?" I asked.

"Why would he do that?"

"I don't know. Maybe he's busy tonight. Or maybe he won't remember us. Could be that he's tired of talking about horses since he's probably been doing it all week. Maybe he's not even in his room. . . ."

I might have kept going, but Aunt Peg had stopped listening to me. Instead, she was making a connection via the hotel phone. Her conversation with Daniel Nash was brief. It was also—much to my surprise—punctuated at one point by what sounded like a girlish giggle.

"I guess he remembered who you were," I said mildly when she'd hung up the phone.

"Of course he remembered us." Aunt Peg's brisk reply

steamrolled right over my innuendo. "And he wants to hear all about Lucky Luna. Daniel told me there's a lovely restaurant across the street named Azur. We'll be meeting him there at six-thirty."

"Just don't forget," I told her.

Aunt Peg paused in the act of lifting her rolling bag up onto a suitcase rack. "Melanie, what are you talking about now?"

"We know that Daniel Nash lied to us. And that for some reason he's chosen to hide his former connection to Miss Ellie from her family."

She slanted me an exasperated look. "So?"

"So he's not the kind of man we want to trust." *Did I really have to point that out?*

When Aunt Peg didn't reply, I added, "And I don't want to hear any giggling over dinner."

"I won't if you won't," Peg snapped.

Just as long as we were both on the same page.

Even at six-thirty on a Tuesday night, Azur was already crowded. In horse country people get up early and they go to bed early. And their socializing habits follow.

Daniel Nash was at the restaurant when we arrived. He had taken a table outside on the patio. The late-March evening was brisk, but heaters warmed the small courtyard to a very comfortable temperature.

Daniel stood as we approached. He had donned a sports coat for the occasion and his silk tie was festooned with tiny flying horses. As the waiter held out my chair, Daniel stepped over and seated Aunt Peg himself. The smile she thanked him with made me want to smack her.

Any minute now, there was going to be giggling. I just knew it.

"I hope this is all right?" Daniel asked Aunt Peg. "I'm visiting from Massachusetts where we're still months away from being able to eat outside, so I couldn't resist giving it a try. But if you think you're going to be cold, we can move indoors."

"This is fine," Aunt Peg replied. "Melanie and I are from the Northeast, too. So this weather feels mild to us."

"Where in the Northeast?" Daniel asked after the waiter had taken our drink order and disappeared.

"Connecticut. Fairfield County," I said. "I live in Stamford and Aunt Peg is in Greenwich."

"Lovely area." Daniel nodded. "I went to college in New Haven."

"Yale?" Aunt Peg asked with interest.

Daniel confirmed her guess. Then he and Aunt Peg spent the next fifteen minutes comparing connections and trying to discover friends, school ties, club affiliations, or even far-flung relations that they might have in common. And repeatedly coming up blank.

For some reason, that initial lack of success didn't deter either of them. I sat back in my seat and watched in silence as Daniel and Aunt Peg continued to spar back and forth. The longer their name dropping game went on, the more it began to seem like a competition.

Several dozen people were brought up and quickly discarded as possible links. But oddly, the only person whose name hadn't been mentioned was the one Aunt Peg and Daniel should have started with: Ellie Gates Wanamaker. It appeared that they were both determined to explore every other potential association first.

I sipped a glass of cool Chenin Blanc and pondered the interesting fact that Daniel seemed to be scoping out Aunt Peg's bona fides with every bit as much attention to detail as she was devoting to his. He had represented himself as a newcomer to the horse industry, but obviously something had already taught him to be wary. I wondered what that was.

"Melanie?"

I tuned back in to the conversation and saw that Aunt

Peg was gazing at me expectantly. I didn't have even the slightest idea why.

"I'm sorry," I said. "What did you say?"

"Daniel was just asking me how well we knew the Gates family."

Well, then. Game on. *Finally*.

"Aunt Peg and Miss Ellie were old friends," I told him. "But I just met her for the first time last week. Although I've been familiar with Miss Ellie's name and her line of Standard Poodles for years."

"Is that so?" Daniel sounded perplexed by my comment. That made him easy to categorize: *not* a dog person.

"Gatewood Standard Poodles," Aunt Peg told him. "In their day, Ellie's Poodles were famous, and justly so. Any student of the breed is well aware of her contribution to it."

"Aunt Peg and Miss Ellie used to compete against each other at the big dog shows on the East Coast," I added.

"Then I must have misunderstood." Daniel turned back to Peg. "I was under the impression that you had horses."

"Just the one, I'm afraid," Aunt Peg admitted. "I unexpectedly inherited Lucky Luna last month. She lives at Six Oaks Farm. Last week when we ran across each other at the training track, I had just come from visiting her for the very first time."

"Yes, I remember that day," Daniel said with a frown. "I had no idea who you were, but I overheard some of what you said."

"Aunt Peg has never been shy about expressing her opinions," I told him. "I hope you weren't offended."

"Not in the least. In fact, I would have been interested in hearing more. But Billy was pulling me in one direction and you disappeared in the other and the moment was lost."

The waiter came to take our dinner order and offer us refills on our drinks. Aunt Peg and Daniel accepted. Mindful of my recent misadventure, I switched to sweet tea instead.

"So you don't have a background in horses," Daniel continued when the waiter had left, "and yet you had a clear preference for one of those two-year-olds over the other. Even more interesting to me, you didn't pick the bigger, more visually impressive horse. Why is that?"

"The bay was a better mover," Aunt Peg told him. "And isn't that what it's all about? Which horse can get around the track the fastest?"

"Simply speaking, yes. Although Billy Gates has been educating me to understand that other factors come into play as well. Things like a horse's ancestors and its preference for one racing surface over another. Not to mention correct conformation which helps promote long-term soundness."

"It sounds like you've learned quite a lot in your short time here," Peg said.

"I'm trying. Although I'm still very much aware of my limitations. That's why I hired Billy to guide me through the sales process."

"And why you were wondering how well we were acquainted with his family?" I asked.

"It never hurts to seek a second expert opinion."

"I'm hardly that," Aunt Peg said. "I wish I were. I'm every bit the newcomer to this business that you are. So if you discover a way to avoid making mistakes, I hope you'll pass that knowledge along to me."

The two of them smiled at each other as if they were already complicit in furthering each other's goals. I stopped just short of rolling my eyes.

Our food arrived and conversation waned as we began to eat. Daniel and Aunt Peg had both chosen the lamb steak. I was eating a restaurant specialty, bourbon fried chicken, so all was right with my world.

"You asked about our connection to the Gates family," Aunt Peg said between bites. "Now I'd like to hear about yours."

"That won't take long," Daniel replied. He ate like a man who wanted to fuel his body rather than one who wished to savor the dining experience. "I was in need of a bloodstock agent and Billy Gates was recommended to me. We plan to do business together at the upcoming Keeneland sale."

Aunt Peg and I exchanged a look.

"I heard you say at the funeral that you'd only met Miss Ellie briefly," I mentioned.

"That's right. I attended the event solely as a gesture of support for Billy. If I'd realized ahead of time what a crush it would be, I might not have bothered. I'm sure my presence wouldn't have been missed."

Aunt Peg tipped her head to one side. She gazed at him as if considering something. "When you were a young man, did you go by the name of Danny?" she asked.

Daniel smiled. "Only occasionally. And only then among very good friends."

"High school friends," I said. "Like Miss Ellie?"

"No, as I just told you . . ." Daniel's voice trailed away. He set down his knife and fork. "I get the feeling this conversation has taken a turn that I don't entirely understand. What are you trying to say?"

"We think you've been lying to us," Aunt Peg informed him.

"I don't know what you mean."

"If you were a better liar, that protest might be more convincing." Aunt Peg sounded almost disappointed. "As it is, I think you might as well save us all some time and come clean."

"We found Miss Ellie's high school yearbook," I told him. "You know, from Foxcroft?"

"As you mentioned earlier, you prepped at Randolph-Macon Academy," Aunt Peg added. "Which, as you know, is also in Virginia."

"Virginia's a big state," Daniel said easily. He appeared to have regrouped. He began to eat again with a studied air of nonchalance. "Of course I've heard of Foxcroft. But I dated a Madeira girl myself."

"Did she write you love letters, too?" I asked.

"Excuse me?"

"Miss Ellie mentioned you in her yearbook."

"She did not." The denial was swift, but not entirely convincing.

"She did," Aunt Peg corrected him. "Did you really not know that?"

"No." Daniel ran his hand over his chin. "She talked about love letters?"

"Yes," I said. "We have the yearbook back at our hotel."

He looked away and I got the impression that Daniel had briefly forgotten all about us. I would have given him a minute. Not Aunt Peg. She doesn't have a sentimental bone in her body.

"We know that you've been lying to us about your friendship with Ellie Gates Wanamaker," she announced. "What we'd like to know is why."

Daniel turned in his seat. "How could that possibly be any business of yours?"

I debated the best way to answer that question. It didn't seem wise to divulge our suspicions regarding Miss Ellie's death just yet. So far, we'd learned very little about Daniel Nash. And I was pretty sure he'd be more inclined to share if he wasn't aware that we doubted his good intentions.

But as usual, Aunt Peg was three steps ahead of me. And heading in an entirely different direction.

"The thing is, Daniel, we don't believe that Miss Ellie's death was an accident," she said. "So Melanie and I find ourselves wondering what it was that really brought you to Kentucky. And what else you might be hiding."

I half expected Daniel to snap out a quick insult. And maybe to shove back his chair and leave the restaurant. He didn't do either of those things. In fact, for what seemed like a very long time he didn't do anything at all except sit and stare at us across the table. He seemed to be working something out in his mind.

And then he finally spoke. His answer was the last thing I expected to hear.

"I'll tell you what I'm hiding," he told us. "I don't think Miss Ellie's death was an accident either. And I have every intention of finding out who killed her."

Chapter 22

I was momentarily speechless.

Aunt Peg recovered more quickly. Indeed she barely looked perturbed by the magnitude of that bombshell.

"I think you'd better start at the beginning," she said briskly.

Daniel did no such thing. Instead, on the heels of his unexpected pronouncement, he ceded us the floor. "Ladies first, please."

"I'm not sure I even know where to begin," Aunt Peg said.

"I'd advise you to start by telling me about your real connection with Miss Ellie," Daniel replied. "And please try to make it sound more convincing than that silly story about you both owning the same kind of dog."

That got Aunt Peg's hackles up. No surprise there. Funny thing though, Daniel wasn't put off by the scowl that settled on her face. Instead he seemed rather pleased by the effect his words had had.

"Obviously you're not a dog person," I said.

"I like dogs just fine," he replied mildly. "I even have one."

"What kind?" asked Aunt Peg.

"A Scottish Terrier."

"It figures."

"Oh?" Daniel looked amused. "And what does my choice of dog tell you?"

"Scotties tend to be opinionated and scrappy," Aunt Peg said. "Does that sound like anyone you know?"

"Several people." Daniel looked around the table with a grin. "Some of them new acquaintances. What personality traits do Standard Poodles have?"

"They're very smart. They're loyal. They're eager to please."

"That sounds like my first wife."

"Poodles also enjoy a good joke," I said.

"Oh, then they're definitely not for Emily. She had no sense of humor at all."

"We seem to have gotten sidetracked." Aunt Peg's tone was a bit sharp. "Miss Ellie didn't just *have a dog*. She developed and maintained a premier line of Standard Poodles. Her dogs were a hugely important part of her life and she traveled over much of the country to exhibit them at dog shows."

"And that's how the two of you met," Daniel confirmed.

"Yes, it was. At first we were competitors, but as time went on we became good friends. Miss Ellie and I spoke often back then. We compared notes on our respective breeding programs, on judges, and on the genetic research that was being done at that time."

Aunt Peg stopped speaking. She glanced down at her plate as if she was surprised to see it still sitting there. Though her dinner was only half-finished, she appeared to have lost her appetite.

"Unfortunately Miss Ellie and I lost touch when she stopped showing Poodles," she said after a moment. "I shouldn't have allowed that to happen but it was an unsettled time in both our lives. And with half the country between us, our relationship simply faded away."

"What about you?" Daniel turned in my direction. "Where do you fit in?"

Good question. I'd often wondered about that myself.

"I teach school," I told him. "Married, two kids, six dogs. I came to Kentucky for spring break."

"Most people head farther south," Daniel said. Once again, he looked amused.

"I'm not the bikini and tequila type. Kentucky seemed like a fine idea until . . ."

I didn't need to complete the sentence. We all knew what I meant.

"Some people seem to think I have a suspicious mind," Aunt Peg said into the silence that followed.

"Some people would be right," I muttered.

Aunt Peg ignored me. Nothing new about that.

"Melanie and I spent time with Miss Ellie on the two days before her death," she said. "She seemed to be in good spirits and in good health. With regard to her family's farm, we were told that Miss Ellie knew every foot of that land intimately. So the thought that she took a tumble that led to her death seems patently inconceivable."

"Perhaps I share your suspicious nature then. Because the same thought seems obvious to me," Daniel agreed.

Our waiter approached the table. Daniel lifted a hand and waved the man away.

"The two of you were acquainted with a side of Miss Ellie that I knew nothing about," he said. "Did she have enemies in the dog world? Is it possible that someone might have wanted to harm her?"

"I asked around at the dog show on Sunday," I told him. "Eventually I was directed to a man named Arthur Ludwig."

"Miss Ellie was involved in a serious car accident with Ludwig a number of years ago." Aunt Peg took up the story. "Her son, Gates, was badly injured in the crash. Ludwig's wife died several days later."

"And he blamed Miss Ellie for that?"

"Yes, and apparently with good reason," I said. "According to Ludwig, she was drunk when the accident occurred."

Daniel frowned. "But if that's true, there would have been legal repercussions—"

"There was no investigation," Aunt Peg told him. "Instead, a settlement was offered and accepted and the matter was dropped. The entire incident was hushed up by the family."

"Ah, yes, the almighty Gates family," Daniel said knowingly. "I can picture that happening."

"It sounds as though you're better acquainted with them than you've previously let on," I said.

Daniel nodded. "As you've already surmised, Miss Ellie and I met when we were in school in Virginia. We were teenagers. We thought we were in love. Hell, we thought we *invented* love."

"And the Gates family put a stop to that?" Aunt Peg guessed.

"We were no Romeo and Juliet if that's what you're thinking. As with most things, the truth is more complicated than that. Miss Ellie had been raised from birth to conform to a set of expectations that were as archaic as they were inflexible. Her parents viewed Foxcroft as a finishing school, a place where Ellie could be exposed to the outside world but within the confines of a rigorously controlled environment. Diploma in hand, she was meant to return to Kentucky, marry a nice boy from a pre-approved family, and pop out the next generation of horse farmers."

"That sounds rather constricting," I said.

"I totally agree. But that was the kind of life Miss Ellie knew—and what she thought she wanted. Of course I wasn't aware of all that when we met. It wasn't until the end of senior year that she told me that there could never be anything serious between us because her family wouldn't approve."

"That must have stung," Aunt Peg said.

"It did. And all the more so because I thought we already had something serious."

"What did you do?" I asked.

"What could I do? It wasn't as if Miss Ellie had left me any choice. She went home to Kentucky and I went on to Yale. For a while I held out hope that she would change her mind but she never did. We continued to keep in touch over the years. Miss Ellie got married. I did, too. Three times."

"*Three?*" Aunt Peg inquired with interest. "You must be an optimist."

"Either that or an idiot," Daniel muttered.

This time when the waiter reappeared, we let him clear our plates. Aunt Peg and Daniel ordered the chocolate torte for dessert. I slipped a finger beneath the unforgiving waistband of my pants and settled for a cappuccino.

"So here we are," Aunt Peg said when he'd left. She stared hard at Daniel. "Two people who once knew Miss Ellie well—one old friend and one jilted lover. After everything you've said, tell me why I shouldn't be suspicious of your motives in coming to Kentucky. You reappeared and now Miss Ellie is dead. That seems like a terrible coincidence to me."

"Except for two things," Daniel said. "First, I'm not the only one who reappeared in Miss Ellie's life shortly before she died. The same could be said of you."

He paused to let that sink in. "And second, the only reason I'm here is because Miss Ellie invited me to come."

The man had a flair for lobbing bombshells. You had to give him that. Which didn't mean that I believed this new information Daniel had suddenly presented us with. Not even for a minute.

"That's not true," I said. "You came to Kentucky to get

a horse. You talked about it at the funeral. You hired Billy. You told everyone that you were shopping at Keeneland for a racehorse."

"That's what you were supposed to think. That's what Miss Ellie *wanted* everyone to think."

I blinked several times. It didn't help. Nothing became clearer at all. I hoped my cappuccino arrived soon. I could definitely use a jolt of caffeine.

"So you're not going to buy a racehorse?" I asked in a small voice.

"Not if I can help it. In case you haven't noticed, this is a totally irrational business. Someone would have to be crazy to want to invest money in it."

Aunt Peg was more on point than I was. She started with the question I should have asked. "You said that Miss Ellie invited you here. After all these years, why would she do that?"

"She needed my help."

"I see." Aunt Peg didn't sound convinced. "And despite the history the two of you shared, you still dropped everything and came halfway across the country at her behest?"

"Truthfully, there wasn't much to drop," Daniel said. "My children are grown. My last divorce is final. I retired last year. I'd never been to Kentucky before. This seemed like as good a time as any."

"And you were hoping that the two of you would reconnect romantically," I said.

Daniel shrugged. "Let's just say that I was open to the possibility. Times change. Miss Ellie was obviously no longer connected with her family—and their mandates—in the way she'd once been. I figured, why not? I've had three unsuccessful marriages. It occurred to me that maybe it was time to go back to the beginning and start over."

"And is that what happened?" I asked.

"No," he admitted. "But I've only been in Kentucky a week and we had other business to attend to first. Sad to say, when I arrived, neither one of us suspected that time to leisurely explore something else between us was the one thing we didn't have."

"Tell us about your *other business,*" Aunt Peg prompted.

We all paused as the waiter served dessert and the after-dinner drinks.

The chocolate torte featured rich, dark cake and vanilla ice cream sitting atop a pool of melted chocolate. It looked divine. Aunt Peg is territorial where sweets are concerned. But she also appeared to be very interested in what Daniel had to say. With luck, I thought I might be able to snag a bite when she wasn't looking.

"Don't even think about it," Aunt Peg said sharply.

Seriously? Was she reading my mind now?

"What seems to be the problem?" asked Daniel.

"Melanie, who didn't have the forethought to order her own dessert, is now coveting mine," Peg informed him.

"Just one bite," I said in my own defense. "Maybe two."

"You may share mine," said Daniel. He handed over a spare spoon and nudged the dessert plate into position between us. "This portion is entirely too large for me."

"Thank you." I scooped up a bite eagerly. "That's very generous of you."

"Indeed," Aunt Peg agreed. She circled her arm around her own plate and pulled it closer possessively. You know, so I wouldn't get any ideas about filching cake from both of them.

"You had business to do for Miss Ellie," Aunt Peg said again. "What was it?"

Daniel didn't answer right away. Nor did he pick up his own spoon. The expression on his face was thoughtful.

"What?" I asked finally.

I might have posed the question with a sliver of his own dessert in my mouth. Damn, that torte was good. If he didn't hurry up, he was going to miss the whole thing.

"I guess I'm debating whether or not I should trust you," Daniel said.

"We've been sharing confidences for more than an hour," Aunt Peg reminded him. "Isn't it a little late to be wondering about that now?"

"Not necessarily. I would hate for anyone to get in the way of what I'm hoping to accomplish." He gave his head a small shake. "But I'm probably worrying for nothing. The two of you don't seem like the most formidable pair."

Aunt Peg stiffened at the veiled barb. Not me. I was too blissed out on cake and cappuccino to take offense.

"Aunt Peg and I don't usually squabble like children," I told him. "We can be quite formidable when the occasion demands it."

Aunt Peg lifted a haughty brow. "*Does* the occasion demand it, Daniel?"

"It might."

He finally lifted his dessert spoon. Daniel then glanced down at his half-empty plate. I'd expected him to look horrified. Instead he simply signaled the waiter to bring us another dessert and returned to the topic at hand.

"It sounds to me like the two of you don't know much about Miss Ellie's family," Daniel said.

"We've met the two cousins who run Green Gates Farm," I said. "And we're acquainted with Miss Ellie's son, Gates. Miss Ellie told me a bit about the history of the farm last week. She said that the land had been in her family for three generations."

"Did she tell you anything about her father?"

"Only that he inherited a share of the farm that should have been passed along to her when he died. But he was pushed out of the family business by his two brothers. I know that Miss Ellie ended up with almost nothing."

" 'Pushed out' is a polite way of putting it. According to what Miss Ellie told me, her father was the horseman of the group, but he had no head for business. He managed the Thoroughbreds and trusted his brothers to take care of everything else. He assumed that they would protect his interests along with their own. That turned out to be a huge mistake."

"That all happened years ago," said Aunt Peg.

"Yes, but Miss Ellie never forgot. How could she when she continued to live right there in the same town, virtually around the corner from everything she'd lost? Miss Ellie considered that land to be her birthright. If anything, her bitterness over the way her father had been taken advantage of only grew worse over the years."

"She mentioned that her father had a drinking problem," I said. "Is that how he lost his share of the farm?"

"Miss Ellie thought the world of her father but in reality Walker Gates was a bit of a scoundrel. Drinking wasn't his only vice. He was also a hardcore gambler. Miss Ellie told me that her father would bet on everything from horses, to U.K. basketball, to the chance of rain when the sun was shining."

"Oh my," said Aunt Peg.

"Walker racked up sizable debts and he needed a way to get money fast. He went to his brothers for help. They agreed to bail him out—but they also told him that there was going to be a stiff price to pay for their assistance."

"So Miss Ellie's father wasn't actually swindled out of his share the farm," I said. "He gave it up of his own accord."

"That's what the legal papers said, but it's not what Miss Ellie believed. She said her father told her that he'd been set up by his brothers. At the very least, she was convinced that her uncles had encouraged Walker down the path to his own destruction. After he gave up his legacy, Walker never recovered. He died a broken man."

"I can see why Miss Ellie would have been bitter," Aunt Peg said. "It sounds as though she'd given up a great deal to behave in the way that was expected of her while the rest of her family was acting like a band of marauding pirates."

"Relations between the family members never improved after that," Daniel continued. "After Miss Ellie got married, she went to her uncles and asked to buy back into the farm. The two men laughed at her. They told her that her lost share didn't matter because she was only a woman."

"Those two sound like a nasty piece of work," Aunt Peg said angrily.

"They were," Daniel agreed. "And the current generation, Sheldon and Billy, aren't any better."

"At least Miss Ellie's cousins gave Gates a job on the family farm," I pointed out.

"Unfortunately that's another source of contention," Daniel said. "Miss Ellie thought that was their way of thumbing their nose at her. They made Gates start at the bottom mucking stalls and told him that if he worked hard enough, he could eventually rise to a position of responsibility. The cousins even dangled the possibility that he might be able to buy back into the family land.

"That was why Gates took the job. He thought it would make his mother happy. But Miss Ellie didn't believe a single word that Billy and Sheldon said. She thought they were just stringing Gates along and that they'd use him up and toss him away just as they had done to his grandfather."

"I feel like I'm in the middle of a Southern Gothic novel," I said, and Aunt Peg nodded.

"You still haven't told us where you fit in," she said to Daniel.

The waiter had delivered the additional torte a few minutes earlier. Now Daniel finally paused to take a bite of the dark chocolate confection. Then he glanced up and smiled. The look in his eyes sent an unexpected chill racing down my spine.

"Never forget that Miss Ellie was born a Gates, too," he said. "She possessed the same ruthless nature as the rest of the family. Miss Ellie plotted her revenge for a long time. She needed my help because now she was ready to fight back. It was finally time for her to regain everything she'd lost."

Chapter 23

"You have our full attention," Aunt Peg said.

That was an understatement. I nodded in agreement. "Please continue."

"How much do you two know about Thoroughbred horse sales?" Daniel asked.

"A good deal more than we did when we arrived in Kentucky last week," I told him. Luckily I'd had a chance to tell Aunt Peg about my earlier conversation with Erin. "Erin Sayre, whom you met at the funeral, works at Six Oaks Farm. She's been educating us."

"Then perhaps you won't find what I'm about to tell you surprising, though I certainly did. According to Miss Ellie, some of the transactions that take place at horse auctions are not as straightforward as someone looking in from the outside might think."

"Erin told us the same thing," I said. "Are you talking about dishonest bloodstock agents bidding up the prices?"

"That's one way for someone to take advantage of a horse buyer. But there are others as well."

"Kickbacks?" I asked.

Daniel nodded. "And more."

"*More?*" Aunt Peg echoed incredulously. She signaled for the waiter to bring our check. "I can see we're going to be talking for a while yet. Let me settle this and we can continue our conversation on the walk back to the hotel."

"You'll do no such thing," Daniel said, reaching for his wallet. "Dinner is on me."

"I can't imagine why," Aunt Peg retorted. "As I recall, you accepted *my* invitation."

"Yes, and I've done little more than grill you for information since."

"What make you think we haven't been grilling you at the same time?" Aunt Peg asked with a sly smile. She snagged the check from the server who was hovering between them, slipped a credit card into the leather folder, and sent him on his way.

"Thank you for dinner and the pleasure of your company," Daniel said, accepting the fact that he'd been outmaneuvered.

"The evening isn't over yet," Aunt Peg informed him. "It sounds as though we still have quite a bit to discuss."

Five minutes later, we were on our way. Once we stepped away from the heaters that warmed the patio, the night air was crisp and cool. I slipped on the jacket I'd brought with me and zipped it up. The dark sky above us was awash with tiny, twinkling lights. Yet another way that Kentucky was different from Connecticut. I couldn't remember ever having seen so many stars in a night sky before.

While I was admiring the scenery, Aunt Peg's thoughts were focused on more practical matters. "You were about to tell us more about the shenanigans that take place at horse sales," she reminded Daniel.

"One scheme in particular," he said. "Apparently it's a tactic that Billy Gates is quite familiar with."

The sidewalk was narrow. Daniel and Aunt Peg led the way, striding out together. I fell into place behind them.

"I'm assuming it was Miss Ellie who told you to hire Billy as your agent?" Aunt Peg said.

"That's correct."

"And he knows nothing about the connection between you?" I asked.

"Also correct," Daniel confirmed. "All Billy knows is that I have money to spend and I want to buy a couple of nice young Thoroughbreds. I've engaged his services with the understanding that I'm a newcomer to the industry and I require his expertise in order to spend my money wisely."

"That sounds as though you've written him a blank check," I said.

"I should hope so." Daniel turned and glanced back at me. "That was the whole point. The day after tomorrow, over a hundred two-year-olds will breeze on the Keeneland racetrack so potential buyers can check them out. Billy and I will watch the workouts together. Later we'll visit the horses back at their barns. Billy has already made a short list of those he likes, so assuming that they work well, those two-year-olds are the ones we'll focus on."

"So far, it sounds as though Billy will be making himself quite useful," Aunt Peg said.

"He will," Daniel agreed. "At least when I'm standing right there next to him."

"And when you're not?" I asked.

"That's when things start to get dicey. Say that he and I end up with several horses we agree we ought to try and buy. For the purposes of Billy's ploy, the most important thing is that the animal's consignor—the person who's selling him—is someone Billy thinks he can do business with. Let's call our first horse-of-interest Dobbin."

"Surely not," Aunt Peg interjected. "Dobbin doesn't sound anything like a racehorse. How about Zeus?"

"I defer to your superior naming skills," Daniel said with a laugh. "Zeus it is. Now the horses breeze on Thursday but the sale itself isn't held until Monday. Over the weekend Billy will approach Zeus's consignor and ask if the horse has had a lot of activity. Have there been many interested buyers looking at him? Most likely, the consignor is going to say yes. Because even if it isn't true, who wants to admit that their horse is unpopular?"

"Nobody who's in the business of selling things," I agreed.

"Next," Daniel continued, "Billy will say, 'So how much do you think he's going to bring?' At that point the consignor might hem and haw, but eventually he'll probably supply either a price or else a range that he thinks the price will fall into. Say he tells Billy he thinks his colt is going to sell for between two hundred and two-fifty."

"*Thousand?*" asked Aunt Peg. "As in dollars?"

"Dollars," Daniel confirmed. "Real money."

Aunt Peg looked shocked. I wondered if she was reevaluating her inheritance.

"Now," Daniel told us, "Billy says to the consignor, 'I'll give you two hundred and eighty for Zeus right now.' "

"I don't get it," I said. "Why would Billy offer more money ahead of time than he's likely to be able to buy the horse for during the sale?"

"I'll get to that part in a minute," Daniel said. "But first we have to finish our transaction. So now the consignor thinks, *Hmmm this guy is offering me more than I think my colt is worth. Maybe I should listen to what he has to say. But is it strictly legal what he's asking me to do? Nope, no way.*"

"Why not?" asked Aunt Peg. "Zeus went to the sale to be sold. Why does it make a difference when that happens?"

"Because the next thing Billy says is, 'I'll buy the horse from you now, but I want you to keep him here in your barn and run him through the sale on Monday just like nothing has changed. This ownership deal is strictly between us.' "

"Uh-oh," I said. I was pretty sure where this was heading.

"That part doesn't sound right," Aunt Peg agreed.

"That's because it isn't. It's called dual agency, and

thanks to laws that were passed in Kentucky several years ago for the express purpose of preventing this kind of thing from happening, it's definitely illegal. Because the next thing Billy plans to do is tell his clueless buyer—in this case, me—'Hey, I think we can get that really nice colt for half a million. That's the next Derby winner for sure. He'd be a steal for that price. So let's take our best shot and hope we can get it done.' "

"Half a million," Aunt Peg said faintly. "If I'm understanding correctly, nearly half of that purchase price will go directly into Billy's pocket."

"Yup." Daniel nodded. "That's how it will work out."

I was equally appalled. "So Billy's clueless client will end up paying double what the horse is worth? That's highway robbery!"

Abruptly Aunt Peg stopped walking. Pausing in a pool of light provided by a street lamp, she turned to face us. "Surely everyone here doesn't do business that way."

"Of course not," Daniel said. "There are plenty of honest people in the horse industry, too. But in a situation like this, the deck is stacked against them. Let's look at this deal from Zeus's consignor's point of view. When he gets the offer from Billy, he can probably guess exactly what's going to happen to Billy's client. He also knows that even though he's not the one who initiated the scam, he will be equally guilty of participating in a fraudulent transaction."

"And hopefully he refuses," I said.

"Suppose he does turn Billy down . . . Is that really the right thing for him to do?" Daniel asked.

"Of course," Aunt Peg snapped.

"Not necessarily. Stop and think about it for a minute. The consignor's first responsibility is to the colt's owner whom he's representing at the sale. It's his job to get that horse sold and for as much money as possible. Not only is this price higher than he'd thought he'd be able to get for the colt, it's a *sure thing*. So one might argue that if he turns Billy down, he's not doing the best he can for *his* client, the colt's owner."

"You must have been a politician," Aunt Peg said unhappily. "Because you certainly know how to argue both sides of a debate."

"I'm just trying to acquaint you with all the different angles that are in play. The other thing Zeus's consignor knows is that there are plenty of other horses in the sale, and that if he doesn't take Billy's deal, someone else certainly will. So his refusal doesn't help Billy's client, it only hurts his own."

"I don't care how appealing you make the transaction sound," I said stubbornly, "what you're talking about is still illegal."

"You're right," Daniel agreed. "And our consignor knows that. Could be that he's an ethical man and he's waffling. So Billy adds one last piece of persuasion. He says to Zeus's consignor, '*I*'m a big man in this industry and I know a lot of important people. If you don't do business with me I'm going to tell all my friends they shouldn't even bother looking at your colt because I've already seen him and he's a train wreck. By the time I get done trashing your horse, nobody's going to want him at any price.' "

"Holy crap," I said. "Somebody would actually *do* that?"

"According to Miss Ellie, they do indeed. Her cousin is a repeat offender but he's not the only one. Everybody's trying to find an edge over the next guy and that kind of trash talk is part of the game. The more people you can turn off a horse you want to buy, the less you're likely to have to pay for him."

"I think I need a stiff drink," Aunt Peg said. She turned and headed briskly across the parking lot toward the hotel. "Either that or a bottle of disinfectant to pour over my head. What kind of business have I gotten myself mixed up in?"

"Horse trading." Daniel grasped the hotel door and pulled it open. "It's not for the faint of heart."

"Or the pure of heart either apparently," I muttered.

As we entered the lobby. Aunt Peg took a moment to survey her options. Then she made a beeline for the bar. I'd had every intention of going back to the room where Faith was waiting for us. But when Daniel strode after Aunt Peg, I found myself following, too. I wasn't about to be the only one who didn't hear how this all turned out.

We were in Kentucky so we all ordered bourbon. Drinks in hand, we settled at a small table in a dark corner. Somehow the setting seemed appropriate to the conversation.

"So now what happens?" asked Aunt Peg. On the way to the table, she'd downed nearly half her tumbler. My aunt is no more of a drinker than I am. I sincerely hoped she had a better head for alcohol than I did.

"Now I go to the Keeneland sale and let Billy believe that I have every intention of buying an expensive horse or two," Daniel said. "Miss Ellie took great pains to acquaint me with everything I needed to do ahead of time, including applying to the sales company for a line of credit. As Billy is well aware, I have a budget of a million dollars."

Aunt Peg and I stared at each other across the table. Even in the half-light I could see the astonished expression on her face. I was certain that mine looked much the same.

"There's a reason why Miss Ellie enlisted me to be her partner-in-crime," Daniel said cheerfully. "Aside from our former connection, I was someone who was in a financial position to be useful to her."

"But you don't actually expect to spend that much money on baby horses," I said in a strangled voice. Even the bourbon's smooth burn couldn't make that idea seem like anything other than lunacy. "Right?"

"As I believe I mentioned earlier, I don't expect to spend a single penny. What Billy Gates believes is going to happen at the sale and what actually happens are two very different things."

Behind the bar, I saw the bartender's head lift. When our eyes met, he raised a hand, pointed his index downward, and circled it in the air. "Ready for another round?"

"Not yet," I told him. "We'll let you know."

"Shush," Aunt Peg said to me. "Stop talking to the bartender. I want to hear about Miss Ellie's revenge and how the rest of this is going to work."

"Now that you understand the basics," Daniel said, "what happens next is very simple. Billy and I will go to the works on Thursday. After that, he and I will narrow down our choices to half a dozen horses that we plan to bid on. I expect Billy to settle on some mid-range colts for me—the kind whose consignors might be getting a little antsy about their prospects as Monday draws near. Then, assuming Miss Ellie's knowledge of her cousin's duplicity was correct, Billy will get to work making deals. With luck, he'll be successful."

"If the numbers play out like they did in your example," Aunt Peg said, "Billy will sink more than half a million dollars of his own money into a pair of horses for you, having every intention of selling those horses back to you the very next day at a substantial profit."

"Precisely," said Daniel. "Except that shortly before the sale begins, I am going to receive a phone call from my financial advisor informing me that my stocks have tanked, or my ships have sunk, or some other financial calamity has occurred. With great regret I will inform Billy that it has suddenly become impossible for me to make such a large investment in the horse industry at this time. I will thank him profusely for his help and offer to pay him a day rate for his services. And of course I will promise that the very minute my finances are back on track, he'll be the first person I call."

"Miss Ellie's plot is genius," I said. "You'll have beaten Billy at his own game. He'll be on the hook for all that money but he won't be able to say a thing, since what he intended to do to you was illegal in the first place."

"That's not all," said Daniel. "The coup de grace was what Miss Ellie planned to do next. As Billy realized the precariousness of his position and was casting around frantically for a solution, she intended to step in and offer to cover all his losses—in exchange for a piece of Green Gates Farm. Poetic justice, wouldn't you say?"

"The perfect revenge," Aunt Peg said with admiration.

"Especially since if Billy refused, Miss Ellie could threaten to take evidence of his duplicitous activity to the authorities," I pointed out.

As usual, Aunt Peg was concerned for the animals. "What will happen to the horses Billy bought before the sale?" she asked.

"I'm guessing that he'll start scrambling to try and undo the deals he's put in place. If that doesn't work, he'll probably go ahead and send the horses through the auction ring as scheduled. Best case for him, they'll both sell to new owners. But even so, Billy will lose money, perhaps a great deal of money, because don't forget he paid a premium for those horses above and beyond what they were worth."

"There's just one last thing I don't understand," said Aunt Peg.

"What's that?" Daniel asked.

"Why are you doing this?"

"What do you mean? I thought I just explained that."

"No," Aunt Peg said firmly. "You explained why Miss Ellie had a grudge against certain members of her family, and why she wanted to get even. You even explained why you wanted to help her."

All at once I realized what Aunt Peg was getting at. "But what you didn't tell us is why you are going forward with Miss Ellie's plan now that she's gone," I said. "What do you hope to gain?"

"I would think the answer to that is obvious," Daniel replied. "Especially to the two of you. In the absence of any official consequence for Miss Ellie's dubious *accident*, I'm seeking my own form of retribution. She deserves justice and I'd like to see her get it. Isn't that the same thing we all want?"

Chapter 24

I parted company with Daniel and Aunt Peg in the lobby after we'd finished our nightcap in the bar. While the other two said their good-byes, I raced back to the room where Faith was waiting. I owed her a long romp and plenty of undivided attention and Faith obviously agreed with that assessment.

Instead of greeting me at the door eagerly, the big Poodle remained lying down on the bed as I came barreling into the room. She merely lifted her head and stared at me balefully. Her expression was easy to read. "*What, you again?*"

The knowledge that I deserved every bit of that rebuke only made me feel worse. I'd brought Faith with me to Kentucky because I couldn't bear the thought of leaving her behind. And yet once we'd arrived, all too often events had conspired to make me do just that.

I sat down on the edge of the bed and ruffled her silky ears. "I'll try to do better," I said.

Faith just sighed. She rose to her feet, slipped off the bed, and gave her body a good hard shake. Before the pom-pom on the end of her tail had even finished lashing back and forth, I was already slipping a looped collar over her head. Faith padded with me to the door. I opened it a crack and looked both ways before slipping us out into the corridor. We quickly made our escape through the exit at the end of the hallway.

Across the road from the hotel was a large, grassy plot of land that hadn't yet been developed like its neighbors on either side. Faith and I spent nearly an hour there, walking, talking, and taking care of business. We both had a great time; Faith because—unlike a human—it never even occurred to her to hold a grudge, and me because I had missed the steady comfort of her constant presence during this last hectic week. It was wonderful to finally have the chance to relax and reconnect again.

When we got back to the room, Aunt Peg hadn't yet returned. *That* was interesting. But not enough to make me desert Faith again in order to go in search of my errant relative. Instead I plopped down onto the bed, pulled Faith up into my lap, and called Sam.

Even though only a day had passed since we'd last spoken, it seemed as though a lot had happened. It took a few minutes to bring him up to speed. I finished by telling him about the deluge of surprising revelations that had come to light during Aunt Peg's and my dinner with Miss Ellie's long-lost boyfriend.

"So you see," I said at the end. "We can't possibly come home yet. We have to stay until after the horse sale and see how it all turns out."

"Remind me again whose idea it was to send you to Kentucky?" Sam asked. I could picture him shaking his head.

"I'm quite certain that was you," I said. "As I recall, I tried to object but you insisted."

"Was I out of my mind?" he wondered aloud.

I figured that was a rhetorical question and stayed mum.

"Kentucky seemed like such a safe place," Sam mused. I was pretty sure he was still talking to himself. "Serene . . .

pastoral . . . Just farms and bluegrass and happy horses. Who could possibly find trouble in a place like that?"

Another rhetorical question, unless I missed my guess.

I looked at Faith and shrugged. She flicked her tail up and down on the quilt. Any minute now, Sam would remember that I was actually on the other end of the phone line and start directing his comments back to me.

"This horse sale you need to attend," he said, finally tuning back in. "When is it?"

"Monday afternoon."

"You're supposed to be back in school on Monday morning."

I'd already thought about that part.

"I'm never absent from my job," I said. "And we'll drive all night after the sale ends, so I'll only miss one day—"

"One day at the end of spring break," Sam pointed out. "Do you think anyone's going to be fooled when you call in sick?"

"Maybe I should say we had a flat tire," I considered. "That might go over better. Besides, I won't be the only one who's out. Half the kids won't be back from their skiing and beach vacations yet either."

Sam chuckled under his breath. "Don't try selling that excuse to Russell Hanover," he advised.

Mr. Hanover was headmaster at Howard Academy. He was a man of dignity and discipline and he was a stickler for the school's rules—many of which he'd put into place himself.

"I'll make it work," I said. "I'm more worried about you than Mr. Hanover. Is everything all right at home?"

"Peachy," Sam replied. "I'd put the boys on to tell you themselves but they're already asleep. I can coast through a few extra days . . . except for one thing."

"What's that?" I asked, even though I was pretty sure I knew. Sam's voice had dropped into that husky register that always makes my insides melt.

"I miss you," he said.

I sighed softly before replying. "I know. I miss you, too."

"Here's a thought," said Sam. "Instead of letting this all play out, why don't you and Peg just drag Daniel down to the local sheriff's office and get him to tell them everything he knows?"

"Aunt Peg and I suggested that," I said. It was the last thing the three of us had discussed before leaving the bar. All to no avail. "Apparently Daniel's already had a conversation at the police department in Versailles. He didn't get any farther with them than Aunt Peg did with the sheriff. The Gates family wields a sizable amount of influence around here and the consensus among law enforcement seems to be that the three of us are outsiders looking to stir up trouble."

"I'd say that's rather short-sighted of them."

"I agree, which is why Aunt Peg and I want to lend our support to Daniel. He's determined to go through with the plan that Miss Ellie put into place. At this point it seems as though we may never know the truth about whether or not her death was an accident. Bearing that in mind, Daniel believes that the best tribute he can offer Miss Ellie is to finish what she started."

"It sounds like you and Peg feel the same way."

I thought about that for a few moments before answering. "I only knew Miss Ellie briefly, but one thing I know for sure is that she didn't deserve what happened to her. I have my suspicions what might have taken place, especially now that I've heard Daniel's story about the acrimony her whole family seems to thrive on.

"But in just a few days Aunt Peg and I will leave Kentucky for good. Our suspicions will remain just that. In all likelihood, no one will ever be arrested, or charged, or punished in connection with Miss Ellie's death. So I guess I agree with Daniel that financial retribution is better than nothing. I think Miss Ellie would have appreciated that."

"Then it's settled." The provocative timbre I'd heard in Sam's voice earlier was gone now. Darn it. "I'll expect you back early Tuesday?"

"That's the plan," I said.

"Stay out of trouble."

"I'll certainly try." It wasn't my fault that I always found that easier to say than to do.

"And keep Peg out of trouble, too," Sam growled.

"No promises on that score. You know Aunt Peg."

We were all well aware of Aunt Peg's propensity to make a bad situation worse. Even Faith.

"In that case, watch your back," Sam said. "I need you home safe."

"Always." My thumb brushed the screen to disconnect. I lowered the phone from my ear.

"Always," I said again. It was a promise.

With time to kill before the works at Keeneland on Thursday morning, Aunt Peg and I spent most of Wednesday playing tourist.

"I refuse to leave central Kentucky having seen nothing more than horse farms and dog shows," Aunt Peg said emphatically over breakfast. She was brandishing a guidebook she'd brought to the table with her. "You have no idea how many things we've been missing out on. There are all kinds of interesting sights to see around here."

"Like what?" I sectioned off a large wedge from my stack of pancakes and popped it in my mouth.

"For starters, the University of Kentucky is right here in Lexington."

"Go Wildcats!"

Aunt Peg looked up from her book. "Who?"

"The Wildcats. They're U.K.'s basketball team. Coach Cal?"

She shook her head.

"Aunt Peg, they're huge. They're *famous*. March Madness? Final Four? None of this is ringing a bell?"

"You're the one whose bells are ringing," she said. "What are you going on about? The university is a *school*. Quite a good school."

Okay, then. *Not a fan of college basketball.*

"Right," I agreed, deflating. "U.K. is a bastion of higher learning. What else have you got?"

"Mary Todd Lincoln's house." She peered at me over the top of her guidebook. "You *do* know who she is, don't you?"

"Of course."

"Because suddenly it occurs to me that perhaps you spent your entire educational life thinking about team sports."

"No such luck," I told her. "Mary Todd Lincoln was born in Lexington, wasn't she?"

"Indeed. Her family home has been restored and it's available to be toured. Along with"—Aunt Peg flipped through several pages until she found what she was looking for—"Shaker Village."

"I remember the Shakers," I said. "Aren't they extinct? Wasn't there some problem with sex? Like they weren't having any?"

Aunt Peg's chin elevated slightly. "I do believe that they adhered to a life of celibacy, yes."

"Which accounts for the lack of Shakers today. Nice furniture, though. Clean lines, built to last. Under the circumstances, that seems ironic, doesn't it?"

Aunt Peg let an eye roll serve as her reply.

Undeterred, I plowed on anyway. "So the Shakers have an entire village here in Lexington? Who lives there?"

"It appears to be more like a museum, actually. Or a historic center."

"Cool. Put it on the list." I took a break to gobble down more pancakes, then said, "I notice you haven't mentioned Keeneland. Since it's one of Lexington's premier tourist attractions, that seems like a curious omission."

"Not at all. I'd imagine we'll be spending much of the day there tomorrow, watching horses run around the track."

"Daniel called it a works show," I said. "And speaking of Daniel, where did you disappear to last night?"

Aunt Peg slid the billfold holding the check over in front of her and signed the meal to our room. "I have no idea what you're talking about," she said.

When pigs took flight, I thought. But just to avoid any confusion, I laid out the facts.

"You didn't come back to the room after we left the bar. And when Faith and I returned from our run and went to sleep nearly an hour and a half later, you *still* hadn't shown up. For all I know, you might have stayed away all night."

"Honestly." Aunt Peg sounded exasperated. She pushed back her chair and stood. "Sharing a hotel room with you is like staying with my mother. Are you keeping tabs on my whereabouts now?"

"I'm merely curious," I said primly.

She stalked out of the dining room. I hurried after her.

"Plus," I added, "Sam told me to keep you out of trouble."

Aunt Peg stopped suddenly and spun around. "I'll have you know that if I want to get into trouble, I shall do so. With or without your permission."

I was pretty sure I'd told Sam much the same thing.

"But . . . *Daniel Nash?*"

"Oh please. Nothing happened with Daniel Nash. He and I simply started sharing fond memories of Miss Ellie after you left. Eventually we found seats in the lobby and talked for several hours. It was all the more interesting because each of us had known the woman at two such very different times in her life. We were rather teary by the end, both of us regretting that we'd ever let our connections to Miss Ellie fade away as we did."

"I'm sorry," I said. "I shouldn't have pried."

Aunt Peg continued down the hallway toward our room. "For heaven's sake, don't be such a weenie," she snapped.

"Excuse me?"

"If you're going to start apologizing for asking personal questions, you're going to spend the rest of your life feeling sorry about things. And what a colossal waste of time that would be."

Trust Aunt Peg to put things into perspective. And manage to make me feel like a whiner at the same time. Just another example of her rare and unusual talents. If only I could persuade her to use her powers for good rather than mischief, imagine what we might accomplish.

Aunt Peg slipped her keycard into the lock. She checked to make sure the hallway was empty and then opened the door. "Now grab Faith and let's go. The day isn't getting any younger and we have sights to see."

Aunt Peg drove. I navigated. Faith supplied the occasional commentary from the backseat. We walked around the expansive U.K. campus, spent several hours at historic Shaker Village, and toured the downtown home where Mary Todd Lincoln had been born. And as if that wasn't enough running around for one day, Aunt Peg decreed that we would end the afternoon by visiting the sumptuous Woodford Reserve Distillery.

It was almost dinnertime when we got back to the hotel. I was tired and slightly sunburned. And I'd devoured more bourbon balls in the previous hour than any sane person should eat in an entire lifetime.

I was looking forward to a shower and maybe a short nap. So when a knock came at the door shortly after Aunt Peg, Faith, and I entered the room, I decided that Aunt Peg, who was still brimming with energy, should be delegated to deal with whatever had come up now.

If only things could ever be that easy.

I was shucking my sweater off over my head a moment later when Aunt Peg stepped back from the doorway and invited Daniel inside to join us.

"Sorry to interrupt," he said. Then he stopped and stared at Faith. "Do you know there's a dog in here?"

"Yes," I told him. "I'm well aware. That's Faith. She's a Standard Poodle."

Daniel's expression brightened. "One of Miss Ellie's?"

"No," I said firmly. "*Mine.*"

"Oh." He turned back to Aunt Peg. "You might find this interesting. There's been a development."

She waved him toward a chair near the window. "What kind of development?"

"Billy just called. He wants to meet with me."

"That doesn't sound unexpected." Aunt Peg sat down opposite him. "Is it?"

"Not the meeting part, no," Daniel allowed. "Billy and I have spoken at least once on some pretext or another every day that I've been here. I think it's his way of keeping tabs on my activities and making sure that I'm not looking into other opportunities that don't include him."

"So how is this different?" Aunt Peg asked.

"He and I already had a plan in place for tomorrow morning. We were supposed to meet in the grandstand at Keeneland at nine-thirty to watch the works. But now Billy thinks we should get together before that. He asked me to meet him at the training track at his farm at seven A.M."

"That's early," I said.

Daniel shrugged. "Horse people. They have no appreciation for the joys of a warm bed. I think everybody in this whole state rises at the crack of dawn."

"Are you going?" asked Aunt Peg.

"Of course I'm going," Daniel replied. "And I think you should come with me."

Chapter 25

"You want me to come with you?"

Had the request been directed to me, I'd have been surprised. Not Aunt Peg. She sounded positively delighted.

And—along with the other interesting developments I was busy making note of—Daniel had reached across the space between them and taken Aunt Peg's hand. I just thought I'd mention that.

"Yes," he replied. "Definitely yes. And we need to think about how to make it work."

"Or why it should happen at all," I said.

As if they'd forgotten I was even there, Daniel and Aunt Peg both turned their heads to gaze in my direction. I was half tempted to waggle my fingers in a wave. Deciding that was too juvenile, I tossed my sweater onto my suitcase, and plopped down on the bed instead. Faith quickly hopped up to join me.

"The *why* is easy," said Daniel. "At this stage of the game, I don't want to make Billy suspicious that something might have changed by refusing to meet with him."

"That explains why you're going," I pointed out. "It doesn't tell us why you think Aunt Peg should join you."

"Two reasons. First, because I want there to be a witness to whatever is said between Billy and me. I'm well aware that this plan is being played out on Gates turf and that Billy definitely has a home field advantage. If things should get messy later—or if something happens that I'm not anticipating—I don't want the situation to turn into a 'he said/she said' impasse."

"I can certainly see that," Aunt Peg agreed.

"The second reason," said Daniel, "is that I didn't enter into this arrangement on my own. Miss Ellie and I were working together as a team. When things came up, or when I had questions, we bounced ideas off of each other and decided how best to proceed. Her feedback was enormously valuable. Obviously that's a resource I no longer have access to."

"Quite right." Aunt Peg gently disentangled her hand and pulled it back to her lap. "When it comes to reasoning things through, two brains are always better than one."

I looked at her pointedly. "Especially if one of those brains is an expert on horses. Which you most definitely are not."

"No, but I do like to think that I possess a good understanding of human nature. Under these circumstances, that might prove to be an equally useful skill." She turned back to Daniel. "What did you mean when you said that we need to figure out how to make the meeting work?"

"Think about it," he said. "It's not as if the two of us can simply show up together. Especially since the first time you and Billy met, you tried to tell him that he was steering me toward the wrong horse."

"Perhaps not my finest moment," Aunt Peg allowed. Her eyes narrowed. "Even if I *was* correct in my assessment."

Daniel ignored that gibe. "How would you feel about a little undercover work?" he asked.

I groaned under my breath. Everyone ignored me except Faith, who laid her head across my lap in a silent gesture of support. Thank God I wasn't the only smart one in the room.

"A clandestine assignment?" Aunt Peg said with relish. "That sounds like a brilliant idea."

Daniel chuckled. "I'm afraid I wasn't thinking of anything that exciting. Rather I was hoping you'd be willing to serve as unseen backup. Actually *under cover,* as it were. You've been to the training track. Do you remember the layout?"

Aunt Peg and I both nodded. Once again, I don't know why I bothered. Nobody was paying any attention to me.

"Billy and I are supposed to meet in the parking lot. What he won't know is that you'll be concealed in the back of my SUV. When I get out, I'll make sure to leave all the windows open. Even though you won't be visible, you should be able to hear everything we say."

That sounded much too simple to actually work. I asked the logical question.

"What if Billy takes you somewhere else?"

"I'm pretty sure he won't. Don't forget, I've spent the last week with him. Billy Gates is a talker, not a walker," Daniel said. "Also, there shouldn't be anything in the barn or on the track that he wants to show me. The horses we're interested in are all over at Keeneland now. I'm betting that Billy and I won't move even ten feet from our starting point."

"It's too bad he's already seen me," Aunt Peg mused. "Otherwise you could pass me off as your cousin from Connecticut who loves horses and wants to invest money, too."

"Because this plan isn't already wacky enough?" I said drily.

"Melanie's right," Daniel concurred. "We should keep things as simple as possible. That way there'll be less chance of anyone slipping up. So you'll help?"

"Of course," Aunt Peg confirmed. "You couldn't keep me away."

The two of them looked inordinately pleased with themselves. How could I be the only one among us who was harboring doubts about the wisdom of this harebrained scheme? And another thing. What were the chances that Aunt Peg would actually follow Daniel's directions?

"I'm coming with you," I found myself saying into the silence that followed.

"*You,*" Aunt Peg told me pointedly, "were not invited."

"Tough luck," I said. "Daniel's plan has a much better chance of succeeding if I come along to make sure that you don't decide to improvise."

"Fine with me," Daniel said with a shrug. "I have an SUV. I'll put the seats down." His gaze drifted over to Faith. "You can even bring the dog if you like."

He laughed at his own joke.

He wouldn't be laughing tomorrow when I took him up on it.

My life is filled with reasons to get up early. A cranky toddler, school bus schedules, and distant dog shows all drag me out of bed before I'm ready to face the day. So rising at six the next morning was easy for me. Less so for Aunt Peg, who was grumbling as she dragged herself off to the shower when Faith and I were on our way out the door for a walk.

By the time we returned, Aunt Peg had made a remarkable recovery. She was dressed and ready to go, waiting outside the hotel next to Daniel's SUV. There was still almost an hour until sunrise and the morning air was both damp and chilly. When Daniel emerged from the lobby a few minutes later, his fingers were wrapped around a steaming cup of coffee.

"I was kidding about the dog," he said, casting us an unhappy look as he used his key fob to open the locks.

"I wasn't." I'd had to leave Faith behind too many times in the last week. I wasn't about to do so again. "Don't worry. She'll behave."

"She'd better," Daniel muttered.

Moisture rising from the area's numerous creeks and streams contributed to an early morning fog that had come down like a low blanket to settle over the outskirts of Lexington. By the time we reached Midway, I could barely see the road ten feet ahead of us. It felt as though we were driving through a silvery cloud. Even with his fog lamps on, Daniel had to slow the SUV's speed considerably.

"This morning mist is nothing unusual around here," he said. "It'll probably lift in a couple hours, but for now it suits our purposes perfectly. We won't have to worry about Billy looking inside the vehicle if he can't even see it."

As we reached the perimeter gate that led directly to the training track, Daniel pulled over to the side of the road. "Let's get ourselves set up before we drive onto the farm. Are you sure that dog is going to be good?"

"Positive," I said. "But I can't make the same guarantee about Aunt Peg."

"All we have to do is listen," she said with a snort. "How hard can that be?"

Indeed.

All four of us got out of the SUV. Daniel and I lowered the backseat to enlarge the vehicle's cargo area. Aunt Peg climbed in and lay down. Faith and I followed. Daniel shook out a dark-colored quilt and settled it on top of us.

"Everybody comfy?" he asked.

"Couldn't be better," Aunt Peg said cheerfully.

"Sit tight and we'll be there in a minute. I'll crack the windows open as soon as I park."

It felt eerie moving along like that in the dark. With nothing to look at, every sound—like the muffled creak of the farm gate as it swung slowly open—was amplified. Divots and ruts in the road caused the three of us to lose our balance and list from side to side into each other. I knew logically that there was plenty of air in the car and we could all breathe perfectly well, but the closeness beneath the quilt felt stifling.

I kept a reassuring arm curled over Faith's back, but the precaution was unnecessary. The Poodle lay quietly with her head nestled between her front paws. As usual, she was dealing with things better than I was.

"I'm almost at the barn," Daniel said in a low tone. "Billy's truck is already there. I'll pull in next to it. Everybody ready?"

"Ready," Aunt Peg and I murmured in assent.

I heard a smooth whir as Daniel lowered several of the windows. The SUV coasted to a stop. There was a click as the key was turned and the engine died.

"Mornin'," I heard Billy Gates say. "Thanks for coming. You need coffee? There's some in the barn."

"I brought my own," Daniel replied. I heard him climb out of the vehicle and close the door behind him. "Where is everybody? Last time we were here, this place was bustling. Now it looks deserted."

"Most of the horses that were here before are two-year-olds that have shipped over to the sale. Only a few older horses in the barn now. No reason to take any unnecessary chances. We won't be bringing 'em out to the track until the fog lifts."

"That's good," said Daniel. "I guess we'll have plenty of privacy to talk."

"That's just what I was thinkin'. Because it seems to me that we need to clear some air between us."

I shifted slightly and stole a look at Aunt Peg. She lifted a brow. We both waited to hear what would happen next.

"I don't know what you mean," Daniel said.

"Oh, I think you do," Billy disagreed. "For starters you should think about filling me in on your relationship with my cousin."

"Your cousin?"

Daniel Nash wasn't much of an actor. He was probably

aiming to sound confused by the question. Instead his voice rose unsteadily. There was a clear undercurrent of apprehension in his tone.

"A'right then," Billy replied. I heard a loud creak and pictured him leaning back against the side of his dilapidated truck. "We'll approach this from another direction. People in other parts of the country sure make a lot of jokes about how everyone in Kentucky is related to everybody else."

"Umm . . . I guess." Daniel sounded relieved by the change of subject. He must have lifted his cup. I heard him slurp his coffee.

"The thing is, what makes that joke so funny is that the premise is partly true. Most of the old families around here have branches spreading all over the place. By the time your people have lived in Kentucky as long as the Gateses have, you're kin to just about everybody."

"If you say so. Look, Billy, I thought you asked me to come out here this morning so we could talk about horses."

"Don't worry, we'll work our way back around to that. In the meantime, let me tell you about my second cousin, Harriet's, boy. Name of Elliot. Bright young kid. Doesn't care much for the horses though. Shame about that."

"Maybe he'll change his mind," Daniel offered weakly.

"Doubt it," Billy said. "Kid's workin' his way through U.K. right now. Biology major, industrious as all get-out. Elliot knows how to keep his eye on the main chance. And how to take care of his own. You wouldn't want to hazard a guess as to where he might be workin', would you?"

"I have no idea," Daniel sputtered. "How would I know something like that?"

"The thing is, you probably wouldn't," Billy said with satisfaction. "Which was kind of a lucky break for me. You see Elliot's puttin' himself through school by workin' nights bartending over at the hotel in Beaumont Centre. That's the place where you're staying, isn't it?"

My head came up. I smothered a startled gasp.

Aunt Peg reached over and poked me with her thumb. My eyes were accustomed to the darkness beneath the blanket now and I could see the expression on her face. It was every bit as horrified as my own.

My thoughts sped back to the conversation we'd had in the bar on the previous evening. And to the attentive way the bartender had kept an eye on us while we huddled around his back table, talking. At the time I'd thought he was merely doing his job, watching so he'd know when our drinks needed replenishing.

But now I realized that the first time I'd noticed the bartender paying attention to us was right after Daniel had mentioned Billy's name. He must have tuned in to our conversation and listened to everything we said after that.

Holy crap, I thought. That was really not good.

My stomach clenched; I felt my insides turn over. Harriet's boy, Elliot, with his eye on the main chance, must have left the bar and brought that damning information straight to cousin Billy. Taking care of his own indeed.

"This is going to be a problem!" Aunt Peg whispered furiously.

"You think?" I hissed in return.

"Come on, Daniel, walk with me," Billy said in a genial tone. "You and I, we have some more talkin' to do."

"Walking?" Aunt Peg's eyes opened wide. "They can't leave now. There wasn't supposed to be any *walking!*"

"I have a feeling none of this is going to go the way we hoped," I said grimly.

We listened to the crunch of departing footsteps on the gravel driveway. Within moments the fog had obscured even that sound, and quiet descended once more. Still lying shrouded, I felt a shiver slip down my spine. The total absence of sensory input from outside the car gave the situation a seriously spooky vibe. I'd had nightmares that were less creepy than this.

Then suddenly I remembered the dream I'd had just before we left for Kentucky. With startling, dizzying clarity those buried sensations came flooding back. Once again I saw myself racing through swirling mists on the back of a fleet-footed horse. The sound of hoofbeats pounded in my ears.

I blinked my eyes and shook my head and the vision abruptly vanished. *Good riddance,* I thought. That damn dream better not have been an omen.

"Now what?" Aunt Peg flipped back the edge of the quilt and poked her head out. "We can't just let them go off on their own. You heard what Billy said. He knows that Daniel intended to double-cross him. We have to do something."

Cautiously I raised myself up and looked out through the nearest window. Outside the SUV, the quality of the light had changed. Though it wasn't visible, the sun must have been rising over the horizon. Here, however, a bank of dense, low-lying fog still covered everything. The big barn was only a hazy shadow in the foreground. I couldn't see the training track at all.

"Doing something wasn't part of the plan," I said.

"Obviously the plan has changed," Aunt Peg snapped.

I fumbled in my pocket and pulled out my phone—and was presented with the downside to all that pastoral beauty. I had no bars at all. Not even one.

"Maybe we should wait for them to come back," I said.

"What if they *don't* come back?"

The ominous thought hung in the damp air between us.

"How dangerous do you think Billy is?" I asked. I wasn't at all sure that I wanted to hear her answer.

"How dangerous do you have to be to shove an old lady to her death?" Aunt Peg retorted. She was already drawing her legs up and reaching for the door handle. "The whole Gates family seems half-cracked to me. Billy's already removed one obstacle from his path. I can't see him hesitating to remove another."

There was only one thing I could say to that. "Then let's go." I swung my legs around and scooched toward the door as Aunt Peg opened it and slid out. "We'll follow behind them and listen. There's no need to make our presence known if we don't have to."

I hopped Faith down out of the vehicle, pulled a leash out of my pocket, and slipped it on. As I straightened, a mask of thick, wet fog swirled around my head. Faith pressed her body up against my leg. We both found comfort in the contact.

"Do you know which way they went?" I whispered.

"Not toward the barn." Aunt Peg pointed instead toward the other side of the small lot. "Over there, I think."

I couldn't see more than three or four feet in front of me. Whatever lay in the direction she'd indicated was invisible now. I seemed to recall from our previous visit to the training track that it was a big, open field containing a herd of curious yearlings. There hadn't been any buildings in that direction, nor people either.

Aunt Peg must have remembered the same thing because she said ominously, "Whatever Billy has in mind, it looks like he wants to get Daniel somewhere off by himself."

I gathered Faith close and the three of us hurried across the driveway. Our footsteps made noise but only for a few seconds. Then we reached the grassy verge on the other side. Aunt Peg and I both stopped to listen.

After a moment, I heard the muted sound of disembodied voices floating in the air ahead of us. "That way." I rested a hand on Aunt Peg's shoulder and turned her in place. "I think I hear them."

We'd only traveled another fifty feet before Daniel's and Billy's voices suddenly became distinct. Now they were raised in anger. Abruptly Aunt Peg and I both stopped moving.

"—don't owe you any explanations," Billy was saying.

"I want to know what happened," Daniel snarled. "You tell me the truth, dammit." It didn't sound like the first time he'd issued that ultimatum.

"Miss Ellie had a blind spot where this farm was concerned," Billy shot back. "That weren't my fault. That woman badgered me and badgered me until I couldn't stand it anymore. She never could leave well enough alone. Sometimes a family has to step up and take care of its own problems."

"*What did you do?*"

"I told you. Miss Ellie slipped and fell. That's the God's honest truth."

"I don't believe you," Daniel snapped.

"I'll tell you somethin'," Billy said. "A horse farm is a dangerous place. Plenty of things can go wrong. Things that people don't even see coming. Sometimes folks get hurt for no reason. Take a city feller like you, for example. You could have an accident and nobody would ever get the blame."

"I guess you'd know all about how that works," Daniel replied.

He'd sounded sure of himself only moments earlier. Now his voice quavered. Then I heard the reason why.

"So why'd you bring a gun out here?" Daniel asked. "Because I'm pretty sure there's no way you're going to be able to pass off a gunshot wound as an accident."

Chapter 26

Aunt Peg and I stared at each other in mute horror. She grabbed my arm and yanked so hard that I almost lost my footing. Together we stumbled backward, retreating until we'd put several additional yards between ourselves and the two men ahead of us.

I wondered whether it was my imagination that Daniel had raised his voice when he mentioned the gun. Was he hoping that we were out here somewhere listening? Had he been trying to send us a warning?

Aunt Peg leaned in close and pressed her lips to my ear. "Whatever Billy has in mind, we have to get Daniel away from him. Now!"

For once, she and I were in perfect agreement.

"I might have an idea," I said.

On earlier visits both Erin and Gates had stressed the importance of keeping dogs away from the farm's flighty Thoroughbreds. Now it occurred to me that unless we'd gotten entirely turned around in the fog, we should be near the pasture that housed a band of rowdy yearling colts. The last thing anyone would want was for an ill-behaved dog to cause those valuable horses to spook.

Unless, of course, one was looking to cause a distraction.

"You stay here," I said to Aunt Peg. "Somewhere ahead of us is that pasture with the colts in it. Faith and I are going to find it and make our way around the other side."

"How will that help?"

"If we make enough of a ruckus out there, I'm guessing that the horses will bolt away from us and head in this direction. Even in the fog, you should be able to hear them coming. Billy's a horseman. That should distract him long enough for you to grab Daniel and run like hell. Billy won't be able to use that gun if he can't see where the two of you are."

"That might work," Aunt Peg considered.

As it seemed to be the only idea we had between us, one could only hope.

I cupped my hand around Faith's muzzle and guided her in close to my side as she and I began to move. Eager to avoid the two men in front of us, I angled our direction hard to the left. Eyes straining for clues that weren't there, ears listening for the slightest sound, I was navigating blind through the soupy mist. Hopefully Faith and I weren't retracing our steps back toward where Billy and Daniel were standing.

Abruptly Billy's voice came floating out of the fog. He suddenly sounded a good deal closer than I wanted him to be.

"Now you're just getting ahead of yourself," he said. "Nobody's going to be doing any shootin'. That would scare the horses, don'tcha know. And that wouldn't be good for business."

The unpleasant cackle that followed that pronouncement raised the hairs on the back of my neck. Faith felt the same way. Her lips fluttered against my fingers as she whined deep within her throat.

"Shhh," I said on a quiet breath. "Let's go."

Only a few steps later the four-board fence suddenly

materialized in front of us, emerging as a dark, solid presence in a world made of silvery shadows. My shoulders sagged in relief. We weren't out of the woods yet. Not even close. But at least we were heading in the right direction.

The fence's highest panel was nearly as high as the top of my head. I lifted a hand and rested it on that upper edge. Now that we had a guideline, Faith and I could move much faster.

We were hurrying through the wet grass when I heard a loud, metallic bang come from somewhere behind us. It sounded like a chain was being rattled or maybe dragged slowly between a pair of metal restraints. Immediately the plots of half a dozen horror movies flashed before my eyes.

Could things possibly get any spookier?

I shouldn't have asked. Moments later a low, moaning shriek shivered through the damp air.

I stopped and spun around, straining my eyes to see something . . . *anything*. There was nothing but a swirling wall of mist.

Then I heard Billy speak again. Faith and I must have moved a good distance away because his voice was fainter now. "There's no need for me to go shootin' anything, Daniel, when you could just disappear. After that, nobody'd ever have to know that you'd been here a' t'all."

I'd barely had time to register the import of Billy's words before a new voice spoke up. This one carried clearly through the low fog that mired everything around us in half-light.

"*I* would know," Aunt Peg said emphatically.

Damn, I thought. That wasn't part of the plan.

"Who the hell are you?" Billy asked. He sounded furious.

He probably wouldn't be comforted to know that he wasn't the only one.

If anyone answered Billy's question, I missed it. Because

all at once I heard the soft, steady thrum of approaching hooves. The herd of inquisitive yearlings must have sensed Faith's and my presence near their fence. They were coming to see who we were and what we were doing beside their pasture.

Seconds later, the first shadowy equine emerged from the haze. A chestnut colt with a blaze that crooked sideways over his nose poked his head toward us and snorted under his breath. Then a bay with a broad chest and an unruly forelock came up beside him. His ears swiveled forward and back as he tried to take in everything around him at once. Several other colts quickly crowded in behind the first two.

The horses weren't the only ones who were curious. Delighted by the yearlings' sudden appearance, Faith hopped her front feet up on the fence and pushed her nose through the opening to have a closer look. Startled by the Poodle's sudden move, the chestnut colt skittered sideways. That maneuver knocked him into the bay. The two colts bounced off each other. Both began to backpedal at once.

That set off a chain reaction of bumping and bucking among the entire group. Finally a large dark colt peeled back his lips and bit the yearling beside him on the crest of the neck. With a shrill squeal, the smaller colt lashed back at his aggressor.

And then a shot ran out.

The crack of gunfire was so loud and felt so immediate that reflexively I ducked down and covered my ears. Faith dropped to the ground beside me. On the other side of the fence, the colts threw up their heads and spun around, suddenly alert to danger.

For a moment, everything went still. Then, in a flurry of scrambling legs and lifted tails, the colts took off and raced away into the fog.

The mists were finally beginning to dissipate but even

so, I lost sight of the herd within seconds. I hoped that the colts could see where they were going better than I could. Because Faith and I were up and running now too, and I still couldn't see a damn thing.

"Aunt Peg!" I yelled out. "Where are you?"

My call was swallowed by the damp air. No reply came back. Even the sound of hoofbeats was gone.

All at once I felt the same wave of half-panicked helplessness that had haunted my dream. Once again I was lost and out of control. But this time instead of racing along, I felt like I was moving much too slowly.

The fence served as a guide as Faith and I ran back the way we'd come. The colts had vanished—as invisible now as if they'd never existed at all—but suddenly I could hear them again. Judging by the rapid, syncopated rumble of their hooves on the turf, the yearlings were moving fast. It sounded like we were all racing in the same direction.

Then I heard a strangled shout. It was definitely a man's voice. *Daniel? Billy?* I had no idea which one.

Almost immediately that sound was followed by a resounding crash. As Faith and I rounded the corner, a weak ray of sunlight made its way through the fog and illuminated a small patch of ground before us.

The hoofbeats weren't just echoing now, I could feel them shaking the terrain. Their movement seemed to rattle my bones. Beside me, Faith skidded to a stop and suddenly sucked back. The leash that attached us to each other whipped me around. The big Poodle pulled me back too, and just in time. All at once the colts appeared out of nowhere.

The yearlings should have been on the other side of the fence, still confined within their pasture. But instead they came bursting out of the fog only feet from where the Poodle and I stood. A dozen Thoroughbred colts swept past us, nostrils flaring, muscles bunching, tails streaming in the wind. They were running free and racing for the sheer joy of it.

There was no time to worry about what that might mean. A stitch in my side begged me to stop but Faith and I had to keep going. We had to find Aunt Peg and make sure that she was all right.

As if on cue, the thinning fog finally began to lift and a tableau opened up in front of us. My gaze swept anxiously back and forth across the scene. For a minute I couldn't make sense of what I was seeing.

The gate to the pasture was hanging open and someone was lying crumpled on the ground nearby. A wave of relief swept over me as I realized that the motionless body wasn't Aunt Peg. She was there too, though. I saw her bending solicitously over the fallen man.

"Are . . . you . . . all right?" I called out when we'd almost reached her side. It took effort to push the words out. I couldn't catch my breath.

"There you are." Aunt Peg stood up. She wiped her hands on her pants. "I wondered where you two were."

Busy panicking, I thought. Running like crazy, and hoping against hope that we'd reach her in time. That was where we'd been.

Aunt Peg meanwhile was cool as a cucumber. It figured.

I looked past her and saw that it was Billy who was on the ground. His body was limp. There was a long, jagged tear in his shirt. His head, facing away from us, was cocked away from his torso at an odd angle. A spot of color nearby caught my eye and I saw that Billy's baseball cap had been trampled into the dirt.

Aunt Peg grasped my shoulders and turned me firmly around. We both walked several steps away. A subdued Faith accompanied us.

"Is he . . . ?"

"I couldn't find a pulse." Aunt Peg crossed her arms

over her chest and pulled them in tight. “Daniel’s gone to the barn to get help. But I think it’s too late.”

“What happened?” I asked. “Who opened the gate?”

“Billy did. He intended to take us out into the pasture. Maybe he thought that he could make us both disappear. But then the horses came running out of nowhere. . . .”

“There was a gunshot,” I said. “That was what set them off.”

Aunt Peg shook her head. “Daniel tried to be a hero. When Billy was unlatching the gate, Daniel jumped him. The two of them began to struggle and the gun went off. Nobody paid any attention when the gate fell open. Daniel and Billy were going at each other like a pair of prizefighters.”

“You’re lucky you weren’t shot,” I said gratefully.

“Even luckier that I wasn’t trampled,” Aunt Peg retorted. “Billy looked up in that last moment. He must have heard the horses coming. He knew what that sound meant even if Daniel and I didn’t. He stopped paying attention for only a second, but when he did, Daniel coldcocked him. Billy dropped like a stone. By the time Daniel and I realized what was happening, there wasn’t time to help him. There wasn’t time to do anything but scramble out of the way ourselves.”

“Horse farms are dangerous places,” I said softly. “That’s what Billy said. He told Daniel how easy it was for accidents to happen out here.”

“It turns out he was right.” Aunt Peg sighed.

The fog was melting away quickly now and I could see the band of loose yearlings. They’d only gone as far as the training barn. The dozen colts were milling in confusion around the open courtyard. Several grooms had come hurrying out of the building to deal with them. Daniel and two other men were running toward us.

As Aunt Peg headed over to meet them, I turned away

and gazed out over the beautiful land that surrounded us. A few remaining tendrils of mist clung to the treetops, giving the scene an other-worldly feel. Suddenly I was so homesick that my breath clogged in my throat.

Faith was close beside me, waiting to see what we were going to do next. I reached down and tangled my fingers in the silky hair of her topknot.

"It's time to go home," I said.

Faith wagged her tail in agreement.

Sheldon Gates was the first to arrive.

By that time the loose colts had been rounded up and put away. The grooms had disappeared back into the barn. Sheldon strode across the wide, grassy tract and knelt down beside his cousin's body. Like Aunt Peg, he checked briefly for a pulse. I was too far away to be sure, but after that it looked as though he slid something out from underneath Billy—the gun, perhaps—and slipped it into his pocket. Then Sheldon walked over to Daniel and pulled him aside to talk.

Miss Ellie's son, Gates, appeared next. His pickup truck came careening much too swiftly down the rutted driveway. Gates stopped near the barn and surveyed the scene from the cab of his vehicle. His gaze went first to the open gate, then to the empty field. Last of all, it rested upon Billy's battered body. When Gates hopped out of the truck, he didn't approach any of us. Instead he went directly into the barn and remained there.

"I feel extraneous," Aunt Peg said under her breath.

"Me, too," I agreed. But having left Aunt Peg's minivan at the hotel, we had no choice but to hang around. We were stuck at the farm until Daniel decided to depart.

The police came, followed shortly thereafter by an ambulance. Two officers climbed out of their patrol car and immediately made a beeline for Sheldon. Despite the fact that he hadn't been present when Billy died, the farm's co-owner now appeared to be the one in charge.

Daniel returned to stand with Aunt Peg and me.

"I told Sheldon what happened," he said. "What he's actually telling the authorities is anybody's guess."

We discovered the answer to that quickly enough. The officers declared themselves to be both shocked and saddened to hear that a second calamitous accident had befallen a member of the Gates family. It was tragic that a group of frisky Thoroughbred yearlings had spooked in the fog and that Billy'd had the misfortune to be in the wrong place at the wrong time.

Nobody mentioned the fact that Billy, a lifelong horseman, would have known better than to allow the pasture gate to swing open wide. Nor did anyone inquire why Aunt Peg and I were there so early in the morning, or what we might have seen. Indeed, although Faith drew several curious glances, no one said anything to us at all.

I decided that was probably just as well. I was in no position to contradict whatever story was being offered up for public consumption. I'd heard mention of a gun but never actually seen one. Nor had I witnessed Billy and Daniel fighting, or the yearlings bursting through the open gate. In fact, now that the fog had cleared and the world around us came into sharper focus, the whole episode was assuming a hazy, dreamlike quality in my mind.

As for Aunt Peg, she waited with a ferocious scowl on her face until Billy's body had been loaded into the ambulance and the vehicle had disappeared down the driveway. Then she turned and strode purposefully into the barn. By that time, Daniel was already heading toward his SUV. Faith and I hurried to catch up. I didn't want him to forget that he was our ride.

Aunt Peg emerged from the barn only minutes later. She

slid into the front seat and reached around to fasten her seat belt.

"What an unholy mess," she said. "I left my contact information with Gates and told him to call me if he needs help getting Miss Ellie's dogs sorted out. As for the rest of it, the entire episode already seems to be covered with whitewash."

"That's for the best. Don't you think?" asked Daniel, sounding relieved.

Neither Aunt Peg nor I replied and we made the rest of the trip back to the hotel in silence. Once there, Faith and I scrambled out of the vehicle and went directly to our room. I had thought that Aunt Peg might want some time alone with Daniel, but by the time I was slipping the keycard into its slot she had already caught up to us.

I opened my mouth to speak but Aunt Peg held up her hand.

"Don't ask," she said.

On the whole, I supposed I would have preferred giggling.

We checked out of the hotel and left Kentucky later that morning. There was no reason to stay for the Thoroughbred sale now, no need for me to miss even a single day of school. Aunt Peg typed our destination into the minivan's GPS and set the cruise control at eighty miles an hour.

Most days, I'd have protested her need for speed. But as we pulled onto 64 and headed east, I didn't say a single word. Instead I pulled Faith into my lap, closed my eyes, and wished fervently for a deep sleep that wouldn't contain any dreams at all.

Faith and I made the last leg of the journey on our own. Driving from Aunt Peg's house in Greenwich to ours in North Stamford, I could already envision our homecoming. When we let ourselves into the house, everyone would come to greet us. The boys would jump up and down with delight. The Poodle posse would rally around Faith. Sam and I would kiss. . . .

That lovely fantasy began to unravel as soon as we pulled in the driveway. The front door to the house flew open and our three-person/five-dog welcoming committee came spilling out onto the lawn. I barely got the Volvo stopped before we were surrounded.

"Mommy's home!" Kevin squealed. "Bring me a present?"

Davey dodged around his younger brother. "Good, you're back," he said. "What's for dinner?"

My answer was drowned out by the sound of barking Poodles. As I stepped out of the car, I was nearly bowled over by Tar. Sam reached out and grabbed me.

He started to say something, then just shook his head instead. He pulled me close and I rested my cheek on his chest as Faith leapt from the car to join the fray. Mayhem erupted around us.

We were home at last. And it was perfect.

Nearly a month later at the end of April, long after spring break had ended and life was once again blessedly normal, Aunt Peg called to say that she had news.

"Lucky Luna had her foal early this morning," she said. "She's a bay filly with a star on her forehead just like her dam. Erin says that she's big, and healthy, and built like a racehorse."

"Oh, Aunt Peg," I said with a laugh. "You can't seriously be thinking of racing her?"

"You never know. I do like to keep my options open. But there's something else Erin told me. Now that Billy's gone, Gates has been promoted. Erin thinks that Sheldon might be grooming him to assume his rightful place in the family business."

"That's wonderful," I said. "Good for him."

"Even better, Gates has given up his apartment and moved into Miss Ellie's house. He and the Fab Four are keeping each other company and getting along splendidly."

I suspected Aunt Peg had been meddling again. But for once, her interfering ways didn't bother me a bit.

"Somewhere," she said with satisfaction, "Miss Ellie is smiling right now."

I liked the sound of that.